"Report!" Domingo snapped.

Strozzi quickly gave assurances to the mayor—and to the hundred or so people who by now were also listening—that the alarm was real. The duty officer hastened to add that the danger to Shubra did not appear to be immediate; he would have called a red alert for that.

"What, then?"

"A robot courier arrived here about five minutes ago from Liaoning." That was another colonized planetoid of the same sun, some twelve hours away at the current orbital positions of both bodies. "The message is that they're under berserker attack there, and they want immediate assistance."

"Attackers' strength?"

"One unit only. But they say it's overwhelming their defenses."

Domingo swore, blaspheming the names of ancient and almost forgotten gods and demigods. "Let me guess."

The duty officer relaxed from the formal posture he had been holding, as if managing any prolonged dialogue that way were too much of a strain. "Guess if you want. They think that it's Leviathan."

FRED SABERHAGEN

BERSERKER
BLUE
DEATH

A TOM DOHERTY ASSOCIATES BOOK

BERSERKER BLUE DEATH

Copyright © 1985 by Fred Saberhagen

First printing: November 1985
First mass market printing: September 1987

A TOR Book

Published by Tom Doherty Associates, Inc.
49 West 24 Street
New York, N.Y. 10010

Cover art by Boris Vallejo

ISBN: 0-812-55329-2
CAN. ED.: 0-812-55330-6

Printed in the United States of America

0   9   8   7   6   5   4   3   2   1

CHAPTER 1

The bright orange lights of the alarm began to flash, as if in deliberate synchronism with the first notes of live wedding music coming from the electronic organ. The lights of the alarm were positioned all around the top of the circular wall, about three meters high, that rimmed the huge domed room, and they extended up against the lower portion of the huge clear dome itself, making it impossible that they should not be seen. The orange lights were eerily beautiful against the driving, rolling whiteness, shot through with distant pastel colors, that seemed to fill all space outside the dome.

In synchronism with the first flash of the lights, the audio component of the alarm came blasting with almost deafening loudness through the rich sounds of the wedding processional. At the impact the organ music trailed and shuddered away to nothing, while the piercing blatting of the alarm itself kept on. And on.

Niles Domingo swore under his breath, invoking gods and creatures stranger than the gods. Reflexively he called on

1

beings he did not believe in, that at most were no more than half believed in even by the people of the farthest and most isolated colonies. He had a sense of last night's bad dream intruding into reality.

At the moment the alarms came on, Domingo was standing with his daughter at one end of the long aisle that passed diametrically under the center of the domed assembly hall. Maymyo's hand first tightened on her father's arm, then slipped away, as if she were determined to leave him as free as possible of personal distraction.

Domingo turned to look into his daughter's dark-brown eyes, at her lovely face framed in the pure white of unfamiliar ceremonial lace. She was gazing back at him trustfully. Her expression said that her father was still her first source of guidance on any problem, on how to deal with a wedding or an attack alarm. Or, as now, both at the same time.

At least the flashing lights around the wall were not bright red, nor was the audio alarm of the shrieking kind that would have proclaimed the imminence of a berserker attack upon the colony of Shubra. Instead the signal was the comparatively less terrible one of a simple orange alert; still, there was no choice about responding to it, and no option for even the smallest delay in doing so.

No option. Yet, for a long moment in the huge room, no one had moved.

Domingo and his daughter were standing together in the rear of the biggest indoor space available for human gatherings on the colonized planetoid called Shubra, satellite of a sun that had never been seen from Earth. Thirty meters away from where father and daughter stood, at the front end of the long aisle, the clergy and the witnesses were waiting. And of course the groom was up there too, Gujar Sidoruk looking even bigger and bulkier than ever in his formal citizen's robes. Gujar was gazing back at his bride-to-be and at her father as if he, independent young man that he was, were also waiting to be told what had to happen next.

That first moment of the alarm seemed to be protracted

endlessly. It was as if the warning had already sounded for a long time, but these people, having committed themselves to a wedding, could not quite make up their minds to respond to it. Before the long moment was over, most of the roomful of people were looking at Niles Domingo, too.

Nine tenths of the population of the colonized planetoid, some two hundred people, were assembled in this hall today. With them were twenty or thirty visiting neighbors, people from other small inhabited rocks within the Milkpail Nebula. A handful of the neighbors lived virtually next door, on Shubra's unnamed moon, but the others had traveled up to a full day to get here, astrogating their way half a billion kilometers through nebular space.

Occupying almost as much floor space in the huge room as the people did was a small forest of plant life, some of the forest's individual components towering over the humans' heads. The permanent flora of the chamber, imported from Earth and elsewhere, had been augmented for today's occasion by extra greenery and a million flowers joyously freighted in from another colony, Yirrkala.

On Shubra, as on most of the other small colonized rocks that revolved around certain suns within the Milkpail Nebula, outdoor ceremonies were rarely practical. The great domed room brought the assembly as close to the out-of-doors as was feasible. Overhead a clear hemisphere of force and crystal held back the whiteness and the sunset clouds of the long winter night, really astronomically distant folds of the nebula that here made up the entirety of sky and space. In only a standard year and a half it would be spring on this portion of the slow-orbiting planetoid's surface.

The night outside was one of atmospheric snow as well as nebular display; the artificial gravity imposed by the colonists upon their rock attracted—among other things—gasses enough to form an atmosphere from this peculiar sky.

Last night a terrible vision, concerning things from the sky, had come to Domingo during sleep. He knew that it had been only a nervous father's dream. A natural phenomenon and, he supposed, common enough, especially on the eve of a daughter's wedding. But this was real.

"Alert stations, everyone!" Domingo called out in a firm loud voice, as the audio warning paused. It had to pause, or voice communication would have been impossible. The alarm had killed all other sounds; in the sudden tomblike silence of the huge room the mayor's order sounded like a shout.

The pause brought on by momentary shock was over. The illusion that there had been any real hesitation about responding to the alarm dissolved. Even before the last word of the mayor's order had sounded through the room, most of the adults present were scrambling for the exits. People went running in every direction, to reach their variously scattered alert stations.

The score and more of guests who had come to the wedding from nearby colonies were as accustomed to alerts as were the citizens of Shubra. The visitors knew their duty and dispersed wordlessly, rushing to the ships that had brought them here.

When the sound of the alarm came back, it was at a more moderate level; people once alerted had to be allowed to think and talk. Giving his daughter's hand one last squeeze, Domingo dropped it and set off at a loping run. He knew—as firmly as a man could know anything—that he would be speaking to Maymyo again within moments, as soon as he had discovered the reason for this damned alarm. Certainly he ought to have at least one more chance to speak to her again before he had to launch a ship.

Running through the familiar corridors of his own small world, first aboveground and then below, Domingo pulled off the formal citizen's robe that custom had required him to put on over his ordinary garments at his daughter's wedding, and bundled it under his arm. He would stuff the garment away somewhere in his ship when he got there, but for the moment it had already been forgotten.

He intended to run all the way to his ship without a pause.

In the small confines of the settlement, neither he nor anyone else had far to go to reach their posts.

The tunnel flashed by him with the speed of his pounding legs. His eyes were fixed ahead, in the direction of the operations deck of the spaceport. He allowed only one thought that was in any sense a distraction to intrude itself upon him as he ran: *The gods help someone, whoever did it, if this turns out to be a joke . . . such a thing,* he supposed, *was remotely possible. Rough humor was still popular out here on the frontier, especially in connection with weddings. Or it could be a simple false alarm, some flaw in human guardian or in equipment, though both types of trouble were uncommon. It was certainly not an ordinary practice drill; no one would or could have called one at this time, at the instant the mayor's daughter's wedding was about to start.*

The cause of the alarm would be brought to light soon enough. Whatever the cause, no one, no colonist anywhere in the Milkpail Nebula, ever failed to take such an alarm seriously or delayed in reacting to it. Everyone who lived in the Milkpail knew, with more than intellectual awareness, what berserkers were.

Still moving at a run, among other men and women still running with him, Domingo entered the great rocky cave of the space harbor. Here too were the orange lights, the pulsating throb of the alarm. In a few moments more the mayor had reached the interior dock where the *Sirian Pearl* was drifting gently, waiting for him. His new ship was a smooth volume of metal, more a flattened ovoid than a sphere, its overall size a trifle greater than that of the huge crystal room he had just left. Still, the ship was small inside the enormous carved-out cave chamber of the port.

Like some of the other more advanced craft nearby, his new ship had reacted automatically to the alarm by altering its own gravitic balance enough to rise up from the dock, starting to prepare itself for launching. The *Pearl,* pearl-colored in the brilliant lights around it, its silent space-warping engines barely energized, was keeping station now

about a meter above the deck. Domingo knew that his ship's
computer would already be counting itself down through the
preliminary prelaunch checklist. It would wait for human
orders before it went beyond the prelaunch phase.

The mayor was not a large man, but he was strong and
active. He swung himself up and into his ship through the
waiting hatchway. Moments later he was throwing himself
into his command chair in the center of the ship. The command chair was centered in a small hollow space whose inner
surface was all pads, displays, controls. The space was physically isolated from the other crew stations, as they were
from one another. In it there might have been room for two
people to stand beside the single chair.

The cushioned, built-in command seat closed its panels
and pads around him as he sat down, making a snug fit. The
manual controls in front of him now were only auxiliary
devices for use in odd emergencies. He reached for a brown
circlet of what looked like cloth that was attached to his seat
by a slender cord. By pulling the band caplike onto his head,
he fitted himself to his headlink, through which he interacted
with the ship.

The ship was now attuned to certain components of the
electrical activity of his brain. Now, essentially by ordered
thought, almost as if by telepathy, Domingo could exert
direct control over all shipboard systems.

He began immediately, turning on, without physical motion, several of the viewing devices in front of him. One of
these presented him with the holographic image of the head
and shoulders of a middle-aged man named Strozzi. Strozzi,
the colony's current duty officer, was now standing somewhere in the Defense Center, deep underground with a wall
of deep gray rock showing behind him.

"Report!" Domingo snapped.

Strozzi quickly gave assurances to the mayor—and to the
hundred or so other people who by now were also listening—
that the alarm was real. The duty officer hastened to add that

the danger to Shubra did not appear to be immediate; he would have called a red alert for that.

"What, then?"

"A robot courier arrived here about five minutes ago from Liaoning." That was another colonized planetoid of the same sun, some twelve hours away at the current orbital positions of both bodies. "The message is that they're under berserker attack there, and they want immediate assistance."

"Attackers' strength?"

"One unit only. But they say it's overwhelming their defenses."

Domingo swore again, once more blaspheming the names of ancient and almost forgotten gods and demigods. "Let me guess."

The duty officer relaxed from the formal posture he had been holding, as if managing any prolonged dialogue that way were too much of a strain. "Guess if you want. They think that it's Leviathan."

When the name was spoken, others among the people listening swore. Domingo scarcely heard them; he was already busy thinking, trying to make plans.

Strozzi went on methodically with his report. He already had the Shubran ground defense system's radio receivers scanning the communications spectrum for more word from Liaoning, but there was nothing coming in. That was not necessarily significant. Between worlds such a distance apart in nebular space, it was usually more surprising when radio communications were open than when they failed. Hence the reliance by everyone in the Milkpail on swift, small robotic courier ships for quick, dependable communication across all but the smallest interplanetary gulfs.

Strozzi also reported that he had already dispatched a Shubran robot courier to the Space Force at Base Four Twenty-five. The duty officer had programmed it to pass on word of the reported attack and had added the information that Shubra planned to respond to the call for help. Their response would probably be taken for granted anyway.

"Very good," Domingo said and began to issue orders. "Put our ground defenses on red alert, Strozzi. But cancel the extra alarm. I'm sure we're all awake already."

"Yes, sir." The duty officer looked away, his hands doing something offstage. "Red alert is now in effect."

Domingo looked at another display inside his armored nest. "All Shubran defense ships prepare to launch, and report to me as soon as you're ready. We're going to relieve Liaoning. Visitor ships, check in with me."

Now the mayor-commander divided his own personal communications display. In one sector before him the faces of visitors appeared, beginning to report as ordered from their own ships. There was Spence Benkovic, organizer of a tiny private colony on a moon of Shubra. There was Elena Mossuril, the leader of the delegation from da Gama, a large planetoid of a different sun. Here came the Mounana people. Someone else, and someone else again, from different planetoids and moons, from very minor and comparatively major colonies, all of them within a day's space travel from Shubra.

The visitors could have elected to remain, to take some part in the defense of Shubra, or to add the firepower of their ships to the relief expedition to Liaoning. But, as Domingo had expected, all of them chose to depart, to carry warning to their own homes. He, in their place, would have done the same thing. All were quickly cleared for launching.

"My own crew, check in."

The lifelike images of their familiar faces appeared one by one on the holographic stage in front of the captain. The stage was again split, leaving room for the simultaneous display of other information, in particular the checklist display showing how far each one of the Shubran ships was from readiness to launch.

Even as Domingo's own crew members reported in, they were already wearing their headlinks, busy running the *Sirian Pearl*'s various systems up to speed.

"Chakuchin here." The stage showed optimistic features

framed in blond hair and beard, the face of a large and solidly built young man.

"Poinsot aboard." Henric Poinsot was a slightly older man, smaller and darker than Chakuchin, at the same time more crisp and businesslike.

"I'm here, Niles." That was Apollina Suslova, a compactly built, attractive young woman, wide-eyed as usual, her wild-tossed hair giving an erroneous impression of disorganization. Like most of the other crew members she had on a mixture of wedding-guest finery and hastily added shipboard gear and clothing.

"Iskander in." This was an old friend of Domingo's, deep-voiced, calm and almost leisurely; his black hair and brows were bold-looking to match the rest of his angular face. Iskander Baza was reclining in his acceleration couch with his broad shoulders turned at an angle. As usual at the beginning of action, he gave the impression that he was not taking any of these matters of routine preparation too seriously, but he was ready to enjoy what was going to follow.

"Wilma checking in. I was aboard before you were, Niles." Then the pretty red-haired wife of Simeon Chakuchin corrected herself in this formal situation. "I mean Captain."

His crew were all aboard, his ship was ready. And the other crews and ships that made up the rest of his little squadron were ready too, or nearly so. And still the final warning of imminent attack had not been sounded.

Neither Strozzi, Maymyo, nor any of the many other people assigned to Ground Defense, probing with their subtle instruments, had yet been able to discover any information indicating that there was any direct berserker threat to Shubra. Nor was there any further word on what might be happening or had already happened at Liaoning.

The powerful detector fields of Ground Defense were ranging out as far as they could into white nebula. But there were no berserkers in sight as yet on the immediate approaches to Shubra. Beyond a few hundred thousand kilometers it was impossible to see; the nebula as always offered cover for potential attacker and victim alike.

One ship after another of the mayor's irregular squadron reported ready to launch, but Domingo held back from ordering a launch. He wanted to keep the squadron all together from the start. And he wanted, before departure, to talk once more to his daughter.

He got through to her defensive post, which was one of the riskier, isolated positions near the surface. Again Maymyo's image appeared before him; this time Domingo had a moment to consider what she looked like. His conclusion was that she looked very businesslike, in spite of everything. Though she was still in her wedding gown, the lace that minutes ago had crowned her dark hair had been replaced by a headlink band. Her father could see the white collar of the dress inside the space armor that regulations prescribed for defenders near the surface. And behind his daughter he could see part of the interior of the little dugout of hardened rock and metal, and some of the panels and readouts there much like those in his ship.

He said to her, softly and quickly: "This will still be your day, sweetheart. Or tomorrow will. We'll get things organized again."

"I'm not worried, Dad." It was a brave, obvious lie, the best that could be expected under the circumstances.

They exchanged smiles. Domingo added: "Your mother would have been . . ."

Maymyo smiled. "What, Dad?"

"Nothing." What had he been about to say? Proud of you? Isabel would have been terrified, and had been, close to the point of helplessness, on several occasions. Not really made for this kind of life. But Maymyo was tougher. "She would have been all right. You will, too."

His daughter nodded bravely.

A moment later, with all available ships reporting readiness to launch, Domingo gave the order that took them all in rapid succession, in silent, unspectacular, efficient movement, out of their docks and harbor and up into low defensive orbit. The small ships, with their crews cushioned from acceleration by interior fields, needed only a very few seconds to do that; the outside gravitational gradient, strongly augmented as it was by buried generators, fell off sharply with increasing distance from the planetoid.

Shubra, below, looked small—as indeed it was, no more than about two hundred kilometers in diameter. It also looked very white, swathed in a snowy rag of atmosphere accumulated over the years of artificial gravity. On the side of the long Shubran day, surface collector grids and harvester machines were working, gathering and sorting through the steady infall of primitive nebular life forms. The crop would be sifted for the desired exotic chemicals, some of which would be processed for shipment to distant worlds. Some of the largest collecting and harvesting machines were barely visible at this altitude. No other planetary bodies, no suns or stars, were directly visible anywhere. The white, giant sun of Shubra that indirectly, through reradiation in the nebula, nourished several colonies was perceptible by a general whitening and brightening, in one direction only, of the eternal pale pastels of the interplanetary mist.

In this whitespace region—another name for the interior of the nebula—it was common for small planets in the several systems to know no real surface darkness, from one day or one year to the next. Large planets had no time to develop life of their own, or even favorable conditions for it, and tended to be uninhabitable for Earth-descended people. Within the Milkpail such worlds existed only very briefly, in terms of astronomical or evolutionary time.

The planetary bodies here, like many outside the nebula, were produced from the occasional exploding suns. In the thicker parts of the nebula, as around Shubra, light pressure from most types of suns was inadequate to produce a stable clear space in which planetary orbits could be stable and long-lasting. Relatively thick nebular material encroaching on a solar system, as it did here, tended to wear out the planetary orbits rapidly, particularly those of larger bodies. Those were broken apart by tidal forces when the friction of the medium through which they traveled had sufficiently constricted their orbits. Worlds as big as Earth, or even Venus, lasted no more than a few million years at most from the time when they first cooled into a solid state. With the nebula interfering so drastically with orbital mechanics, it was not unheard of for a small planet within the Milkpail to switch suns, effecting a sudden change in allegiance after a few hundred thousand standard years of orbital loyalty.

The portion of the Milkpail Nebula immediately surrounding Shubra offered good screening for a sneak attacker and thus contributed to the danger; but in another way the nebula was an aid to the defenders. An attacking force had a hard time trying to scout out the defenses of a world, just as the defenders found it difficult to observe an enemy's approach.

Now, via tight-beam communications, a discussion began among the captains of the orbiting ships as to how the situation might have developed since the courier was sent from Liaoning. There was some debate among crews and spacecraft commanders as to how best to respond to the cry for rescue, whether to approach Liaoning from two sides or in one small squadron. People voiced their views openly, the mayor making no effort as yet to squelch dissent.

Let them talk, he told himself silently; that much at least was their right. When they had finished talking, he would tell them: We stay in one squadron. He was in charge, and everyone knew it, but still he could expect nothing like the discipline of a Space Force fleet. There were moments—no more than that—when he would have been glad to have it.

Poinsot suggested: "We could split up, come in from different directions at slightly different times. They said there was only one unit attacking."

Domingo spoke sharply. "They said maybe it was Old Blue. We stay together."

"What's all this Old Blue? I thought someone said Levia-

than, whatever that is. I didn't get that, either.'' The speaker
this time was Chakuchin, a comparative newcomer to the
Milkpail.

"It's a particular berserker," said Domingo, and fell silent, sighing faintly.

Chakuchin, who had fought berserkers before, outside the
Milkpail, paused, trying to figure it out. "But still only one
of them, right? And I thought they couldn't get any of their
really big units into the nebula." That was not strictly true; a
machine or ship of any size could be brought in among the
tenuous clouds of interstellar matter and eventually manage
to make its way around and through them. But any vessel or
machine above a certain size, perhaps twice the cross-section
of the *Sirian Pearl*, would be unable to move through those
clouds at a speed great enough to allow for effective action.

Iskander took a try at explaining. "Leviathan is a special
berserker. It has three or four names, actually. Some call it
Old Blue, some something else.''

"Why special?''

"Partly because it's a damned tough one. Weapons from
one end to the other. And it has a way of coming up with
something new.''

"Huh.''

"And partly because it behaves erratically. Even for a
berserker. It's been around the Sector for generations, and
attacking Milkpail colonies for the better part of a century.''
Iskander's sardonic voice made it sound as if he might be
making up grim jokes.

Simeon, sounding not all that much enlightened or impressed, muttered something vague. Domingo, listening in on
the conversation, could hardly blame him. Few people, thank
all the gods and godlings, had Domingo's own experience or
anything like it. You had to at least have lived here for a few
years, on one or more of the colonies, to understand . . .

His own thoughts returned to more current problems. He
could not rid his mind of the people he was leaving behind,
the abandoned ceremony. And Maymyo in particular, spend-

ing her wedding day at her battle station, virtually alone. But there was a job to be done, and quickly. Once more he issued orders.

Now the little squadron led by the *Sirian Pearl* moved into a higher orbit. And now it quickly left the small globe of Shubra behind, hurrying to a neighbor's aid.

Domingo wondered how much help, how many ships and what type, would be on the way to Liaoning from the other colonies. Probably Liaoning had tried to dispatch couriers to some of them, too, but he could not assume that those messengers had ever reached their destinations or that more help would be forthcoming. If it was coming, it might of course arrive too late. But whether it was much or little, in time or too late, his own duty and that of his fellow citizens was clear.

Leviathan. He put down—tried to put down—old personal memories and feelings. He had to look at this as a military strategist, a logical commander.

It would be something, it would really be an achievement, if they could surround the damned thing in space with this many fighters and settle a lot of old scores for a lot of colonies and ships.

"Maybe we'll get out of the milk a little way, have a chance to see a few real stars." That again was from Chakuchin, the newcomer on the crew who was still somewhat homesick. Domingo had been here in the Milkpail for twenty years, with only occasional peeks outside. By now he'd almost forgotten what stars out in clear space looked like.

The little ships had built up speed. The folded whiteness of the Milkpail was passing over and under and around them continually, almost like atmospheric clouds flowing under and around a speeding aircraft, gatherings of whiteness and subtle color flickering with the velocity of their passage. Lungs trying to breathe this stuff would labor vainly, on what to Earthly life was no more than a good vacuum. But when the brightness was seen millions of kilometers deep, it looked thick and practically opaque.

"Something out there to our right, Captain."

"I have it. Thank you."

Even as the crew watched on their individual viewing devices, the three-o'clock detectors confirmed that something moved out there to starboard, something that was independent of the inanimate currents and surges that worked perpetually within the nebula itself. Life of a kind that never visited a heavy planet's surface. A school or shoal perhaps of microscopic bodies, half matter and half force. Life throve here in the nebula, in themes that were unknown anywhere else in the modest portion of the Galaxy that had been visited by Earth-descended folk. It flourished, unbreathing life in wide variety growing in the light gravity, mild pressure and plentiful energy that obtained here.

Something out there absorbed energy, ingested material food—that same gas, far too thin to sustain a human breath or insect's wing—metabolized, and lived. It might be one of the more or less familiar nebular life forms, the types that were harvested on and near the surface of Shubra and the other active colonies. It might be something not yet encountered by the colonists; right now it was too far off for Domingo to be able to tell, and he had no time to stop and look.

"Damn, but this is a peculiar place!" Chakuchin said it with admiration, with the pride of a new but authentic resident.

CHAPTER 2

When necessary, all of the major systems of the *Sirian Pearl* could be driven by the agile thought of one skilled pilot working alone. But the ship served its human masters most precisely and reliably when it was operated by a crew of six, who could divide its several functions efficiently among them. The five crew stations other than the pilot's, all separated in different parts of the ship, were now filled with Domingo's friends and fellow colonists. He congratulated himself, as the voyage of the relief force got under way, that days ago, even with wedding preparations and mayoral duties competing for his attention, he had made himself take time over the final selection of the crew for his new ship and for a couple of test-and-training flights.

Domingo himself now held the helm. He was sitting in his armored chamber near the center of the ship, still wearing some of the good clothes he had put on for his daughter's wedding. On his forehead rested the spacecraft commander's mindlink control band; it was a physically light weight, but he well knew that it could be as heavy as any crown.

Without moving a finger or even blinking an eyelid, the captain personally held the *Pearl* on what he considered her best course for Liaoning—close to, but not identical with, the best course as simultaneously calculated by the ship's computer. He still considered the human brain, particularly his own, superior to hardware at the most difficult parts of the incredibly complex task. There was some feedback from the equipment to the optic centers of the brain, making the control a partly visual process, trickily akin to imagination—inexperienced pilots often got into trouble imagining that there was no difference.

The autopilot, teamed with the ship's computer, might have managed to conduct the flight just as well—or almost as well—as he could, but right now the captain preferred to drive his new ship himself. The *Pearl* boasted new engines and improved protective fields—at this speed inside the nebula you needed protection against collisions with mere molecules, there were so many of them. Domingo might have raced well ahead of the five other ships in his small squadron, but he did not. Urgent as was the need for speed, he calculated that it was a still more urgent need that his force stay together in the face of a certainly formidable and possibly superior enemy.

Leviathan. The captain had a personal score to settle with that particular legendary foe—whether or not it made sense to feel a personal enmity toward a machine. But he couldn't be certain that he was going to encounter Leviathan this time. All he could really be sure of was that he was leading his people against berserkers.

The berserkers were robotic relics of some interstellar war that had been fought long before the beginning of written history on Earth. They were, in their prime form, vast inanimate spacegoing fortresses, moving lifelessly across the Galaxy in obedience to their fundamental programming command that all the life they could find must be destroyed. In all the centuries of expansion of Earth-descended humanity among the stars, berserkers were by far the greatest peril that they had encountered.

Still without stirring himself physically, Domingo could have called up on any of several screens or stages the image of whitespace whipping by outside. But after making the checklist test of that function shortly after launching, he forebore to use it. Instead, during the first hour of the flight, Domingo called up human faces, those of his fellow colonists aboard the other ships, coming and going on his screens and stages. In this way he held conversation fairly steadily with the other units of the relief squadron. There were five other ships in all, including the craft commanded by Gujar Sidoruk, and Niles Domingo, as commander of the relief force, wanted to make sure that when the combat zone was reached they would all continue to follow his orders.

That willingness established to his satisfaction, as well as it could be before the fact, he ordered intership conversation to be broken off and imposed complete radio silence.

Desultory intercom conversation continued aboard the *Sirian Pearl*. There was no reason why it should not.

Some of the crew, talking now among themselves, expressed concern for people they knew on Liaoning, and speculated on the strength of the berserker force attacking there. It was possible that the report of only one berserker was outdated, that more attackers had come in later, after the courier was sent. If the enemy force at the scene proved to be overwhelming, the relief squadron would have to turn and run for home again—if it was still able to do even that much. Everyone understood that, but no one mentioned it.

Domingo took little part in the rambling intercom chatter, but he listened to it with more than half an ear even while his mind went its own way, watching the instruments before him and trying to make plans. As it was with the captains of the other ships, so it was even with his own crew: He knew some of them better than he knew others. The population of Shubra was small, but it was far from stable. People moved on- and offworld frequently. Some of the present population were almost strangers to the mayor. Some were combat veterans and some were not. Domingo, who certainly had earned that status, wanted to monitor the nerve, and assess the probable behavior under pressure, of those who had not.

It would have been an excellent thing, of course, to have the *Pearl* manned by an all-veteran, picked crew; but in this militia organization, rank had no such privilege. The available pool of experience had to be shared out among all the crews.

The veterans on the *Pearl*, besides Domingo himself, included Iskander Baza, Wilma Chanar and Henric Poinsot. That left two rookies on the team.

Apollina Suslova had not been many months on Shubra and was really still a citizen of Yirrkala. On being assigned to Domingo's crew—every capable adult had an alert station somewhere—she had told him that she had been briefly under bombardment at least once, on yet another colony, but she had never known the strain of helping to control a ship in battle.

Domingo suspected she was becoming attracted to him, and he found the idea not displeasing. If it should turn out that way, though, he'd have to get her off his combat crew. In his experience the two kinds of relationship didn't mix. A married couple aboard ought to be different. He hoped so, at least. Not that he himself had any intention of getting married again.

Simeon Chakuchin, unlike his wife Wilma Chanar, was a comparatively new settler, but all indications were that he was psychologically strong and capable. Not everybody who reached the frontier colonies fit those criteria, though you'd think they might.

The captain's meditations were interrupted by the voice of Iskander Baza on intercom: "I've got Liaoning on the detectors, Cap. Still at extreme range."

The captain switched one of his own display stages to take the forward detectors' signal. Even to his trained perception, the solid-looking image was no more than a vague mottled blur. The planetoid that was the destination of the relief force was in an orbit not greatly different from Shubra's. The two bodies moved in long slow orbits around the same almost-hidden sun, a giant of a radiation source. Its fierceness, dulled by intervening clouds, still turned the atmospheres of its inhabited planetoids, as well as much of nearby space, into a white veil of sometimes glaring brightness.

The nebula not only made interplanetary observation difficult, but it rendered the faster modes of space travel totally unattainable within itself. There was no possibility that human ship or berserker machine could ever achieve effective faster-than-light velocity through these vast, attenuated clouds of matter. Therefore all of the colonized planetoids were separated by long hours or days of travel time, as if they had been light-years apart in more ordinary space. Now, to Domingo and the others watching their own progress as charted by their onboard computers on holographic models of the intervening nebula, their best attainable motion was a painful crawl.

But eventually, long hours after the relief mission had begun and minutes after Baza's first claimed sighting of their goal, the computer-enhanced image of Liaoning ahead was beginning to show a definite change behind the thinning veils. The image was becoming just a little clearer, something marginally better than a blur.

Domingo ordered: "Cut the chatter, everyone. To stations. We're getting near."

With all six ships on full alert, the small relief squadron at last prowled within clear instrument range of its goal. The nearly spherical ball of Liaoning, slightly prolate, showed more and more clearly against the ubiquitous milky background. Still the instruments revealed no sign of the attacking enemy.

"Tight beam, Wilma. Tell them we're here."

The message went out on radio, aimed precisely at the

planetoid ahead; no receiver anywhere else should be able to pick it up.

The seconds passed that should have brought an answer, but they did not. And then at last the *Pearl* was close enough to see the settlements on Liaoning's surface.

To see, rather, the places on the surface where those settlements had been.

Domingo's crew, and those of the other relief ships, in almost silent shock, gazed down at a scene of total devastation. Not a building had been left standing, not a settlement was still recognizable.

They hurtled closer.

Questioning radio beams probed the scorched-looking land below. Still there was no response of any kind. No sign that any berserker still lurked in the area or that the death machines might have been inefficient enough to leave anything still alive behind them when they departed.

The marks of the terrible enemy weapons became plainer and plainer on the surface below, as the *Pearl* drew nearer and nearer to the planetoid. There appeared to be no survivors.

Hours ago, Domingo had silently made plans for what ought to be done in this worst case. He implemented those plans now, issuing terse orders. There was a small spacegoing launch aboard the *Pearl*, and he selected three of his crew members to go down to the surface of Liaoning in the launch and directly investigate the death and ruin at close range. The captain himself remained where he was, at the helm of his fighting ship.

Iskander Baza was the first crew member detailed to go down. Polly Suslova, who the captain thought could use the experience, was second. Henric Poinsot, steady and reliable, was the third of the crew to be chosen.

When the launch ejected itself from his ship, Domingo could feel nothing through the *Pearl*'s metal frame or through the field of artificial gravity maintained within the ship, a field usually set, like that of their home planetoid, at Earth normal strength. But he could see, on the stages and screens in front of him, how the long, narrow shape of the smaller vessel dwindled rapidly away toward the scorched surface of the planetoid.

Minutes passed, minutes that brought an almost continuous stream of progress reports from the swiftly receding launch below. The relayed observations added little but detail to the horror already known. So far there was no sign of any survivor out of the hundreds of colonists who had lived here. Now, with Domingo's permission, other ships in the relief squadron sent down launches of their own, descending to different areas on the blasted surface.

The launches landed, one after another, at separated sites. The first reports direct from the surface confirmed the catastrophe. One crew reported finding a small wrecked berserker unit, an automated lander—ground defense here had not been totally ineffective.

At last one of the searchers picked up a faint tone from a survival radio. In less than an hour the launch crews were able to uncover first one human survivor and then another from isolated hideouts. Briefly the rescuers' hopes rose. But that was all. No more people were found alive.

The two survivors were brought up into space and taken aboard one of the other ships of the relief squadron. Then Domingo, while his own crew and others listened in, questioned them on tightbeam communications. He spoke with special gentleness to one of the two, a young girl. In his mind he kept seeing Maymyo in her place.

Both of the people who had been recovered alive were injured, and both of them had tales of horror to tell. The two survivors had been isolated, in deep separate shelters. They were numbed and shaken by what they had been through. They murmured disjointedly of incredible dangers, of being stalked and bombarded by death, and of miraculous escape.

Domingo asked: "How many of them were there? How many berserkers? I don't mean landers. How many of the big machines in space?"

One of the survivors had no idea. The other had heard a report that there had been but a single enemy.

"Leviathan? Old Blue?"

"I don't know. Somebody said that it was . . . that one. People always say it's that, when there's only one . . . I don't know."

A medical person who was on the ship with the survivors and trying to treat them now intervened. The captain ought to cut his questioning as short as possible. The patients were both in a bad way, with shock and other problems.

"I'll keep it as brief as I can. Which way did the enemy go from here? Have you any clue as to that?"

But the survivors, not surprisingly, were able to offer their rescuers no clue. Neither of the stunned humans had seen the enemy approaching their world or attacking it, even on instruments, much less observed its departure.

The captain let them go.

How had the defenses of Liaoning been overwhelmed so quickly? The two numbed, quivering humans had been able to give him no information on that point. The recording devices that were supposed to register combat action might tell the story, but the indications were that none of the ground stations containing those recording devices had survived.

Domingo now ordered his own shipboard instruments turned away from the planetoid, and with them his crew diligently scanned the thin surrounding clouds of white emission and reflection nebula. In the clouds the instruments could find disturbances that told of the recent passage of sizable objects moving at high sublight velocity, as fast as was prudent and maybe a little faster for something that big moving within the nebula. Berserker tracks were left in the nebular fog that was thin enough to count as a fair vacuum. Had there really been only one of the enemy, or more? The disturbances were too fragmentary to tell. And the scanners and computers could find no dependable indication of which way the tracks were leading.

A clamor began to reach the commander from people on the other five ships. Each colonist in the rescue squadron had

begun to fear that his or her own family and home on Shubra
was now in greater danger than before, perhaps at this very
moment already under attack.

"We better get home, Chief."

"We will. We're going home right away, don't panic."
Then Domingo reminded them calmly—and some of them
began reminding each other—that the automated defenses of
Shubra were strong, stronger than those of Liaoning had
been, and that they ought to hold, even without their squadron's support, for several days, especially against attack by
only a single enemy.

Of course at one time, perhaps only hours ago, the people
of Liaoning had probably felt confident in their automated
defenses too.

Had those people been given time to get any of their own
ships into space? It was impossible to determine the answer
to that one conclusively; what had been the Liaoning space
harbor, an underground facility much like Shubra's, was now
an inferno of nuclear fire. If any ships had been launched,
they were nowhere to be seen.

Still, the known power of the Shubran planetary home
defense systems gave the people from Shubra a positive
thought to cling to, something with which to reassure themselves during the return trip to their own world. That trip now
began without further delay.

Domingo saw to it that the two people his squadron had
rescued from Liaoning were kept aboard a ship other than his
own. There was one ship whose crew included a couple of
people that one of the survivors knew, and the two were
placed on that. He hoped it might make things a little easier
for them. The captain-mayor also wanted to make certain that
his own craft was as close as possible to perfect readiness for
combat. Having refugees aboard would not contribute to that
end and might detract from it. His new ship was the best
fighter in the squadron, he was sure, even if it was still
untested in battle.

If the trip out from Shubra had seemed long, the journey

back again was endless, filled with largely silent horror and impatience. Domingo still held the squadron together, for the same reason he had done so on the journey out. When a berserker had achieved one such successful attack, another one soon, somewhere, was very likely.

No one on his ship wanted to voice the common fear of what they might find on their arrival home, but neither could anyone stop thinking about it. All logic said it was unlikely. There was no reason to believe the berserker had gone from Liaoning to their world rather than somewhere else. But . . .

Polly Suslova, at least, thought that she could sense a faint, silent accusation in the air: that Domingo had guessed wrong. His tactical gamble had failed. It was an unfair accusation, of course. There was nothing else the Shubran ships could have done, under any commander, but respond as they had responded to the urgent distress message from their neighbor colony.

But the response had failed. Instead of intercepting the berserkers, saving Liaoning and putting a stop to the menace for the time being, all that had been accomplished was to save two shattered people and to weaken the defenses of their own home for more than a day.

It would be bad luck indeed if the enemy were to mount a heavy attack on Shubra within that time. But the absence of bad luck could never be relied upon.

And at last the trip home was almost over.

"I've got an image of home on the detectors now, Captain. Maximum range."

Good, thought Domingo. Now within thirty seconds or a minute I will get a further detector report, observation of some surface features, some activity, the beginning of reassurance that all is well at home. There would probably not be any open radio transmissions to pick up. A red alert, which meant radio silence, had been in effect here since the squadron's departure. Those conditions could soon be relaxed somewhat. There was a wedding to carry on with, however Maymyo and Gujar wanted to do it. Any celebration today or tomorrow would have to be severely restricted. It was going to be a while at best before the alert could be canceled completely. Until communications were exchanged with the Base. Until . . .

The thirty seconds had passed, and then thirty more, and the silence on all the instruments was beginning to grow ominous. The visuals were getting clear enough to see now, to allow recognition of something of the familiar surface, anyway . . . but still only ambiguous spots were coming through. There was so much surface cloud, ice crystals blowing . . .

Two seconds later he had to admit it to himself. The surface of Shubra ought not to look like that.

The defense frequencies were not detectable. But they ought not to be, could not be, totally silent at this close range. They could not be, unless the unthinkable should intrude here and now into the actual.

And that could not be happening. No, not that.

Unless . . .

There was no single moment in which the terror became reality. Rather there were minutes in which the members of the relief expedition slowly found their worst fears realized. There was now ruin on Shubra, almost the equal of that they had left behind them on Liaoning.

There were spontaneous outcries from the people aboard the *Pearl*, and then stunned silence.

The silence did not last long; there followed frantic efforts to communicate with someone, anyone, below. The attempts were as futile as they were desperate.

Still there might be, might be, survivors. The rush to investigate was frenzied. This time Domingo landed the ship, crudely and clumsily; he put the *Sirian Pearl* down directly on the surface, because here, just as on Liaoning, the space harbor had been effectively destroyed, turned into a gaping wound whose jagged mouth resembled that of a volcano. The deep center of Defense Control had to be gone, too; it could not have survived that cavitation.

As Domingo landed his ship, the other ships of his squadron were coming down as well, landing on the surface close around the *Pearl*.

The crews all disembarked and then milled around beside their ships, looking for some kind of hope, some indication of human survival. But it was a strange and unfamiliar world on which they stood, protected by their suits and helmets of space armor. The rocks of it still roared and shuddered underfoot. Every building had been wiped away. The atmosphere was poisoned. Fresh snow and black smoke blew together across a cratered, shattered, alien landscape. The artificial gravity was weakening already. The deeply buried generators that created it had doubtless been damaged, and soon the smoke and the snow would be gone, along with all the air . . .

Domingo was commander still, and still mayor of whatever might be left. He had to spend the first minutes giving orders, trying to prevent the disintegration of his crew and the other crews, instead of running in a frenzy to see what had happened to his daughter. An organized search for survivors was begun.

It was only minutes after the search started when the personal news reached him: The bride-to-be, his daughter, along with all her comrades in Defense, was dead.

Duty forgotten, Domingo commandeered the only ground vehicle available—it had come down aboard one of his squadron's ships—and rushed to the scene.

Maymyo's small defense position had been as well protected as any of the other posts near the surface. The only access to the position from the surface was through a bank-vault door set under the overhanging brow of a hardrock cliff. But her nest, like all the others, had been scorched and blasted open. The massive door hung ajar, half torn from its great hinge, the inner and outer surfaces of it alike sagging where they had begun to melt, radiating red heat.

Domingo, protected in his armor, ran in through the unprotected doorway. Enough light came in through it, into the small chamber of steel and hardened rock, for him to see.

The poisoned snow was drifting in before him, with him, after him. Her body was almost completely destroyed. At least the pitiful thing, scorched flesh and bone with snow already drifting on it, was assumed to be her body, because here it was at her post; but whoever it was was not wearing space armor, had not been wearing it at death. Chunks of the armor lay nearby, more durable than almost anything else amid the ruin.

When Domingo had jumped into the groundcar and roared away without waiting for Gujar, the younger man had climbed back into his own landed ship and taken off, only to land again almost immediately here by Maymyo's cave. Now, screaming and ranting, his duty and his crew forgotten, he came running into the gutted dugout, past Domingo, to throw himself down at the scene of death. He spent a minute of incoherent grief with the man who was to have been his father-in-law.

Then Gujar gathered up what appeared to be the shreds of wedding gown and, moving at a staggering run, took them back into his ship. On his suit radio Domingo could hear him, muttering half coherently about some kind of positive identification test.

The stricken father remained kneeling in front of the ruin of what had been a human being. All he could think was: Why no space armor? Maymyo would not have taken her armor off in combat. So the blasted body before him was not hers after all. Anyway it was impossible that it should be hers.

Another report was brought to Domingo, who somehow was still numbly functioning. On Shubra, unlike Liaoning, one of the military combat recorders, deeply embedded in the surface of the planetoid, had survived. Enough information had already been extracted from the recorder to confirm the fact of a single attacker. It had been Old Blue, Leviathan, rearmed with improved weapons and with new force-shielding that successfully resisted the weapons employed by Ground Defense.

Leviathan. Standing now in the doorway of the ruined cave, Domingo looked up into the howling sky.

Overhead another ship, a small one, was approaching the surface, coming down to a gentle landing beside the six that had already landed, following their squadron commander. Presently the newcomer's markings could be identified. It carried one of the wedding guests returning.

The small ship landed quietly only fifty or sixty meters away from the cave, and its owner got out of it, alone, and approached the little crowd now gathered around Domingo. The new arrival was Spence Benkovic, who had his own small colony on the only moon of Shubra.

Benkovic was a lean, dark-bearded, youngish man. He had a handsome face and large, expressive eyes. Staring without comment at the small shattered shelter, the covered body, he gave what news he could to the stunned people standing around him.

"When the alarm went off, I thought I'd take a look around myself," he began in a numbed voice. "All I've got is that little one-seat battler. Not real good for a real fight— but I thought I'd see what I could see." A couple of hours later, he reported, he had been patrolling out at maximum detector range, several hundred thousand kilometers from Shubra, hoping to be able to observe any approaching berserkers in time to give warning to the world of the enemy's approach.

"I should have let you know what I was doing, I guess . . ." No one commented; there was no reason to think it would have made any difference.

"Then I thought I saw something, moving in the nebula. Too fast to be just a shoal of life. But it wasn't a berserker, either."

"What, then?" someone was curious enough to ask.

"A drift, maybe." After shoals, drifts were the most common kind of formation in which the local primitive life forms tended to approach the planetoid, where the selective collectors waited for them. "But—so fast. And then I thought

that on the detectors it looked like some kind of spacecraft—
one ship, or two close together. I don't know whose ship it
would have been. But it wasn't berserkers, either, not then,
because whatever it was didn't come on to attack.''

"Berserkers just scouting? Small units."

"Maybe." Benkovic didn't sound convinced. "Then—
Leviathan must have come in on Shubra from one direction
while I was off scouting in the other. Didn't take it any time
at all to take out the ground stations; it couldn't have taken
any time, because in a matter of minutes I was back, close
enough to see what was happening. Then . . . I could see it
dropping small units right here . . . in this area of the surface."

Domingo raised his head. It was as if he were really seeing
Benkovic for the first time. "Leviathan," the captain repeated.

"Yeah. Yeah. I saw Ol' Blue once before, a long time
ago. I've been in a fight or two. . . . It put its little units
down, right here, directly on the surface, or hovering over it
so close as makes no difference . . . there was nothing I
could do. I didn't stay close enough to watch. My little
battler, hell, there was nothing . . . I went back to my moon,
to try to get my own people out. But it had already been
there, too."

After a little pause, someone asked: "Who was up there on
the moon besides you? I never heard, exactly."

"Three people. Three women. Only one's still alive. Then
I tried to broadcast a warning, but the whole area, the planet
and moon and everything, was under some kind of jamming.

"Then when I took off and looked around for Old Blue
again, it was gone. Missed me somehow, coming and going.
And there was—this." Benkovic made an expressive, sweep-
ing gesture encompassing the dead landscape around them.

Domingo turned away from him, looking in another direction. Gujar, still moving like a sleepwalker, was coming back
from his own ship. There were still scraps of white material
in his hands. In an alien-sounding voice the bridegroom said
that he had made a final identification of the wedding gown
fragment as Maymyo's. There could be no mistake. There

had been exotic fibers woven into it, plant material from his
own mother's distant homeworld.

Benkovic looked sick.

Domingo was suddenly sitting down, on a snow-drifted
rock, staring at nothing. His face inside the clear plate of his
helmet was ghastly. Polly Suslova caught him as he fell.

CHAPTER 3

Polly had been married once, but her husband had moved on, leaving the two children with her. She and Karl had for the most part enjoyed each other's company. But now, looking back on their relationship, she had the feeling that she had unintentionally and in some nonphysical sense worn him out.

The only close relatives Polly now possessed in the universe, besides her two children, were a sister and brother-in-law who were caring for those children now. At present they were all four elsewhere in the Milkpail, riding another colonized rock called Yirrkala, the planetoid from which the flowers for Maymyo's wedding had been imported.

As the magnitude of the Shubran disaster became plain, as the reality of the destruction of her friends' families and homes established itself, Polly's thoughts were increasingly occupied not with the ruin before her eyes, but with her two children, whom she had not seen for several months. It was not so much anxiety she felt, or overt fear that Yirrkala was also going to be attacked. Rather she felt a vague satisfaction that she had planned the disposition of her children properly, had done a good job of seeing to their safety. They were both still very young and it was difficult being separated from them, but Polly's job had required her to move to Shubra for half a standard year. She was a specialist in a field that was sometimes less and sometimes more esoteric than it sounded, the relationships of machines with the environments in which they worked. The job also kept her unpredictably busy. Whenever she had thought about it rationally, even before disaster struck, there had been no doubt in her mind that the kids were currently better off with her relatives on Yirrkala.

Polly had been getting along well enough with the Shubran colonists as she lived among them, but she had made no deep personal attachments on Shubra. Except, as she now had to admit to herself, for one. The destruction of the Shubran colony, devastating though it was, was the second such shock of mass tragedy to hit her in a little more than one day. It found her already somewhat numb. Empathic feelings for the grieving survivors did not strike her with overwhelming personal force.

Again, with the same one exception.

She was standing near enough to the captain, and watching him closely enough, to try to catch the inert mass of his suited body when he started to fall. In the failing artificial gravity—fields dying with the blasted generators under the ground—she was successful. Inside his faceplate Domingo looked more dead than alive; pure shock, Polly supposed. She had got the impression that much of his life was wrapped up in his daughter. She eased him to the ground and sent someone else running to the *Pearl*'s landed launch for a first-aid kit. When the kit arrived, she administered a treatment for shock through one of the inlet valves thoughtfully provided in suits of space armor for such emergencies.

She watched the victim's reaction as under the chemical stimulus he began to recover. In the busy minutes immediately following, minutes largely taken up by an intense and

futile search for more survivors, Polly stayed with Domingo
as much as possible, wanting to keep him in contact with
humanity if nothing else. The shock had hit him so intensely
that for a time she was worried for his life.

The captain spoke to no one for almost an hour following
his collapse. For the first few minutes he was deeply stunned,
almost paralyzed. His crew gave him what modest medical
care they could. After that he showed signs of awareness but
remained for a considerable time in his state of silent shock.
He sat on the ground speechless and essentially alone except
for Polly, while around him his few surviving fellow citizens,
in the intervals between their futile efforts to find other
survivors, acted out their own grief and outrage in various
ways.

The next stage of Domingo's recovery, when it came, was
rapid. And as it progressed, it became—to Polly at least—
frightening.

It began when he broke his hour-long silence. He at last
said something. A short statement; none of those near him
could quite make out what it was.

Two or three minutes after speaking those incoherent words,
Domingo was on his feet again, brushing aside Polly's attentions and other people's questions and issuing harsh orders.
He came out of shock, seemingly without transition, into
grim, purposeful rage, driving her and the others of his crew
to get the *Pearl* back into space. If there were any survivors
here on the planetoid, he told his people brutally, they would
have been found by now. Already they had checked out all of
the defensive posts, the deep refuges that would have offered
the only real chance of survival.

Another ship's captain, tears running down his own cheeks,
approached Domingo on the ground, stressing the hopeless-
ness, the pointlessness, of any immediate effort to lift their
ships. It was too late to retaliate. Amid the shrieking wind,
the driving, poisoned snow, the other captain's voice came
over the personal communication channel. "Don't you un-

derstand, Domingo? It's all over . . . the berserkers have got
away. They're gone.''

Domingo glared like a madman at him. "Leviathan hasn't
got away yet. We'll get it. Get those ships up!" His voice
was hoarse, almost unrecognizable.

And Domingo's own crew, who a moment ago had been
trying to nurse him back to some first stage of recovery, now
felt the lash of his words and had to get themselves aboard
the *Pearl* and get ready to lift off.

Polly at first had the feeling that what he was doing to his
crew and the others was wrong and useless, but she did not
dare to try to stop him.

Demanding data, Domingo bullied everyone. He got them
moving back to their duty stations, their shipboard instruments. He made them provide him with fresh observations,
reports of ionization trails and other recent disturbances in the
nebula nearby. These reports indicated that the destroyer
machine—the readings confirmed that there had probably
been only one berserker—was not long gone, probably no
more than a very few hours.

Domingo raged at them all. The burden of his ranting
seemed to be that so much time had been wasted on the
ground.

Someone protested the injustice. "You were in shock,
Captain. You were—"

"*You* weren't in shock." He glared at the questioner.
"Were you?"

They gaped at him.

"If you could move and I couldn't, you should have
dragged me back on board."

They were all back on board now, and working. It was
almost as if the still-smoldering pyres and gutted caverns of
their homes below had already been forgotten. There was a
quotation in Polly's mind from somewhere, something about
letting the dead bury the dead. That was all right, a healthy
attitude, but to carry it to this extreme . . . she continued to
observe Niles Domingo worriedly. When he first got to his

feet again, she felt relieved that he was recovering from the shock, rebounding from the initial blow more completely if not faster than the others who had suffered tragic losses. But Domingo's energy had returned to him too suddenly, his grief had been transformed too rapidly and efficiently to rage.

Polly Suslova was sure that it was a false recovery.

But so far it was sustained. And it was pulling the others along with him. They were all bereaved to one degree or another, and almost as shocked as Domingo was. They actually benefitted from being dragooned aboard ship again, shouted at about their duty, hooked by the alpha rhythms of their brains into their crew stations and coerced into giving him reports. The necessity of routine, of following orders, formed a kind of support for them in their own shock; at some level they all understood this, and so far they had submitted to it willingly.

Such was the compulsion he exerted on the other people of his squadron that all six ships, with all their crew members aboard, had launched obediently within a few minutes of his order.

The six ships rendezvoused in orbit. From this altitude, their homeworld looked not much different than it had before life was expunged from it. There was a radio silence. This time silence had not been imposed by order; it was just that no one at the moment could find anything to say.

Then Polly had an exchange of intercom dialogue with the captain.

She asked him: "Where are we going?"

The features of Domingo's face, viewed individually, looked the same as they had before fate in the form of a berserker had struck him down. Yet his face had altered, she thought, all the same. It was as if someone had got in under the flesh with a chisel and had done some carving on the bones.

He answered her: "Where do you *think* we're going? We're going after that damned thing." Like his face, his voice had altered. The chisel had worked angles in it, too.

Someone else broke in: "We can't . . ."

The protest was never finished. Nor was it answered. The captain left it hanging in the air, and told them to get busy. And no one else had yet dared to take up the banner of rebellion.

Polly wished intensely that she could get a direct, in-person look at the captain's countenance. She could call up his intercom image before her whenever she liked, but it was not the same.

The radio silence was broken again. Some voices of dissension, mingled with pure lamentations, were calling in from other ships, questioning this hopeless pursuit.

Domingo paid little heed to the dissenting voices or to the lamentations, either. He was again busy driving his ship. The few words he spoke to the captains of the other ships conveyed essentially the message: *Follow me or not, just as you like. Where else are you going to go?*

He drove the *Pearl* into nebular space again, looking for the berserker's trail. The five other ships came along. None of their captains—so far—was persuaded that it would be better to give up and turn away.

Covertly Polly continued to watch his face on intercom whenever she was not fully occupied with her own job. She had given up hope, for the time being, of being able to guess just what was going on inside his head. Continued shock, of course, and grief. But—what form was it taking? What were his thoughts?

In fact, at the moment the captain's only conscious thought was simply that his ship ran well. Better than that, it ran superbly. For the time being, for the moment, he was able to lose himself in the beautiful running of his new ship. He was momentarily content, even cheerful. There was no need for him to consider—to consider anything else at all.

Outside, whitespace flowed by, smooth and at the same time intricate, like ruffling wedding lace.

I have been so proud of this ship, Domingo thought, serenely watching instruments. *Ever since I got it—not long ago, I admit—it's been everything I ever hoped for in a ship.*

For ten years I've wanted a new ship, because—

"Did you say something, Captain?" That was Polly's voice on intercom. Had he spoken aloud? He hadn't meant to.

"Nothing," Domingo said. Then he ceased for a time to think at all. He only calculated how to get more speed.

When he had the problem of speed settled, for the time being, he could think again. He was going to catch up with the berserker, the one that ten years ago . . . and now again . . . he was going to catch up with Old Blue.

Yes. And then . . .

But soon it was obvious that the ionization trail was becoming painfully difficult to follow. He was as experienced at trailing as anyone—it was a valuable peacetime skill in the nebula, one ship trailing another just to keep from getting lost, or simply as a game—and he knew that the trails in the nebula sometimes faded, suddenly and inexplicably.

He heard again from some of his own crew. They were watching the trail too, and his increasingly labored efforts to follow it. Henric and Simeon were now wondering pointedly if it was still possible to go on with any hope of success.

The captain pointedly ignored their wondering.

Some of the people on the other ships were less impressed with him than his own crew was. More of those other people were speaking up now, talking reasonably to him and to each other, forming the nucleus for a gentle and sad revolt. The berserker was gone, was the gist of what they said. This wasn't really a trail any longer. Perhaps some day the damned thing could be hunted successfully and destroyed. But right now they, the survivors, had to take time to come to terms with themselves, with their own grief and loss.

The reasonable, nonviolent view nearly prevailed. The other ships of Domingo's squadron were all turning away now, the people aboard them voting that it was time to go to the Space Force for help.

The *Pearl* moved on, along the fading trail—some of her

crew arguing that the trail had already been lost—with Domingo still piloting.

"Captain. Where are we going?" This time it was Iskander Baza who said it. The same question had already been asked aboard the *Pearl*, but now it had a new context and was posed in a practical tone that deserved an answer, if anything practical was going to get done.

Domingo's reply was only slightly delayed, as if he were being thoughtful about it. And when it came it sounded perfectly rational. "All right. Set a course for the base, then. For Four Twenty-five. Iskander, you take the helm for a while."

Polly breathed a faint sigh of relief. That made sense. Base Four Twenty-five would have help to offer. As much of any kind of help as anyone in the *Pearl*'s squadron was going to get anywhere right now, as much as the universe could possibly have available for people who had lost all that they had lost. And if the hunt was still to be pursued, the base undoubtedly offered the best chance of obtaining information about where the berserker—Leviathan—had gone now.

She had not even had a good chance yet to offer the captain her condolences on his daughter's death. Right now she was afraid to try.

Domingo's crew, still suffering from shock, were largely silent as their journey to Base Four Twenty-five began. But as the flight proceeded they began slowly to talk among themselves again. They had all been friends and neighbors once, just yesterday when they had lived in a community together. And they were certainly more than neighbors now. They were survivors together.

Polly wasn't sure that Niles Domingo was still a friend and neighbor of the others. All those others were perhaps too involved right now with their own grief and shock to notice the transformation. But Polly doubted that he was even listening to them any longer, that he was even living in the same world with the other people aboard his ship or in his squadron. Some of those people had certainly lost children too, some had lost whole families. But none of them had collapsed the way Domingo had—not yet anyway—or recovered in his way either.

In what kind of hideous, private world he was living—existing—now, she couldn't guess, much less try to share the experience with him. But she swore to herself that she would be ready when the chance came to help.

Base Four Twenty-five was fairly near though in a different system from Shubra, on a planetoid that had remained otherwise uncolonized, and had no commonly used name of its own apart from the base. It was a barren rock, considerably smaller than Shubra, that supported a Space Force installation of modest size and virtually nothing else.

Base Four Twenty-five was about a day away. It was going to be a long day for them all.

The *Pearl* glided slowly into one of the row of berths built into the section of the shielded underground docks that was reserved for civilian visitors to the base. Other ships of the ill-fated orphan squadron were coming in behind the *Pearl*. None of the other ships had been quite as fast as Domingo's *Pearl* in getting here, but he had not been deliberately trying to outrace them, and they were already catching up. As the other craft arrived, they entered nearby berths. The crews of all six vessels disembarked, almost together. All of them were moving slowly, a reluctant step at a time; it was as if the act of leaving their ships now might take them yet farther from everything that they had lost.

The people of the *Pearl*, first to arrive, were also first to step out. Several Space Force people known to Domingo and to most of his crew had already come into view, standing on the dock, waiting to greet the arrivals sympathetically. The squadron had radioed its grim news ahead.

At the head of the welcoming committee was the base commander, a man named Gennadius, tall and hollow-cheeked, looking chronically worn down as if by his job. Polly had seen him only once before, at some function a couple of years ago, and she knew that in the past he had fought at Domingo's side against berserkers. It was obvious now from the commander's behavior that the two men were old friends.

Gennadius said "Niles" as the other approached, and followed with a one-word question: "Maymyo?"

Domingo looked at the tall man in front of him as if he had trouble comprehending the question. "She's dead," the captain said at last. It was as if he were talking about someone he had barely known.

The base commander winced, with a more than social reaction. Polly made a mental note to herself that as soon as she had the chance she would ask this man for advice and assistance in helping the captain.

Gennadius asked him: "How about you? Come and rest. I want to have the medics look you over."

With a gesture Domingo brushed the notion aside. "They can look over some of my people if they want to be looked over. I'm all right. What I want is to get to your operations room and see your current plot."

When one of the base medical people tried to be firm with him, Domingo pulled his arm away with a flourish that seemed to threaten violence. "Let me see the plot!"

Gennadius, with a much more modest gesture, called the doctor off. Then he led his old friend Domingo toward the operations room. Polly and a few others followed. Others of the bereaved crews sat down exhausted where they were, milled around lamenting afresh or accepted medical examination.

The operations room, on the next level above the docks, was a large ovoid chamber, perfectly lighted, big enough for forty or fifty people to gather inside it at one time. In the approximate center of this chamber there was a computer model, itself the size of a small room, illustrating the explored portions of the Milkpail.

A color key for the model was displayed nearby. After Polly had studied it for a few moments, she understood the essentials of the presentation. This was evidently what Domingo had called the current plot, indicating where within the Milkpail Nebula berserker attacks had recently been reported, and which additional colonies and installations were now considered to be at high risk. The model also showed the locations to which the battlecraft at Gennadius's disposal, about twenty of them in all, had been dispatched, in an effort, Polly supposed, to try to intercept the enemy's next attack. She couldn't interpret all the symbols on the plot; for one thing, she was unable to tell just how many ships of which kind were supposed to be where.

One wall screen in the operations room showed the scene down in the visitors' dock, where it appeared that three or four additional ships were now arriving, more or less together. Polly did not recognize them. Someone standing near her in operations said that they came from Liaoning. Having arrived home to find that their world had been destroyed, they had turned here to the base as the Shubrans had.

Domingo handed over to Gennadius the recording on which Old Blue could be identified as the attacker. Then he demanded that the base commander tell him his plans for hunting down the berserker that had destroyed the Shubra colony.

"I'll have to take a good look at this first," Gennadius said wearily, juggling the recording in his hand. "There might be some useful information, even if it doesn't help us immediately. We'll do an analysis."

"Piss on your analysis." That expression was, by local custom, a much uglier way of swearing than to profane the names of half-forgotten deities and demigods. Polly had never before, in the months she had known the captain, heard him use this kind of language. It disturbed her to hear it now, more than she could logically explain.

Again he demanded of the commander: "I want to know what you're going to do about Leviathan."

Gennadius stood solidly, with folded arms. "I'm going to

run my command. To give as much protection as I can to the people in this district. I appreciate how you feel, Domingo—"

"Do you?"

"Yes. But my prime function is not to hunt Leviathan. It's not the only berserker around, you know."

Domingo was silent. The base commander (Polly got the definite impression that he was making allowances for his bereaved friend) went on in a tired, methodical, soothing voice, explaining his current plans. From what Polly, who was no military expert, could understand of it, his basic strategy seemed to be more defensive than offensive. He wanted to detail the *Pearl*, with other ships from Shubra and Liaoning, as soon as they and their crews were ready to go out again, to guard duty over other colonies. There were perhaps twenty more Milkpail colonies still out there, potential targets for the berserker enemy. Gennadius intended to get as many armed ships as possible, including those of the bereaved colonists, out there to protect them.

Domingo said, in his new hoarse voice: "At least you think those other colonies are still there. Still in existence. You don't really know."

"That's right." Gennadius, under strain himself, no longer sounded like an old friend. But he was still trying. "As far as I know, they're still alive. Will you help them stay that way?"

Domingo spoke in the same voice as before, with no more or less expression. "Say there are twenty places to be guarded. If I take the *Pearl* to do patrol duty at one of them, I have one chance in twenty of encountering Leviathan at the next attack. That's not good enough."

"Not good enough." Gennadius repeated the words, as if trying to understand what they might mean. "Not good enough for what? What are you proposing instead?"

"My ship goes along with your fleet, when you set out to hunt Leviathan."

"It's not going to work that way, Domingo."

"Then I hunt the damned thing alone."

"That would not be wise."

Domingo's monotonous voice pointed out that the *Sirian Pearl* was undoubtedly his ship, his private, personal property to do with as he chose. He was not going to have his ship assigned to guard duty anywhere. Speaking slowly and calmly, as if explaining to an idiot, he said that he intended to take the *Pearl* in pursuit of Leviathan, by himself if necessary. He felt confident, with a little preparation, of being able to follow and find the berserker anywhere in the nebula.

Some of his own crew looked doubtful when they heard that announcement.

The base commander meanwhile gazed off into the distance, as if trying to calculate something, or maybe to invoke some exotic technique of self-control.

Polly tried to remember the version of interplanetary law obtaining in this sector. She thought it was technically true that even now, in this state of emergency with colonies being crushed like anthills under an iron heel, the military had no right, or had only a very doubtful right, to give orders to a civilian captain or to the mayor of a colony. But anyone as grown up as Domingo ought to know that being technically in the right could lead to disaster; Domingo of course would know that, if he were in his right mind now.

Gujar now joined the group in the operations room. The huge, bulky man looked totally exhausted.

The bereaved bridegroom was completely on Domingo's side in the argument; Gujar wanted to press on with the chase, too. But the ship he had been piloting was not his own, and the woman who owned it was going to use it to get out of the Milkpail right away; she was giving up. Gujar was unhorsed.

Gennadius had returned to the argument with Domingo: "All right, maybe technically I can't give any of you orders right now. But I tell you I need help. And I would strongly suggest that you and anyone else who's looking for a fight should take the *Pearl* and whatever other ships you have, and provide some cover for people out there who need it badly. Leave the hunting to us.''

"You've just told us that the Space Force doesn't plan to do any hunting."

"I've said nothing of the kind. Let us do it in our own way."

But Domingo wouldn't listen. When one of the officers in the background thought aloud that the *Pearl* would have no chance alone against Leviathan, he turned on the woman and argued, without anyone being able to prove him wrong, that the *Pearl* was the equal in nebular combat of anything the Space Force had locally available; and in fact superior to many of their ships.

He argued too that his own ship was probably superior to any of theirs in this one task, hunting down and destroying a rogue berserker like Leviathan. Domingo had designed the *Sirian Pearl* himself, and at enormous expense had had her built—at the Austeel yards—primarily for that very purpose.

"Really?" asked someone who didn't know him, and therefore didn't believe it.

"For ten years I've wanted a ship that—" He broke off that sentence and plunged into technical detail. The *Sirian Pearl* also had superb new weapons systems on board. Since the events of ten years ago, Domingo had been planning and working to equip himself with a ship that would not have to run from anything it might encounter in the Milkpail.

Someone grumbled in a low voice that in the Milkpail, at least, it was still insane to go out with only one ship, whatever she was like, against *any* berserker, let alone that one.

Iskander Baza put in: "Leviathan may have taken a lot of damage in those raids; it must have taken some."

Domingo argued also that his ship had speed; it had beaten all of the other ships here to the base, although most of them had started for it sooner. And it had, in himself, a veteran commander. And, he told the military people again, he was not convinced that they intended ever to hunt this enemy seriously, hunt it to the death.

The response from Gennadius was stony silence. Domingo and his crew left the operations room. Polly stayed close to him and watched him glowering as he paced the corridor outside.

He looked around at her and at the four other people of his own crew. "We're not lifting in the next ten minutes. But I am going after Leviathan as soon as I can get a hint of where to look for it. Those of you who don't like that idea had better drop off the crew right now."

Iskander stood beside his captain, looking at the others, as if such a suggestion could not possibly apply to himself. There was no question that he was on the crew, no matter what.

"I'm staying on," said Polly, and wondered at herself, though not as much as she would wonder later. Simeon and Wilma looked at each other, then both tentatively signed assent. Right now there were not a whole lot of choices about what else to do, where else to go.

There was a pause, then Poinsot sighed. "I'm dropping out, Domingo. You have to play it the way you see it. But so do I. I can still see some kind of future life for myself. I've still got people, my sister and her kids, who are going to need me."

Polly recalled that Henric's brother had been on Shubra too, in Ground Defense, but the brother's family had been visiting elsewhere.

"Drop out, then," said the captain.

Henric walked away. Gujar Sidoruk came out of the operations room, swearing at Gennadius, at the commander's refusal to order a general hunt for Leviathan immediately. In a minute Gujar had officially signed on the crew as Poinsot's replacement.

CHAPTER 4

Four days after the attack on Shubra, the entire crew of the *Sirian Pearl* was still at Base Four Twenty-five, as were a number of the people from the crews of the other Shubran ships. The rest of the Shubran survivors had taken their ships out to patrol as Gennadius had requested, putting aside their own grief to help guard some of the twenty or so other colonies that still survived within the nebula.

Domingo still refused to consider doing that. He calculated that flying guard duty around a colony somewhere would give him at the most one chance in twenty of encountering Leviathan, and that was not enough.

Polly had the impression that Gennadius thought the captain would come round in a little while and be willing to take the *Pearl* out on a defensive mission. But Domingo did not come round. Too full of vengeance to care about helping others, he waited at the base, along with those who were too shattered to care what happened to the other colonies, and a few other people who were too obsessed with the idea of immediately starting to rebuild, regaining what they themselves had lost. The military would shelter them all as refugees as long as necessary, feed them and provide them with spare clothing, but they could not remain its wards indefinitely. Eventually even the shattered ones would all have to go somewhere else, live again somewhere else, do something else with the remainder of their lives. It would be a matter of starting over, essentially from scratch.

After the first three days at the base, a few of the Shubran survivors had approached their mayor, wanting him to take some initiative in finding a place or places away from the base for his few remaining citizens to settle, at least temporarily.

But Domingo had no interest now in making that kind of effort. There was now only one subject that had any attraction for him at all.

He gave Gennadius a strange smile when the base commander raised the matter of resettlement. Domingo answered: "A place to live? What does 'to live' mean?"

Gennadius looked at his old friend rather grimly for a few seconds, then turned and walked away.

Domingo called after him: "What's new on the operations plot?"

The question got no answer.

Polly wanted to take Niles Domingo in her arms, to let him weep away some of the bottled grief that seemed to be driving him coldly and quietly insane. But he gave no indication of wanting to be in anyone's arms for any reason; and trying to picture him shedding tears made her want to giggle nervously. She had never seen a human being who looked less likely to weep than Domingo did now.

She waited for some change, for better or worse, in his condition.

Polly had been able to piece together Domingo's story, more or less, from scraps of conversation and from talk overheard, both at the base and earlier on Shubra. He had arrived in the Milkpail about twenty standard years ago as a very young man, accompanied by his timid young bride, a girl named Isabel. By all accounts he had loved Isabel deeply. Then about ten years ago his wife—she had never got over being easily frightened—had died in some kind of ship crash. Polly had never heard whether that disaster had been somehow related to berserkers or simply an accident. Two of Domingo's three young children had died in that crash, too. He had not remarried. When Polly first met him a few months ago he had been a kindly man, though somewhat remote from everyone except his surviving daughter.

Kindly was not the word that came to her mind now when she looked at him or listened to him. *Grim*, certainly. There were probably more ominous variations on that word that would fit his present condition even more exactly, but right now Polly had no inclination to try to find them.

At least the refugees at Base Four Twenty-five had plenty of room. The visitors' quarters here at the base were extensive, because in more normal times they got a lot of use. But now everyone who still had a home had gone scrambling to defend it, and the remaining refugees had the place practically to themselves.

For her own use, Polly had chosen a small single room next to the one where Domingo had indifferently allowed himself to be billeted. She saw little or nothing of him during the nights, but everything was quiet next door, as far as she could tell. So quiet that she began to doubt that he was ever there.

Worried about Domingo on the first night after their arrival at the base, Polly had gone next door to look in on him, planning to make up a reason for the visit as required. Her brisk tap on his door remained unanswered, even when she repeated it. She called his name, then tried the door, which was unlocked. He was not in the little room at all. One of the flight bags he'd had with him on the ship was sitting unopened on the narrow bed. There were no other signs of occupancy.

Polly thought for a moment and found her captain in the

next place she looked for him. He was back in his ship, wide awake, hunched over some instruments in the common room. On a wall screen a copy of that last surviving Shubran ground-defense recording was being played back, reenacting the destruction of his life. The ugly angular shape that was Leviathan came drifting in slow motion across the screen, dragging its blue glow under magnification that was still not enough to let it be seen very clearly. Weapons flared on the berserker, and beneath it the landscape exploded into dust. This was evidently before the landers had been dropped, the smaller machines that must have dug out and sterilized the small shelters like Maymyo's, for there was no sign of those devices here. The scene ran for only a few seconds, then automatically started over again. And yet again, as Polly watched, Domingo kept studying it intently, critically, as if the recorded onslaught represented no more than an engineering problem. Meanwhile the *Pearl*'s computer was working away in busy silence, constructing a colored holographic model of the whole nebula, one that Polly recognized as a smaller version of the plot on display in the operations room.

When she came into the room, Domingo took his eyes from the screen just long enough to glance at her for identification purposes. "What is it, Polly?" he asked her absently.

She delayed answering the question, but the captain didn't even notice. The screen and model in front of him had immediately reclaimed his attention. Eventually it did dawn on him again that she was there, watching. He looked up again, with more awareness in his eyes this time. "What is it?"

The excuses she had been mulling over, all suitable for dropping in on a friend in the next room, suddenly did not seem adequate to justify breaking in on a ship's captain in the middle of a combat-planning session.

So Polly blurted out part of the truth: "I was worried about you."

That at least appeared to get the captain's full attention.

Was that expression on his face intended to be a smile? He said: "Don't. There's not enough left of me to worry about."

"I don't believe that—I see a lot of you still there."

He had no real reply to that. He grunted something and sat waiting.

She said: "You're still determined to go after that berserker." It was hardly a question.

The captain nodded abstractedly. He was still looking at her, but his attention was already slipping away again.

Indicating the model, Polly asked: "Is that going to be a big help?"

His eyes returned to the holographic construction, and this time they stayed on it. He sat back with folded arms. "I think it will."

She moved a little closer to him and sat down on one of the built-in padded benches. "Tell me about it."

"It's just a matter of trying to get into Leviathan's brain and predict what he's going to do next." Domingo made that task sound almost easy. His eyes were still aimed at the model, but she had the impression that his gaze was focused far away.

He had said *he*. What *he's* going to do. Polly filed that information away for the moment. She asked: "Is there any way I can help you?"

Eventually his eyes came back to her. Sizing her up, he nodded, slowly and thoughtfully. "Yes. Of course you can help. When the time comes, I'll need help. I'll need a good crew. But right now . . . right now it's just a matter of my getting this modeling done as accurately as I can. I think I prefer to do that myself. I want to know it perfectly."

She resisted the strong hint that the best help she could offer him at this moment would be to get out of his way. Instead she leaned back in her seat, as if she were comfortable. "That looks very much like the model in the operations room."

"It should."

"Has Gennadius given you access to the base mainframe computer? Everything it has in memory?"

Domingo nodded. "He and I are still talking to each other. I told him I needed it, and he's a reasonable man, up to a point at least. He wants all the fighting ships in his district as well equipped with information as they can possibly be."

Polly had more questions to ask; but Domingo grew more restless, answering in monosyllables, staring at his slowly growing and developing model. She prolonged her stay only a little longer, because he so obviously would have preferred to be alone. She wanted her presence to be welcome.

On the morning after that talk in the control room—base time was coordinated with that of some of the larger colonial settlements on nearby rocks—Polly was up at about the same time as most of the Shubran survivors. After eating breakfast in the common mess, she found a general discussion going on among a group of Domingo's fellow citizens and sat in on it, listening.

The group that had settled into a small meeting room after breakfast comprised some twelve or fifteen Shubrans, all of them crew members from the various ships in the orphaned Shubran relief expedition. Some of them were already well into the formulation of determined plans to reconstruct their lives, talking about going back to Shubra as soon as possible and rebuilding there, starting the colony over.

Others in the group declared that they had had it with Shubra and never wanted to go near the place again. The two factions were not really trying to convince each other, Polly thought, and it seemed unlikely that the whole group could ever agree on any single course of action.

While this discussion was in progress, Gennadius came to the door of the meeting room. The Base Commander looked somewhat happier than he had yesterday. "I have some good news, people. A manned courier ship has just come in from Sector. They're responding fully, just as we had hoped, to the Liaoning disaster. I think we can take it as guaranteed that the response of the government will be the same in your case when they hear about it. Disaster funds should be available from Sector Government for resettlement on Shubra, too, or anywhere else in this district where they're needed.''

The people in the little group looked at each other. Both factions, the resettlers and those in favor of moving on, displayed generally pleased reactions. Someone asked hopefully: "You think we can depend on that, Commander?''

"I think so. As far as I can see, Sector still plans to have the whole Milkpail colonized some day. Even if now that looks like a rather distant goal.'' Gennadius added: "And I want to see it, too. The more people there are living in my territory, the easier my job gets.''

"Colonies can do well in the Milk,'' someone offered, trying to be optimistic. "We've just got to protect ourselves better. Nebula's still full of life.''

"A thousand-year career for busy berserkers,'' objected one of the survivors who was ready to give up. No one among the optimists reacted noticeably. *Cash in your chips if you want to; we're going on living.*

The discussion, informal but earnest and substantial, continued. The future of Shubra, Polly thought, was perhaps being decided here and now. Without the uninterested mayor. And without the high proportion of the Shubran survivors who were out in their ships, trying to protect other people's lives and homes. Well, she wasn't going to worry about it—she had enough to worry about already.

When Commander Gennadius left the meeting, she tagged along with him.

He glanced sideways at her and, without breaking the rhythm of his long strides down the corridor, opened the conversation with his own choice of subject. "I've got another roomful of people just down the hall here.'' At that moment Iskander Baza passed them in the hall, exchanged nods with Polly, and looked after them curiously as they

marched on. Gennadius continued speaking to her: "These
are not refugees, for once. These are incoming, potential
colonists, just in from Sector. Naturally their ship diverted
here to base when her captain got word of our alert. I want to
have a little talk with them before they start hearing everything about our problems at second hand. You're welcome to
sit in, if you like. I'm not trying to whitewash the way things
are."

"Thank you. I'd like to sit in."

With Gennadius she entered the next conference room,
where the atmosphere was vastly different from that in the
one they had just left, though about the same number of
people were present. The men and women assembled here
looked different from the psychically battered colonists in the
other room. These newcomers were obviously nervous but
still healthy, without the indefinable appearance of victims.

By now the newcomers had heard the full official announcement of the multiple disasters, which was a recital of
bare facts, accurate as far as Polly could tell. And in the short
time they had been on the base they had almost certainly
heard more than that, from survivors and at second hand.
They were, naturally enough, worried and uncertain.

As Polly followed the commander into the conference
room, one of the group was standing in front of the others,
talking to them about berserkers. The speaker was one of the
older people present—none were more than middle-aged—
and her voice carried sincerity if not necessarily authority.

"When berserkers move in, people move out. It's that
simple. Trying to live in a sector where they're active is like
sticking your hand into a shredder. It's just about as sensible
as that, and as brave."

The speaker glanced over her shoulder, saw Gennadius
looking at her, and finished defiantly: "I've been through
this before. I know what I'm talking about!"

Polly could see the base commander pausing, deciding
silently that this called for a more serious speech than he had
first intended.

Gennadius made no attempt to hush the woman, but let her finish. Only when she had returned to a seat did he himself take over her position at the front of the room.

He looked out over his small audience calmly and gravely, letting a little silence grow. Then when he judged he had the timing right, he said: "All right. We've had a very severe problem in the nebula the past few days. A series of disasters, in fact. But as you can see, this is a very strong base, secure against attack. Starting from here, and with the support of Sector, we're prepared to take back what we've lost—in terms of territory, at least. So there's great opportunity in the Milkpail right now, the opportunity that I assume you've all come here to find."

Gennadius went on, delivering an encouraging message without in the least fudging on the catastrophic facts of recent history.

"Sure, we've had severe problems, on the scope of some great natural disaster. But I—" The commander appeared to grope for words. "How can I put it? We are not facing some kind of demonic monsters here. I don't know how many of you hold beliefs of any kind in the supernatural, or what those beliefs are. But never mind that, it doesn't matter. What we are confronted with here are machines, just like— like this video recorder."

While he was talking, the door to the corridor had opened quietly, and Iskander had come in, with the captain right at his shoulder. Their arrival was in time for them to hear the base commander's philosophy regarding berserkers.

Domingo spoke one word, in a soft voice: "Leviathan." He said it as if it were the answer to some question that everyone in the room had been groping for.

"Welcome, Captain Domingo." Gennadius nodded toward the new arrivals. "A man who has had a very recent and very tragic experience with berserkers. He has—"

The captain smiled. It looked to Polly like a madman's smile. "Not just with berserkers, Commander. With one particular . . . machine. That word's inadequate, though, isn't it? *Machine.* And the experience, as you call it, was not simply tragic. No. Tell them the truth.''

Gennadius was exasperated now. ''Your world was attacked by one machine that people have given a name to, as if it were some great damned artificial pet. Or god, or idol. Well, it's none of those things. Why is the word *machine* inadequate? That's what a berserker is.''

''Oh, is it? Tell me more.'' Domingo's voice was still quiet.

''There's not much more to tell. Essentially. If you want to know the truth, it and the others are no more than overgrown, out-of-adjustment machines.''

Domingo had no comment on that for the moment. He listened in silence as the base commander continued his efforts to encourage the potential new colonists. With all the news of berserkers in the air, Gennadius said, he wanted to dissuade them from the idea that the obstacles were just too overwhelming. ''Some people get the notion that the berserker problem can never be managed. That's wrong. They're machines, that from our point of view happen to be malfunctioning. That's all they are. And if we can keep a sun from going nova, as we sometimes can, then we can ultimately manage a few machines.''

Domingo broke in at that point. ''You think Leviathan's only a machine? That it just happens to be out of adjustment?'' He paused. ''I'd like to show you what it is. I'd like you to be there when I pull out its heart.''

Gennadius coldly returned the captain's burning stare. ''You've had a hard time, Domingo, but you're not the only one who has. I respect what you've done, and what you've been through, but getting revenge on a piece of metal is a crazy enterprise, in my opinion.''

Polly sucked in her breath audibly. She sensed that the commander's words were a deliberate shock tactic, but she didn't think that it would work.

The would-be colonists were watching and listening very, very intently. Their heads turned back and forth like those of spectators at a match.

"Only a piece of metal. You think that?"

"That's what they are. You have some kind of evidence to the contrary to present? I'd like to see it."

"Is my body a machine? Or yours? Or was my daughter's? What was her body, Commander? What was it?"

There was a pause that seemed long. At last Gennadius said: "In a manner of speaking, I suppose we're all machines. I don't see the point of looking at it that way, though."

"I can see that you're a machine," said Domingo, looking at the commander speculatively.

Polly could feel her scalp creep. Not from the words; something in the tone.

The potential colonists were still watching and listening with great attention.

The commander, she could see, was working hard at being almost casual and even harder at being tolerant. Polly supposed he did not want to freight this madman's behavior with importance in the eyes of the others watching. "If you have tactical suggestions to make, Captain, I'll be glad to listen to them up in the operations room. Meanwhile there's something else I wish you'd work on. You're still mayor of Shubra. Some of these people might be interested in going there. I think it's your place, your duty, to talk to them and—"

"If I'm still mayor of any place, it's hell. As for your rebuilding, I want none of it."

"As mayor, you—"

"You want my resignation?"

"It's not my place to accept it. Talk to your citizens." Then the commander softened. "We've all lost, Niles. Not like you, maybe, but . . . we've got to start thinking of where we go from here. There are decisions that won't wait."

"I know what won't wait." Domingo looked at the commander, and at Polly. She could get no clue from his eyes as to what he expected her to do. A moment later he had left the room. When she followed him into the corridor, a few moments later, he and Iskander were already out of sight.

CHAPTER 5

The *Sirian Pearl*, along with the other ships of the Shubran civilian relief squadron, had seen no actual fighting and had sustained no damage while shuttling from one disaster to another. Such minor refitting as was required to get her perfectly ready for action had already been taken care of at the base. The Space Force had been eager to help with the maintenance. Gennadius wanted every human ship in the nebula to be as fully armed and equipped and ready for combat as possible.

More combat was expected soon, though with berserkers you never knew. Anyway, it was certain to come eventually.

The *Pearl* was almost alone in the docks, except for a few Space Force ships, a couple of them undergoing routine maintenance, a couple of others being held in reserve as transport and for defense in the unlikely event of a berserker attack on the base itself. Four Twenty-five had truly awesome ground defenses. From the enemy's point of calcula-

tion, there had to be more tempting targets out there in the
nebula, colonies only lightly defended now after the years of
relative peace and quiet.

Domingo's ship was solidly down in dock, with Gujar
Sidoruk and Iskander Baza walking and climbing over and
around her, giving everything on the outside a looking over,
probing with tools and fingers into missile-launching ports
and tubes, field projectors, the snouts and nozzles of beam
weapons. The checkout was really unnecessary, but Gujar at
least was nervous enough to need something to do. Iskander
had come along, and they talked while they conducted an
extra inspection.

Iskander, hands on hips, stood tall on the uppermost curve
of hull. He said: "You know, Sid?"

"What?"

"I'm really looking forward to taking this ship into action." He sounded more serious than usual.

Gujar straightened up from a beam nozzle and looked
about restlessly, swinging his electronic probe in one huge
hand. He responded that he himself was not looking forward
to anything. Going after Leviathan was just something he had
to do, and he wanted to get it over with.

Sidoruk was not as familiar with this ship as the other crew
members were. He had a few questions to ask about the new
weapons and systems Domingo had insisted on having built
into his ship.

Gujar had been taking it for granted that the *Pearl*'s
armaments were adequate for the formidable task Domingo
was planning. But now it seemed to him that, in answer to a
couple of his questions, Iskander was slyly trying to raise
some doubt in his mind, as if just for fun.

Gujar was still frowning in vague puzzlement when the
two men heard footsteps approaching, clomping up a flexible
ladder that curved around the curve of hull. Presently Polly
Suslova's head and shoulders came into sight. She greeted
the two men and asked, "Where's the captain?"

Baza smiled at her. "He's aboard. I looked in half an hour ago and he was sleeping."

Despite the smile, she had the feeling that this man was hostile to her, that somehow he felt possessive about the captain. Baza, as far as she was aware, had had no family anywhere, even before the Shubran massacre.

"Good," she said. "I'll let him sleep. He needs the rest." She looked at Gujar, who was leaning against the railing of the curving stair, gazing glumly into space. He didn't appear to be listening to the conversation, but it was hard to tell.

Polly faced back to Iskander, as the second-in-command asked her: "You think the captain's unhealthy? I don't."

"Have you seen him like this before?"

"Like what?" Polly could read no feeling in Iskander's smooth voice. "He's ready to hunt berserkers. If that makes him crazy, there're a lot of lunatics around."

"I'm sure there are. The point is that until a few days ago he wasn't one of them."

"He'll be all right, when he gets Leviathan." The broad-shouldered man sounded very confident.

That woke up Gujar. "If he can get it."

"He can."

Sidoruk turned around, frowning. "I thought you were just telling me our weapons might not be good enough."

Polly asked Iskander: "Do you think that's what Domingo needs?"

"He thinks so." Baza started to move past her to the ladder. "Excuse me, ma'am. It's time I went to operations and took a look at things."

Polly moved out of Iskander's way, but she had another question for him before he left. "You've known the captain a long time. Were you with him when that crash almost wiped out his family ten years ago?"

"I was. But you'd better ask him about that." And with a lightly mocking little salute, Iskander was gone.

Gujar Sidoruk had roused from his unhappy reverie enough

to pay attention to Polly's latest question. "What do you want to know about the crash?"

"I was wondering if berserkers were involved in that, too." Ships disappeared, sometimes, in every part of space, even without berserkers' help.

"Yes, I remember it well. It wasn't just berserkers. It was the same damned one."

Thinking of Domingo, Polly let out a little wordless moan of empathic pain. She sat down on the curve of hull—carefully; the metal tended to be slippery and there was a considerable drop. "Tell me."

"Well. His wife—her name was Isabel—and two of their three kids were on a ship coming back from somewhere, I forget where, to Shubra. The ship managed to send off a courier before she crashed. Her captain thought Leviathan was chasing them, and the courier message said he was just about to take some risky evasive action. That was all that anyone ever heard from that ship. Either the berserker got them, or he wrecked his ship trying to get away from it. Tried to go too fast in a cloud, or whatever. No lifeboats ever showed up anywhere. No survivors."

"I see," Polly murmured again.

Again someone's feet were clanging solidly up the ladder. In a few moments Simeon's head came into view. "There you are—some of you, anyway. There's news. One of Gennadius's squadrons is supposed to be straggling back in here to the base, all shot up. They tightbeamed a message ahead, saying they've just fought a battle."

"And?"

"Mixed results, apparently."

Polly grabbed for the ladder. "Coming, Gujar?"

He shook his head slowly. "You go ahead. I want to look over a few more things here. Whatever the news is, I expect we'll be launching before long."

Polly descended the ladder quickly. There was someone else who would certainly want to hear the latest combat news the instant it became available. Iskander had said that Domingo was asleep. She debated briefly with herself, then opened the nearest convenient hatch and entered the ship.

The captain was not in his berth. Well, she supposed it had been foolish to look for him there, no matter what Iskander had said. She found Domingo in the common room again, sitting slumped over and motionless at the console beside his computer model, almost on top of it. His face, with the reflected colors of the glowing model playing over it, was turned toward Polly as she entered and she was worried for a moment; he looked absolutely dead.

A closer look reassured her. Domingo was breathing deeply and comfortably, getting what was probably one of his first real sleeps since the disaster. But Polly, sure that he would want to know the news, decided to wake him anyway. She shook him by the shoulder.

The captain's eyes opened at once, and he saw her without apparent surprise. He was glad to be awakened for the news, grim as it was, and was on his feet at once. Pausing only to shut down some of his equipment, he moved toward Operations with purposeful strides, Polly tagging along.

They were in time to be present when Base Commander Gennadius greeted the arriving crews.

The newly arrived military ships had brought with them another item of related news: yet another berserker attack upon a colony, the third in recent days. This time the target had been Malaspina, a planetoid of a sun that was relatively distant within the nebula. Malaspina was known for the foul "weather"—nebular turbulence and activity—that usually afflicted both its atmosphere and its surrounding space.

Before the returning fleet had fought its recent battle, its ships had picked up some peculiar radio messages from the direction of the colonized planetoid Malaspina, messages reporting the sighting of strange ships or objects in the nebula near Malaspina. Very shortly after picking up the radio transmissions, the fleet had been found by a robot courier from the attacked colony. The courier brought an urgent and now horribly familiar message: Colony under berserker attack.

Gennadius, as he listened to this story, appeared to be trying to remember something. "Malaspina. Wasn't there another report of some really peculiar nebular life forms around there just a standard month ago?"

Some of his aides standing nearby were able to confirm this.

"That's not all," said one of the exhausted ship captains who had just arrived. According to later messages received by the rescue fleet, some of the people at the third colony were reported to have behaved bizarrely during the attack.

"Hysteria," said someone on the base commander's staff.

"I suppose. Anyway, one of the radio messages we got said they were acting crazy—tearing off their clothes, singing. Running around wild, I guess. Those were about all the details we heard."

"You have recordings?"

"Of the action we just fought? They'll be along in a minute, Commander."

Others among the people at Base Four Twenty-five, who were now trying to evaluate events, at first attributed the reported bizarre behavior of the people at the colony, during the attack and immediately following it, to the effects of some virus.

The task force, responding with all possible speed to the courier-borne report of that attack, had arrived at the battered colony in time to save it from destruction.

The combat recordings were now being brought into the operations room. Polly retreated into the background, but no one cared if she and the other colonists present stayed to watch.

The light in the large room dimmed slightly, and a stage brightened. The ranking officer of the task force that had just arrived introduced the combat recordings, which told the story.

When the powerful Space Force battle group had appeared

on the scene, the berserker raiding fleet had broken off its assault on Malaspina and retreated. The Space Force had arrived none too soon; the battle had been going badly for the human side until then. Three or possibly four berserkers had been engaged in this latest attack.

A staff officer swore. "Look at that; some kind of new shielding. Cuts off the defensive beams from the ground as if they were flashlights."

"That explains how they were able to overrun Liaoning and Shubra so fast and easy."

When the berserkers retreated from their attack on the Malaspina colony, the human task force had pursued and engaged them again after a chase of about an hour.

Again, disengagement by the enemy and pursuit by the Space Force. This time the human squadron had promptly run into a well-executed ambush. Loop back on your own trail within the nebula—if you could manage that—and ambushing a pursuer came within the realm of possibility. Shortly thereafter, having suffered a reverse and again lost contact with the enemy, the commander of the Space Force battle group turned back to protect Malaspina.

Gennadius nodded. "You say you'd already left a detachment there."

"That's right."

Gennadius now tried to decide where he could get ships to relieve the ones now on duty at Malaspina. The enemy was enjoying such success that he had to think of the defense of the base itself. "The best I can do is send some Home Guard ships to Malaspina—if I can come up with enough civilian volunteers." He switched the direction of his gaze. "Domingo?"

Domingo, who had been listening intently, ignored the question. He asked the returning officers: "Was Old Blue there, at Malaspina and afterward? There was a unit that looked like it in that recording, but I couldn't be sure."

Some of the men and women exchanged looks. "Oh yeah," said one. "No doubt about it."

"You didn't destroy it." It was more a statement than a question.

"No. We didn't."

Polly thought she saw her captain's shoulders slump slightly, as if with relief. Domingo said: "I'd like to see the rest of your gun-camera records as soon as possible."

Another look was exchanged among the haggard captains of the surviving task force: *Who is this guy?*

Gennadius seconded Domingo's question.

"Coming right up, sir."

Soon additional records had been brought in. These confirmed conclusively, and in stop-action detail, the presence of Leviathan in the action off Malaspina.

It was Polly's first good look at the thing called Old Blue—the fragmentary recording from Shubran ground defense hardly counted. Here there were views from several angles, in different wavelengths. Imaging techniques corrected for the exaggerated Doppler effect of high-speed combat. This was about as good a look at Leviathan as anyone had ever had and survived. Polly and the others watching with her now beheld a great, ancient, angular and damaged shape, with some blue coloring about it; she had heard that the color was thought to be the result of some emissions from some defective component of the drive or other peculiar system on board.

Polly watched. *That is his special enemy, and therefore it is mine. If I can't turn him from his purpose, maybe I can help him to achieve it. Maybe then . . .*

They were frightening pictures, but to her, Domingo's face as he studied them was more frightening still.

Gennadius, without taking his eye from the new recording as it played again, beckoned an aide over to him. Polly heard the base commander issuing orders to pass on word of what he saw as a disastrous battle to Eighth Space Force headquarters, at the Sector capital. A manned courier, recently arrived at Four Twenty-five, was about to head back to headquarters and could carry this bad news with it.

Gennadius was now asking the crew of the courier if there was much chance of his getting any reinforcement from Sector Headquarters in the near future.

"Wouldn't count on that, sir. There's berserker trouble in other districts, too, and Sector's chronically spread thin."

"Yes. Damn, damn. That's about what I thought; maybe even a little worse than I thought." Gennadius turned his gaze to the big display. "We're just going to have to mobilize all the colonies in the Milk as best we can."

"Yes, sir."

The commander addressed himself to another aide. "Next courier we send to Sector, I want to tell them I'm invoking martial law over the whole Milkpail district. Get that in print for me to sign."

Then his eyes swiveled to Domingo. "Niles, I want you to take your people, all of 'em that are ready to fight and all your ships, and stand by for Home Guard duty. Might be at Malaspina, might be somewhere else."

"I've told you where I stand on that, Gennadius. Captains who want to do that can. I have other plans for my own ship. And for as many of my crew as will come with me."

"Oh. And what plans are those?"

"I'm hunting for Leviathan."

The room was quiet enough for Polly to hear the sigh Gennadius let out. "With one ship. That doesn't make any sense. I've told you what I need done. If you won't do that, then just go home and stay there."

"Home. Oh yes, home. Where is that?"

"Go somewhere and stay out of my hair, then. Sorry, Domingo. But other people are hurting, too. And this time it *is* an order. I'm invoking martial law."

There was a long pause before Domingo spoke. His answer when it came was surprisingly meek. "All right, Gennadius. I'll be out of your way from now on."

Domingo summoned his crew to him with a look around the room, and they followed him when he went out quietly. When they were gathered around him in the corridor just outside operations, he announced quietly that he wanted to have a crew meeting in his ship immediately.

A minute or two later the six of them were gathered in the common room aboard the *Pearl*. The captain looked around the little group and told them he had allowed the Space Force people to think he was obeying their orders meekly, that he would go home and see what could be done to make Shubra livable and defendable again.

"But if any of you actually thought I was going to obey that order, forget it. This ship is going on with the hunt just as before."

Henric Poinsot had joined the others in their gathering outside operations, and he had accompanied them to the ship, saying he wanted to remove a few personal things that he had left aboard.

But Poinsot now came into the common room and asked the captain: "What about the other people from Shubra?"

"What about them?"

"I mean that we have about twenty of our fellow citizens still here at the base who'll want to know what the hell you're doing, Domingo. About Shubra, if nothing else. You're still officially the mayor."

"I'll nominate you to take a message to them. They can have my formal resignation, if they want it. If any of you get tired of gazing at the wreckage where you used to live, you can try to join me later. But I'm not waiting for you."

The captain spoke coldly and contemptuously. The people who knew Domingo best, better than Polly had yet had a chance to get to know him, were gazing at him strangely. If he was aware of it, he gave no sign.

Iskander Baza watched his captain narrowly and then exchanged looks with Polly. She wondered if the message was that he intended to be her ally or her rival.

Henric Poinsot said: "You're disregarding the commander's orders, then. I'm making no promises to keep any of this secret, Domingo."

"Tell who you like, and be damned to you. It'll save me the trouble of leaving a message somewhere else."

Poinsot looked around at them all, started to speak again, thought better of it and went out.

Domingo looked around at them all, too. "Anyone else? Now's the time."

"I'm hunting with you," Gujar Sidoruk said.

"Good. Polly?"

"I'll go," she said at once. It came to her as she said it that her chief fear at the moment was only of being separated from him. She was more afraid of that than of berserkers. When she tried to think of her children, all she could know of them at the moment was that they were far away and safe.

"Iskander—? I guess in your case I don't have to ask. Wilma, Simeon, what about you?"

The married couple spoke haltingly. Taking turns speaking, looking at each other between phrases, they said that they had lost heavily to the berserkers and wanted revenge. Polly got the impression that there was more to their decision than they were saying.

The *Pearl* was already gone when Poinsot told Gennadius of Domingo's decision. The base commander, his mind heavily engaged with other matters, only nodded and sighed. Knowing Domingo, he was not all that surprised.

All Gennadius said was, "Well. We've each done what we had to do, I guess."

Regretfully he removed the *Sirian Pearl* from his roster of Home Guard craft. He would have to remind himself to count it as lost from now on, and it was going to make his job just that much harder.

CHAPTER 6

The *Pearl*, with Gujar Sidoruk now aboard her as a member of her crew, departed Base Four Twenty-five without filing an official flight plan.

Her captain set a course and then turned the flight controls over to Iskander Baza, his second-in-command. After a few words with Baza, Domingo headed for his cabin berth—his tiny padded cell, or womb, was more like it, he thought—to try to get some rest. Getting to his berth was easy. He had only to crawl through the short, narrow padded tunnel that connected the captain's duty station with the captain's private quarters, the latter only a hollow, padded cylinder, no roomier or more luxurious than the berth of anyone else aboard the ship.

The captain's quarters, like the other berths aboard, had room enough to house only one person comfortably, and that only by the standards of a military ship. Still, two people had been known to occupy this cabin on occasion.

There would be no cabinmate on this voyage. Domingo

removed some of his outer clothing, turned down the intensity of the cabin lights and the various displays and settled himself to try to get some sleep if possible. If he couldn't sleep, he would take something . . .

There was no need for him to take anything. His exhaustion was greater than he had imagined. Almost immediately, Domingo slept.

And dreamed.

Never, in the course of the deathlike sleeps that overcame him in this last epoch of his monstrously altered life, had the captain dreamed of Maymyo his murdered daughter, flesh of his flesh. Nor had he ever, before or after the obliteration of the Shubran colony, dreamed about berserkers.

Such visions as had come in sleep to Domingo since that disaster were few and seemed meaningless. But now, riding his new ship in pursuit of his mortal enemy, he knew the recurrence of a particular dream that he had not had for years. In this dream he was near Isabel, his wife, and the two of his three children, all little ones then, who had been with her when she died. Maymyo, his third child, had no part in this dream; she had somehow been wiped away, as if she had never existed. In this dream the ship carrying three members of his young family had come home to Shubra after all. The reports of its destruction had been only an accident, a great mistake, now satisfactorily explained away.

In the dream he, Domingo, was back on Shubra, working peacefully outdoors under the pearly sky, and Isabel was somewhere near him. Though he could not see her, he knew his wife was there, somewhere just out of sight, and he knew she had the two little children safely with her. He felt so sure of Isabel's nearness, her availability, that he was not even worried because she was not visible. It was no problem for Domingo that he still could not see her moment by moment as the dream wore on.

In this dream he himself was always busy, trying to do something, accomplish some task. What the job was, he could never remember when the dream was over. But while the dream was in progress, this work, whatever it was, kept him too intently occupied to even try to look at Isabel . . .

She was there, and at any moment now he would complete his work and be able to go to her.

He awoke from the dream alone in his berth on his new ship, aware of the light-years of emptiness just outside the hull.

On departing the base, Domingo had not turned his ship immediately in the direction of Malaspina, as some of his crew had anticipated. He hoped and expected to be able to pick up a fresher trail than that.

About two days after leaving Base Four Twenty-five, the *Sirian Pearl* arrived at the scene of the last fight reported by Gennadius's battered squadron. More often than not, solid Galactic coordinates were almost impossible to determine inside the Milkpail, but there could be no mistaking the still-widening disturbances that had been left in this region by the weapons used in the recent battle. Shockwaves expanding at kilometers per second for a number of days had made quite a conspicuous disturbance.

"Figure it out," Iskander said to Simeon, to whom most of this business of searching and trailing in the nebula was new. "Say an expansion rate of ten kilometers a second; then in a little more than a day you have a bulging cloud about a million kilometers across." Such a disturbed cloud was still a tiny tumor in the guts of an object the size of the Milkpail, big enough to contain a dozen known solar systems and perhaps a few more that had not yet been discovered.

Quite apart from the battle's gaudy traces, this region of the nebula was a place of unearthly beauty, of scenery remarkably spectacular even for nebular space. Sharp variations in nebular density, of unknown cause, suggested titanic pillars, domes and other architectural features. Some of the fantastic shapes could be interpreted as halls and mansions, built on a scale to contain planets.

The *Pearl* moved steadily on through these and similar vistas.

Wilma said once, looking into a screen that was almost like a window: "Some people used to think that heaven looked like this. All white clouds and marble halls."

No other ships had joined Domingo in his hunt, and there was no reason to think that any were likely to do so. Most of the *Pearl*'s crew were worried by that fact, but Domingo never seemed worried now, by that or anything else.

Except for one thing: that something might keep him from getting at Leviathan.

Simeon and Wilma began to wonder aloud what their friends who had declined to take up the chase were doing. The captain ignored their wondering, as he ignored much else.

Now the obsessed man displayed fanatical patience. He briefed his crew carefully on exactly what he wanted, then ordered two of them into their space armor and sent them out in the launch to begin a methodical investigation. The idea was to sift as minutely and carefully as they could through the thinly scattered debris of this battlefield, gathering samples of microscopic dust and thin gas, looking for material that would convey information of any kind about the berserkers, particularly Leviathan.

More precisely, of course, the idea was to find the trail of Old Blue's departure. To this end, the *Pearl* circled the volume of space in which the battle had taken place, stopping at intervals to let out the launch and the suited collectors. This process continued for half a day until they had closed in on what Domingo considered the most promising place to start a really detailed search. And to augment the human crew, a couple of service robots were put to work in space.

The nebula here was still torn and mottled by the contending energies that ships and machines had spent against each other. Most of the battle-distorted clouds were still expanding, at meters or tens of meters or perhaps even greater distances per second, fading and intermingling with other material as they swelled. But emission clouds, red-shifting now as they cooled and contracted, were splashed like blood through the contorted whiteness. That these particular clouds were contracting was a hopeful sign; shrinking clots of murk would not hide a trail as still-expanding clouds might easily have done.

Whatever departure trails might exist here were already badly blurred out with the passage of several standard days since the battle was fought. The natural movements of material in the nebula were wiping the traces away. But Domingo stubbornly urged on the search.

Polly continued to observe her captain whenever she had the chance. She had tried to convince herself that she was accompanying him on this mad expedition at least in part for the sake of her children, to rid the Milkpail of the horror called Old Blue so that these little worlds would offer safe places in which her offspring might grow up and live. That would have been a worthy goal, but in her heart she knew better. She was doing this because she could not really help herself.

The man I love, she thought, gazing again at his intercom image and wondering about him and about herself. She had no history of falling as drastically as this for men. Particularly for men who showed no special interest in her. She wondered also if her feelings were obvious to others. Probably they would be, she decided, if everyone weren't moving around in a state of benumbed shock just now, if all this hell weren't going on. Maybe then her attitude would have been noticeable even to him.

Now she wished that she had managed to talk to Gennadius about him before they left Base Four Twenty-five. But she hadn't. There hadn't really been time, for one thing. The base commander had been continuously busy. And Domingo had seemed strong and capable again—as he still did—and he and Gennadius had obviously been at least temporarily at odds with each other.

She wanted to have a real talk with Iskander sometime, too; she thought she didn't understand him at all. But so far she had somehow not been able to arrange it. She thought that Baza was now closer to Domingo than anyone else was, though the relationship did not seem to fall into any neat category.

Her worry about Domingo was as intense as before, though now, active in the chase, he looked stronger and more capable than ever, and his behavior since they had left the base had given her no new cause for alarm. He seemed buoyed up, energetic and almost happy, as long as he could keep driving toward his goal of vengeance. Vengeance on a piece of metal, as Gennadius had described it at one point. But Polly was worried by Domingo's happy energy. *He's going to snap*, she thought. *Or something. He hasn't had time to grieve over his daughter properly yet. Coming on top of what happened ten years ago, the shock of Maymyo's death has turned him away, somehow, from being human.*

There were periods, sometimes of hours, more often only of minutes, when she almost managed to convince herself that her fears were wrong, based on a mistaken assessment. He was just an extraordinarily tough man, and he had survived the blow of his daughter's death. Naturally he was still enraged at the universe, and challenging his bitter fate. Eventually he was going to be all right.

But the conviction could not last for long; her fears returned.

Carrying out the search for microscopic evidence just the way Domingo wanted it done was not an easy job. In the common room, at the daily meeting for discussion and planning, Gujar Sidoruk protested: "We need a fleet to do this properly."

Domingo paid little attention to the protest. "Well, we don't have a fleet. But we're going to do it effectively anyway."

Several more standard days passed while the search went on. The *Pearl* prowled slowly. She was beautifully designed for almost any type of nebular work, built by the almost legendary teams of master artisans and computers working in the orbital yards of faraway Austeel. She glided forward steadily, a huge silvered egg, at the center of the little formation of people and machines that searched the nebula around her, all of them continuously taking samples, testing, seeking patterns.

Polly had her own suit of custom-designed space armor, a tool that came in handy fairly often in her regular job. Now she was out of the launch, working in what was sometimes called milkspace, searching. And trying to keep from being distracted by the scenery. Not that the environment outside a ship was anything new to her; she had been born on one planetoid within the Milkpail and raised on another. But still her opportunities to get a direct look at a region of the nebula as exotic as this one had been few and far between.

She was not watching the view of marble halls and eternal sunrises on a holostage connected to her instruments now, or on a screen, but looking at the nebula itself through the transparent solid of her faceplate. It was difficult for the eye to interpret the pictures that presented themselves under these conditions, the subtly different hues of pearl and bone, milk and chalk and fine-grained snow. Just how big was *that* particular cloud formation, how far away . . . ?

And visible within the clouds at times there was movement, not all of it inanimately caused. Life grew here, and sometimes it swarmed in profusion. Creatures of microscopic size could alter the shape of a cloud or change the quality of light when they moved in sufficient numbers. The changes did not signify intelligence or sentience; those qualities were apparently more than the ubiquitous energies of life could organize within matter this attenuated. But on the microscopic and near-microscopic level, there was a rich variety of life.

The discovery Domingo had been trying for, of a departure trail that might be followed, so far had not been made. Bits of evidence would be very easy to miss, here among the distractions of beauty and danger and strange life.

"You're going to need all your luck, Cap," Iskander Baza told him.

"Luck?" Domingo squinted at Baza. "What does this

have to do with luck?'' Leviathan itself was surely not a matter of luck; the malevolent purpose of the ancient Builders flowed in its circuits as surely as the life flowed in any human being's veins and nerves. Whatever else it might be, it was no accident. Nor were his own encounters with the damned thing accidental. Domingo was sure of that now, certain on the deepest possible level. He could close his eyes and feel it.

The hoped-for trail might still elude discovery, but the search had also already yielded information of another kind about the berserkers. Computer analysis showed that certain inhuman, unusual organic traces were to be found in the nebular material where the battle had been fought. In itself, organic matter in the nebula was nothing very unusual. There was, after all, an industry devoted to harvesting and processing it. But here, in one sample, the ship's computer was able to detect evidence of deliberate genetic manipulation, laboratory work performed on the molecular level.

"I'd say that's the kind of debris you'd get from micro-microsurgery. Whatever the process was, it must have been performed on a large scale for us to be able to pick up traces of it now.''

"It can't be from one of the Space Force ships, then. Are berserkers starting to do surgery?''

"They've been known to engage in biological research.''

"Well, true, it wouldn't be the first time in history they've tried it. But maybe the evidence is misleading. This could be just berserker parts and parts of some human researcher's equipment and results, all mashed into the same cloud.''

"What human researcher would that be? Working out here?''

No one could come up with an answer for that.

For the berserkers to attempt biological warfare against ED humanity by means of microorganisms was nothing new. Historically the death machines had rarely had much success with the tactics of spreading disease. If they were trying it again, probably they had calculated some new variation.

But what was it?

Alternatively, the theoretical and practical problems of disease and how to spread it might not be what suddenly interested the berserkers in the field of biology.

But, what was it then?

The main computer on the *Pearl* announced that it now had a sufficiency of data; it was ready to present a model of the battle.

CHAPTER 7

The common room on the *Sirian Pearl* was the only place aboard ship where six people could meet face to face and still have a little central space to spare. The greater part of that central space was presently occupied by a holostage, and on that holostage the ship's computer was currently engaged in building an elaborate image-model of the local disturbances within the nebula. For the time being the other model, the one that showed the whole Milkpail, had been tucked back into the data storage banks.

Not that the six people of the crew were very often in the common room at the same time. At least two were usually at their duty stations, on watch. And each of them had a private cylindrical cabin adjoining one of the six duty stations. Like Domingo's cabin, the five others were little more than large padded barrels furnished with cots, communications and plumbing. Polly, like several other people, spent a fair amount of time in the common room, sitting beside the stage and watching the construction job with interest. With even greater interest, but less openly, she also watched Domingo, who was fanatically intent upon the model.

When the model displaying current local conditions was completed, the computer, on the captain's order, ran it through an extrapolation back in time. The dispersed explosions that were only dimly detectable in the nebula itself became smaller and clearer in the model as the extrapolation progressed. The tentatively charted tracks of disturbance assumed a sharper, more definite form. Now it was possible to have a much more precise view of what had happened here some days ago in the battle between the Space Force and the berserkers.

Here, at this side of the display, was where the Space Force ships had been during the first moment of confrontation. And over there on the other side had been the enemy, four or possibly five berserkers in all, strung out in a jagged line some hundreds of kilometers long that might or might not have been meant as a tactical formation. That much, the positions before tactical movement started, could be confidently read from the reconstructed cloud disturbances and the distributions of trace elements in the clouds. So could the positions at the start of fighting. The opposing types of weapons, when fired, and even the drive engines had left subtly different flavors in the resultant expanding gasses.

Combat maneuvers must have begun immediately when the opposing forces sighted each other—indeed, the human survivors had so reported. The course of events after the fight had started was harder to reconstruct. Domingo called for more sampling in selected areas. Armored people went out into space again, and the computer kept working.

Gujar, who had been so eager to sign on, began grumbling. "Why is he doing this? Has he ever told us exactly why?"

Iskander smiled faintly. "He's looking for a trail. Domingo knows what he's doing."

"Does he? I can see scanning the area for that. Not that there would be much chance of finding anything. But what difference does it make what the exact positions were of all the units?''

"We'll see." Iskander still sounded confident.

When the additional data gathered by a few more hours' work in space was fed into the computer, the pictured past became visible in greater detail. Two Space Force ships, as reported by the crews of the surviving vessels, had blown up with all hands lost. A couple of berserkers had also been destroyed—their climactic finishes were plain to see, marked by radii of flying debris. And at least one more of the enemy had been badly damaged.

The battered berserker had got away. It must have done so, because it was nowhere in the immediate vicinity now, and no image of its annihilation in a death-blast had been imprinted on the clouds. Evidently the other surviving berserkers had departed unhurt or only lightly damaged. There were faint and fading tracks for them, too attenuated to try to follow. But the badly damaged bandit had gone its own way, and it had certainly left a spoor behind it—a thousand times too thin for the eye to see, but evident to the technique of computer-analyzed sampling. A staggering trail of particles, a skein of what would have been smoke in atmosphere, a fading blaze of heat and radiation, led off toward an unexplored portion of the Milkpail into the heart of a white knot of nebula as wide as the orbit of the distant Earth.

"That's it! That's it. By all the gods, we'll get one of them now." The captain's voice was a hoarse whisper.

As soon as he had accepted the conclusion of the computer model, Domingo recalled those of his crew who were still outside the ship engaged in the task of gathering more data. Only two robots, attached to auxiliary power and shielding systems that let them cruise at a sufficient speed in space, remained outside still working at that task. The two mobile robots, Domingo calculated, should be enough to sniff out the trail, now that its origin was located. The moving fields of the ship would drag the small machines with her as she advanced.

The *Pearl* moved out again, running a little faster than before, hunting now with weapons ready. The model in the common room was continuously updated as the robots continued to take samples at distances of up to a few hundred kilometers from the moving ship and to telemeter the results in to the *Pearl*'s main computer.

Excitement grew. Polly took her brief periods of rest grudgingly, afraid of what discoveries she might miss. Between rest periods she observed Domingo, snatched bites of food, stood watch in her turn and otherwise helped out where she could. She had seen an effort vaguely like this search attempted once before, by someone else, and not successfully. That time the quarry had been a lost ship, presumably willing to be found, not a berserker.

She said to him once: "You really know how to do this, Captain."

At the moment he looked happy and, despite the long hours of concentrated effort, almost relaxed. As if, Polly thought, everything were normal.

He said: "Better than the Space Force, anyway."

Following the trail was slow, hard work from the start. Within the first hour the track of the enemy became blurred, but the robots worked tirelessly and it was not lost. Gradually the job became easier, the gradient of increasing density of certain battle remnants in the nebula becoming better and better defined. The speed of the chase increased until at last it began to seem possible that they would someday catch something—unless, of course, their prey were to increase its speed as well.

The *Pearl* was already a billion kilometers into unmarked whiteness, far off such charts as existed for this portion of the nebula. Determining the location of the ship within it, even roughly, was no longer a trivial problem. Even the brightest suns could no longer be located with any certainty amid the thickening, muffling clouds of white, off-white and gray, the ever-changing pastel shades of perpetual interstellar dawns and sunsets. It was not unheard of for ships to simply vanish in the Milkpail, even in regions where no berserker activity had ever been reported.

There followed another blurring of the track, leading to a more prolonged slowdown. But this delay too was temporary, the trail firming again within a standard day.

Time passed quickly, at least for Polly, working, sleeping, watching. People off duty still took time for conversation in the common room, watching the model transform itself. And Wilma and Simeon still thought aloud, at least in the captain's absence, that the pursuit would ultimately prove hopeless.

But within two more days it was unarguable that they were still following the berserker's trail, and at an increasingly effective speed. The trail seemed fresher now, which meant that the enemy was probably no longer as far ahead as it had been.

That fact sank in. When the crew had begun this voyage, they had all still been in something of a state of shock. But by now that was wearing off. They had started to think about what they were doing: chasing a berserker.

And the pursuit could no longer be considered hopeless. Polly began to wonder what would happen when and if they actually did catch up to the wounded thing they were pursuing. Certainly the *Pearl* was heavily armed and her crew capable. But still.

Were they closing in on Old Blue? Polly, like most colonists in the Milkpail, had heard the name many times, and some of the legendary stories. She had a healthy respect for berserkers, but like Commander Gennadius she had never considered one of them more terrible than another just because someone had given it a name. Now, though . . . there had been something disturbing about the jagged, illogical-seeming shape of Leviathan in the recordings and the theatrical blue glow. But the blue light could be reasonably explained as an accidental effect of some kind of radiation. And as for the jagged form, who knew why berserker machines were sometimes built in one shape, sometimes in another? Ran-

domness, that was always said to be one of their important
concepts . . .

Whatever the reason for its peculiarities, it still seemed to
Polly that one berserker, any berserker, just because it had
acquired a name, ought not to be necessarily more frightening than another. Not that she had ever actually fought any of
them, but . . . and whatever type of a machine it was that
they were chasing, it was certain that it had already been
seriously damaged; and that was reassuring.

Domingo had the six people of the crew divided into two
watches now: three driving the ship, manning the weapons
and studying the computer-modeled trail while the other three
rested and slept and talked and waited for their turns on duty.
In this way the hunt kept going hour after hour, one standard
day after another.

The captain seldom slept or rested now. Polly, watching
him, saw the chiseling of his face grow sharper; otherwise he
seemed unaffected by lack of rest.

The folds of nebula flowed ever more thickly around the
Pearl. This did not slow the progress of the ship, already
limited by the need to find a trail and stay with it. But it did
raise the possibility of ambush.

Gujar, operating the forward detectors on his watch, excit-
edly called in a sighting, and Iskander at the helm slowed
forward progress. But the sighting proved to be a false alarm.

When the object appeared at close range it was seen to be a
peculiar thing, some kind of natural life-construct, with
stalactite-like formations protruding from it in all directions.
It throbbed, faintly and slowly, with the working of the life
within it. Not a single organism, the instruments indicated,
but some kind of a composite form. The thing, or creature, or
life-swarm, or whatever it was, appeared next on the close
forward detectors and finally on the direct-viewing screens.
Then it drifted by the *Pearl* at a range of only a few kilometers. It was vastly bigger than the ship. There was no indication that it was aware of the ship at all.

Relative to the nebular material immediately surrounding

it, the object was moving at a significant fraction of the
velocity of light, a speed that any ship or machine of equal
size would have found practically impossible to attain.

No one on the ship had seen or even heard about anything
like it before. At any other time the humans would have
turned aside eagerly to investigate. But not now.

When the living conglomerate was out of sight, Simeon
and Wilma made a tentative and ill-advised attempt to per-
suade the captain to turn around and go back to Base Four
Twenty-five. They argued that the crew of the *Pearl* could
now report to the Space Force what they had found regarding
the berserkers and consider they had done a creditable job.
Gennadius would thank them.

Domingo did not thank them for the suggestion.

The truth was that most of his crew, everyone but himself
and Iskander, were growing increasingly uncomfortable in
this weird place. Even to people who were more or less at
home in the uncanny environment of the Milkpail Nebula,
this thickening, curdling, mottled whiteness, engendering new
monsters, was extraordinary. Among the uncomfortable majority the opinion was subtly gaining strength that it was, or
ought to be, the job of the Space Force to carry on with this
kind of pursuit.

Domingo was inflexibly opposed to any change of course
and overrode the hints of opposition. He even touched in
passing on the laws of mutiny. In port a crew might, and his
usually did, have the right to vote on big decisions. In deep
space the captain's word was law, and the law applied with
redoubled force when the berserker enemy was near.

The captain did agree to send off one of their two expensive robot couriers, directed to Base Four Twenty-five, before
he continued his pursuit of the damaged berserker.

The courier departed silently, carrying word of their discoveries, their present location and their intentions to Base
Four Twenty-five. They hoped. The chance that it would
succeed in getting there was hard to calculate.

Now there was only one usable courier left aboard. Here in

clouds where radio was hopeless, it represented the only
possible means of communication with the rest of humanity.

The pursuit of the wounded berserker resumed. More hours
passed, adding up to another day. Tension grew aboard the
ship as the trail became stronger, more clearly defined than it
had ever been. Whatever was leaving the trail was undoubtedly closer ahead now than ever before. Sizable bits of
debris, even fist-sized chunks of this and that, began to show
up in the scans still being telemetered in from the outrider
robots.

"That's berserker stuffing." Domingo said it softly, with
obvious enjoyment.

A powerful blast centered somewhere ahead sent a silent
but more-than-detectable shockwave through the white nebula.

Chakuchin made a relieved sound. "It's blown itself up.
That's it."

"We'll see." Domingo's intensity did not alter.

Inside the *Pearl*, whose forward velocity, even here within
the buffeting whiteness, could be conveniently expressed as a
fraction of the speed of light, the enormously slower shockwave
could be studied on the detectors for some time before it
engulfed the ship.

But whatever might be, or might have been, at the center
of the shock to cause it still could not be seen.

Domingo ordered acceleration. And more acceleration. Particles of matter, molecule-sized, pinged dangerously against
the shielding fields that so far were managing to protect the
hull from microcollisions at relativistic speeds. Indicators glowed
with warning signals.

The captain ordered: "Give up the trail. Head for the
center of that shock." The location of the center could be
determined from the automatic recording of the event.

"Double alert for an ambush. Just in case."

On the screens of the forward detectors, the image of an
object considerably bigger than the *Pearl* took shape and
rapidly solidified. It was angular, irregular and metallic,

about at the upper limit of size for effective travel within the nebula.

"Hold your fire!" the captain ordered sharply.

Whatever kind of a machine it was ahead of them, it was not Leviathan. The shape was as jagged as Leviathan's, but still totally wrong for that, if any of the descriptions and recordings of the monster were correct. Polly heard the captain sigh, a sound that might have come from the lips of a disappointed lover.

The second most obvious characteristic of the object they had just caught up with was the remarkable amount of fresh damage that it had sustained. The ruin looked too genuine and extensive to be any kind of trick. As they approached the wreck ever more closely there was hard radiation, too, wild and irregular in both intensity and kind, but always enough of it to suggest that there might be a small-scale nuclear meltdown in progress somewhere on the enemy.

It appeared that secondary explosions, delayed battle damage—or more likely a deliberate destructor charge, set off in anticipation of capture by the forces of life—had left this particular berserker unit, whatever it was exactly, drifting in a helpless condition.

The humans aboard the *Pearl* observed the enemy warily from a thousand kilometers' distance; then from a hundred; and then again from ten.

Simeon said, with the air of someone trying to establish an assertion as undoubted fact: "Now we've got to go back and report."

Polly, watching on her intercom, saw Niles Domingo's eyes turn to the big young man, one image glaring at another. The captain squelched Chakuchin's effort immediately: "We can't. We'll lose it if we do. Do you expect that we, or anyone else, will be able to find the way back to it again in this fog?" In another day or so the trail they had followed would have been completely dispersed by random drifting and other natural movements. There were currents in the nebula; it was at least as dynamic as an ocean of water on the surface of a planet.

"All right, then I suppose we finish it off. We have our missiles armed."

"They'd better be. But don't use any of them just yet."

"But what else can we do?" Chakuchin paused, as if realization had just come to him. "Are you expecting to send some of us over to board that thing? It may just be waiting to use its main destructor charge until something living comes close enough to be wiped out in the blast."

"I think it's already used whatever destructor charges it had left. And I'll lead the boarding myself, if that's what's bothering you. Can I talk two other people into suiting up with me? If not, I'll go alone. Polly, what about you?" The captain's eyes looked out from the little intercom screen and into hers. "We could use your technical expertise."

"I'll go," Polly heard herself agree at once. Then she trembled, thinking of her children. But she could not unsay what she had said. Not to Niles Domingo. She could silently curse the unasked-for fate that bound her to him, but it was her fate still, and she would not have changed it had she had the power.

Iskander, as usual, had not much to say, but he was plainly ready, even eager, to go where his captain led.

Gujar repeated Simeon's suggestion: "We could just fire away at it . . ."

But Domingo was silent this time, and this time the suggestion died without argument. The objections to it were too plain. Self-destruction was doubtless what the berserker had wanted to achieve, but something had gone wrong with the destructor charges.

That it had tried to destroy itself when capture by its enemy seemed imminent at least suggested that there was still something aboard that might constitute a valuable secret, perhaps even a clue to where the berserkers attacking the Milkpail colonies had their repair and construction base.

Conceivably there might even be human prisoners still

living on that wreck. That there could be seemed doubtful, but berserkers did take prisoners sometimes for the information that could be gained from them, for living bodies and living minds on which to experiment.

Domingo was continuing to study the helpless-looking enemy, switching rapidly from one instrument of observation to another and back again. This was not Leviathan in front of him, but it represented the only immediate chance he had of getting closer to Leviathan. He mused aloud in his newly intense voice: "This is too damned strange. It's not like any berserker I ever saw or heard of before now. We can't miss the chance, we've got to go over there and see what we can find out from it."

Simeon suggested: "We've still got one courier. Let's send it off first, at least. Tell people where we are. Get some help out here."

Iskander shook his head. "I don't think so. If we launch our last robot courier here, we don't know that it's going to be able to find Base Four Twenty-five. Or that it'll ever be picked up by the Space Force anywhere. I'd say myself that the odds are pretty poor that a courier message from us here is going to get through." He smiled faintly. "Besides, couriers are expensive." It was the punch line of a standing joke.

Gujar said: "I agree. We might need the courier worse later on. I'd even say it's chancy as to whether we'll be able to find our way out of this ourselves; at least in any comfortable period of time."

And Domingo again: "Maybe a courier would be able to find its way to the Space Force somewhere. And if it found them, they might not be too busy to come and look at this thing. And if they did decide to come, and they did find their way here and saw it, they might be smart enough to realize its value. Or they might not. No, thanks. We're going to handle this ourselves. Even if they did agree it was valuable, they might still decide it would be better to fire away."

There was general agreement among the crew. People out here in the Milkpail depended, often enough, on the Space

Force for their very lives. They also tended not to be overly impressed with that organization's abilities and accomplishments.

Simeon wavered. ''Well, if you put it that way . . .'' Wilma was silent.

''I do put it that way. Let's go.''

CHAPTER 8

Inside the cramped ventral bay where the *Sirian Pearl* carried her only launch—a small craft that also served as her only lifeboat—Niles Domingo, Polly Suslova and Iskander Baza were clambering into the bulbous suits and helmets of space armor. They were speeding up the procedure by calling checklist items back and forth.

Polly saw Iskander watching her as if he found something very amusing in her way of managing the checklist. She gave him a sharp look in return, and he turned away.

As soon as they had their suits on and tested, the three of them gathered up personal weapons and kits of tools and entered the launch, carefully maneuvering their mechanically enlarged bodies, one after another, through the tight hatchway of the smaller vessel.

The launch was a cylindrical craft, half as long as the *Pearl* herself but not much bigger in diameter than the height of a tall man. Its hatches were sealed now, and the bay around it evacuated. Then the ventral doors of the bay were opened to space. With Domingo in the pilot's seat of the launch—his armored helmet had a built-in headlink—the small vehicle separated from the *Pearl* and drove toward the damaged berserker.

Normally the controls of the launch, like those of the larger ship, were operated through a direct linkage to the electrical activity of the human pilot's brain. The system used on the launch was less sophisticated than that aboard the *Pearl*, but adequate for the less complicated craft.

One advantage of the launch was its real viewports, through which people inside could look out. In one direction, nearly astern now, hung the *Pearl*, her gun hatches open, her weapons ready. In almost the opposite direction, suspended against an endless background of distant white billows and luminous pastel columns, the enemy machine was a construction of dark gray planes and angles, torn by blackened holes, lighted from time to time by fitful internal fires—none of which were blue.

The berserker was substantially bigger than the *Pearl*, and through the viewports it appeared subjectively enormous as the three humans in the launch got their first direct look at it. The enemy loomed even larger as Domingo drove closer. Still, the launch's radar instruments assured its crew that the machine ahead was by no means of an unusual size for a berserker. It rotated slowly in the eternal sleet of this nebular space, spurting more fumes and debris from ragged, open wounds, emitting an occasional flare of light in one color or another. Polly, looking at the broken, uneven outline the berserker presented, decided that almost its entire outer hull was gone. And yet it had continued functioning, at least well enough to retreat this far after the battle.

The enemy unit appeared to be taking no notice of the *Pearl*, or of the more closely approaching launch. Possibly it was now completely blind and deaf. Possibly that last explosion, whose shockwave the *Pearl*'s instruments had detected at a distance, had originated in a successful destructor charge, and the berserker's electronic brain, or brains, with their possible secrets, had now been totally destroyed.

Of course it was also possible that the enemy still had additional destructor charges aboard, only waiting to be set off. Or that it still possessed other weapons and was now aware of human presences nearby and was biding its time, calculating how to optimize the last chance it would ever have of carrying out its prime programmed directive.

"Ever get this close to one of them before?" Polly asked the question in a small voice and of no one in particular. Crew stations on the launch were not separated; all three people aboard were riding in the same small compartment. The captain, seated at her elbow, was continuing to ease the launch nearer to the foe at a speed of only a few meters per second.

Wordlessly Domingo shook his head. He seemed to be indicating that he had no time for questions now; Polly bit her lip.

"I was, once," Iskander murmured. Polly turned her head and looked at him, but he was not looking at her, and he offered no details.

The central thought in Domingo's mind right now was that this was not Leviathan in front of him. Still, it was one of the enemy, the only one of the enemy that had yet come within his grasp. The sight of the ongoing damage aboard, the nuclear and chemical reactions eating away at it, offered him a definite, savage satisfaction. The feeling was mingled with an urgent worry that the information he had hoped to find here, the knowledge that would somehow give him an advantage, lead him to his true foe, was being destroyed before his eyes in the same fires.

He willed the launch forward more quickly. The safety fields of his chair shielded him and his shipmates from even feeling the acceleration, but they all saw on instruments how sharply the craft responded.

The storm of radiation, which had to be emanating from somewhere within the enemy, grew stronger as they neared the hulk. Still the armored suits ought to be sufficient to shield them from the radiation when they went out as boarders, unless the flux should increase by a considerable factor even above its present level.

They circled the enemy once in the launch, at a distance of no more than half a kilometer. Then Domingo drove his little craft closer again, slowing at the last moment, without warning taking them right inside the damaged hull, as Polly muffled a gasp. The launch entered the enemy's hull through a great rent that had been torn either by some Space Force weapon or by a secondary explosion. The hole was so big that it seemed to Polly that half of the pastel sunset billows making up the nebular sky outside were still visible after they had entered. But she still found herself holding her breath, with the sensation that gigantic jaws were about to close on her and crush her.

Inside the enemy's battered hulk, patches of heated, glowing metal were visible in every direction. When the glow of the hot metal was augmented by that from the nebula outside, there was enough light to keep the bowels of the berserker from being really dark. Not satisfied with this erratic illumination, Iskander sent searchlight beams stabbing out from the launch. The lights, playing back and forth at varying angles, revealed more twisted metal along with other objects, shapes and textures, some of which remained unidentifiable. At places inside the berserker, the continually outgassing fumes from internal damage were thick enough to interfere with vision, even with the launch's searchlights on.

Running one last time through the operator's checklist of her armored suit—quite unnecessarily, but it gave the mind something to do—Polly knew terror, remembered her children and asked herself why she was doing this. The answer to that question was not hard to find—Domingo had asked her to do it. But that answer, she reflected, was the kind that did you no good when you had found it.

Now that the launch was completely inside the berserker, their communications with the *Pearl* were almost entirely cut off. Radios stuttered and rasped with static. Domingo had been expecting this problem. He got around it by maneuvering the launch back to the lip of the wound through which they had entered the enemy's carcass and pausing to set up a small robotic relay station there. He had to get out of the launch in his armored suit to do so.

Waiting for him inside the launch, Polly and Iskander held their craft in position. They were too busy watching for signs of enemy activity to talk, beyond the minimum of necessary communication, or even to look at each other. But the metal body of the enemy around them, dead or dying, still had not reacted to their presence. Polly could begin to breathe again.

The EVA lock cycled; Domingo came back in. Sitting in the pilot's seat again, the outer surface of his suit frosting over lightly with the cold it had brought in, he exchanged a few words with the *Pearl*, confirming for himself that communications had now been solidly reestablished.

Next, driving the launch very slowly, he moved it deeper inside the largely hollow body of the enemy and with a magnetic grapple secured the prow of the small craft to a central projection within the ruin.

Then Domingo once more unfastened himself from his seat and stood up, drifting. The artificial gravity in the launch had not been turned on, conserving that much power against sudden need. He said: "You both know what we're looking for. Keep in contact with each other at all times."

"One more thing," said Baza. "We're locking up after us. Don't want any mice getting in while we're out." Iskander grinned mirthlessly. "Hatch reentry code will be Baker Epsilon Pearl. Okay?"

The two people with him acknowledged the code. Now the three explorers were ready to begin serious investigation. Domingo disembarked first and looked around before the others came out. Then he beckoned them. Baza, last one out of the small vessel, closed and sealed the hatch. Then the three separated, moving away from the launch in three different directions.

On first touching the metal bones of the berserker, Polly could feel, through the gauntlets covering her hands, how those structural members quivered faintly with the ongoing throb of some machinery. Everything here was not totally dead. But the hulk seemed basically stable, and getting around inside it proved not to be difficult, at least at the start. When necessary the boarders used the small jets on their armored suits to maneuver. But most of the time, in the effective absence of gravity, they were able to scramble readily from one handhold or foothold to another. Each member of the party carried sample cases and nets, means of gathering samples of gas, of debris, of anything that looked like it might represent a clue as to the purpose of this huge construction.

Repeatedly Domingo's voice came on the suit radios of his two companions, urging them to hurry the investigation, not to waste a moment. It was possible that secrets were being destroyed around them every minute. Polly wondered, but at this late juncture hesitated to ask, how they would be able to recognize a real secret when one appeared.

Already Iskander was jabbing boldly with a long, telescoping staff at some wreckage near the launch. "Someone else ought to look at this," he said on his suit radio. "This looks to me like biochemistry lab equipment. Maybe your hunch is right, Cap. About there being something here worth finding out."

Polly, pushing aside incomprehensible alien debris, went to join Baza. The stuff he was digging into looked to her like industrial equipment, pieces from some kind of factory.

Domingo had started his own search some distance away. Over suit radio he informed the others that he had already come upon the remnants of similar equipment.

The three of them, all keeping moving while they talked, discussed the situation with Simeon and Wilma and Gujar back aboard the *Pearl*. As Iskander had said, it looked as if Domingo's instinctive decision to board the wreck might be justified.

From the ship, Wilma's voice came sharply, interrupting the discussion: "We're starting to get some readings that indicate activity aboard that piece of junk."

The captain's voice snapped back: "What sort of activity? What do you mean?"

"It looks to me like physical movement. By objects approximately the size of people, making sudden starts and stops. It's not you; we can distinguish your movements from this other stuff."

The faces of Polly's shipmates were hard for her to see inside their helmets. Domingo's voice came calmly: "If there were any independently functioning, programmable machines still here, I think they would have let us know already. What you're detecting might be drifting bits of stuff."

"Might be. It's hard to read anything accurately under these conditions. But to be on the safe side maybe you'd better get back to the launch."

"Scratch that. This whole operation is some distance from the safe side, anyway. We're going on with what we're doing."

Polly heard her captain's fearless indifference, swallowed and went on with what he wanted her to do. Iskander naturally was doing likewise.

The radio voice came again, relayed from the ship. "All right, acknowledge. We'll continue to stand by." The three people who were still aboard the *Pearl* would be ready to provide what help they could for the three boarders in case of trouble; or, in the worst case, they ought to be able at least to get away with the ship and carry the news of a disaster. The people on the ship also had the task of recording data as it was transmitted from the trio of explorers.

Exploration proceeded as rapidly as was feasible.

Like her two companions, Polly jumped and jetted and clambered about the wreckage at a speed that she would have thought utterly reckless had it not seemed even greater folly to spend more time here than absolutely necessary. Still, she was sure that they were not going to be able to explore the entire hulk.

The explorers were undoubtedly accumulating a lot of raw information. How much usefulness that information had, if any, would have to be determined later. Hand-held video units recorded whatever passed in front of them. Faceplates in armored helmets expanded the spectrum in which the human eye could see, even as they protected the eyes from overloading brightness.

Drifting and clambering through this ruin filled with disorienting shapes and unfamiliar objects, Domingo saw no recognizable weapons and no vast stores of power such as would have been required to energize most types of the space-warfare weapons with which he was familiar. In this portion of the berserker too, some of the things he was finding looked like lab equipment. In fact, a lot of it looked like that. Yes, it had to be.

But what was all the rest of this? The components of a miniaturized factory for the production of some kind of biological materials, as Polly had already suggested?

Still, the only discovery Domingo really felt confident about as yet was that most of this was not weaponry, or direct support for weaponry, at least not any type with which he was familiar. He grew more certain of that the more he saw. There was no question that there had been some weapons on this thing once; on a berserker there always were. But the armament, especially if it were limited in quantity, would have been mounted on or just inside the outer hull, and very little of that hull was left. He hadn't yet taken a close look at the remnant of surface that still existed, thinking secrets more likely to be found inside.

It was amazing that any machine, even a berserker, could have taken a beating like this and still function well enough to propel itself this far.

The strength of malevolent purpose . . .

He moved around a shattered bulkhead, finding his way into yet another bay. Here were massive cylindrical objects—

field generators, he thought, and of some complex kind. Not the usual type of generators that were used to create defensive fields or artificial gravity for human ship or inanimate killing machine. No, these were intended for something else . . . and they were clustered together oddly, as if in an effort to produce some kind of heterodyning . . .

And what had all *this* been, here, inside? Tanks, pipes, equipment for doing something chemically. Producing something, in quantity, he supposed. Beyond that it was very hard to guess.

The problem of determining functions was only partially a result of the extensive damage and the alien design. Difficulty also lay in the fact that there was simply too much volume here, too many *things*, too much material for three harried, frightened people to assimilate or even to record on video in any endurable length of time.

Vibrations in the berserker's framework had been perceptible to the explorers ever since they had left their launch. Now the rumbles and shudders were growing stronger and running almost continuously through the enemy's metal bones, for all Domingo knew presaging another and finally catastrophic blast.

Now, every time Domingo touched a solid part of the berserker, his grip was shaken.

Instruments attached to the captain's suit registered another increase in the flux of radiation. No one spoke up about the increase, but everyone must have made the same observation he had. The readings were still within tolerable limits for the suits, but Domingo feared that they were high enough to make it hard for his people to concentrate on the job at hand.

The captain himself had no trouble concentrating. What he was doing was necessary. He looked around him, making an urgent effort to get some overall sense of where he was, to form a picture of what this entire structure must have been like before the Space Force weapons had blown half of it away. This unit didn't seem like a ship, in the sense of something built primarily for travel or combat. It was, to begin with, he thought, more like some kind of space station, built to stay more or less in one place, working on some job. And the body of the station—call it that—was heavily compartmentalized, or at least it had been before it had been wrecked. The implication, as Domingo saw it, was that different experiments, or possibly different production lines, would have been going on in the separate compartments.

He and the two people with him had as yet explored only a comparatively small portion of this unit. The whole berserker was perhaps twice the cross-section and eight or nine times the volume of the *Pearl*. But so far Domingo had seen no evidence that it had ever held any human prisoners. Not Earth-descended, not Carmpan, not of any of the other known themes among the several recognized varieties of living Galactic intelligence. There was no trace recognizable of the life-support systems that would have been necessary to keep such prisoners alive. Nor were there signs of any cells, rooms or passageways where living victims might once have been held. Nor even of anything that looked like animal cages.

He called his two fellow explorers on radio and questioned them. They had seen nothing of the kind, either.

"Cages?" Polly asked. "Why should there be cages?"

"I don't know. It seemed a possibility."

Iskander, drifting closer from a distance, had a comment. "It's not a prison, not an ark and not a zoo. But it *is* some kind of developmental lab. I'll bet my next chance to own a ship on that."

Domingo was keeping his hands busy while he conversed, putting fragments of drifting material into a sample case. He answered: "I don't know that I'd be willing to go that far. But this is certainly not a fighting unit. We've been through enough of it now to be sure of that."

Iskander, hovering close to his captain in effective weightlessness, seemed to shrug inside his armor. "So far we've given it a light once-over only. But I suppose you're right, Cap."

"Assume I am correct." Domingo snapped shut his sample case. "Then why was this unit traveling with a berserker raiding party?"

"Probably berserkers have their logistic problems, too. Maybe they're moving their laboratory from one planetoid or system to another . . . how should I know?"

Polly put in: "I've got a bigger question for both of you. Why are berserkers cultivating life? Are they experimentally trying to produce new forms?"

In the reflected glow of the launch's searchlights, she could see Domingo's face inside his helmet; the captain seemed to be staring at the question as if his life depended on it. At last he answered. "I don't know. But it would be a good idea to find out." He looked around at the other two, who at the moment were both close to him. "And meanwhile, while we're sitting around thinking things over, it'll be a good idea for us to continue to survive. I think we've got enough information for a start. Let's get ourselves back into the launch."

No one argued with that decision or hung back from its execution. And a moment after they had closed the hatch of the launch behind them, they were heading out of the berserker's belly and back toward the *Pearl*.

CHAPTER 9

A matter of minutes later, the *Pearl*'s entire crew was safely back inside the ship, and the ship had been withdrawn to what Domingo considered a prudent distance, nearly a hundred kilometers from the drifting wreck.

The captain called his crew into a conference. Everyone was wearing shipboard coveralls now, while out in the ventral bay three suits of space armor, along with the launch, were still undergoing a thorough precautionary sterilization.

Some of the sample cases brought back to the *Pearl* had already been processed through the sickbay diagnostic machines, where they had been discovered to contain microbial cultures. Those cases had been resealed by remote control and were being saved in sickbay for further investigation when they could be taken to a real laboratory.

Gujar said thoughtfully: "It's really simple."

"How's that?" Polly asked.

"Berserkers aren't intrinsically interested in science."

Domingo nodded. "Agreed."

"And producing new forms of life is against their basic programming, which is to kill. So if they're experimenting with biology, producing some modified forms of life—that's the suggestion, isn't it?—they have an overriding reason for doing so. It's part of an effort to achieve some larger goal."

It was Wilma's turn to nod. "Of course. And their goal is no doubt their usual one, of wiping out ED humanity. We're their big stumbling block, probably all that stands in the way of their sterilizing the whole Galaxy. We have been, ever since they met us."

"Exactly. And so the most likely interpretation of all this bioresearch material is that it represents a serious attempt to produce—what? An antihuman poison?"

Polly said: "There are a lot of poisons around already that can kill people. It wouldn't take any great amount of research to find out about them. I don't think it's that. But . . . an antihuman something, certainly. Maybe a virus?"

The captain was thinking very intently. "Historically, down through the centuries, they've already tried a number of times to use disease organisms against us. But that kind of tactic has never worked very well for them, as far as I know. People have been doing research on human diseases a lot longer than berserkers have; we're ahead, and we're not about to let them catch up."

"But suppose they have caught up?" Iskander wondered. He appeared to find possibilities of amusement in the idea.

"Well, we can feed what information we've been able to gather so far into the computer, along with that hypothesis, and see what we get."

Wilma and Simeon got started doing that while the others watched.

Simeon was ready to continue the discussion as he worked. "I assume you've all heard about the Red Race."

"Sure." Iskander raised his eyebrows. "Don't tell me they're involved."

Chakuchin ignored that dry joke; the Red Race, the berserkers' original targets, had been dust and radiation as long

as the Builders themselves or perhaps a short while longer.
"Then no doubt you've heard about the *qwib-qwib* too."

"Sure. So what?" In that lost age, sometime before the
beginning of ED history, the Builders' opponents, with almost their dying effort, had constructed machines that were
designed and built and programmed to do nothing but seek
out and destroy berserkers. Or so went the theory most
favored by present-day ED historians. Unfortunately for the
Red Race and for Galactic life in general, the *qwib-qwib*
machines had appeared on the scene too late to cope successfully with the berserkers.

"Legendary," said Iskander, smiling faintly.

"Like Leviathan itself." Domingo was not smiling. "But
whether something is legendary or not is not the point.
Simeon's point, as I see it, is that the berserkers might now
be doing something analogous to what the Red Race did
with machines. I mean they might now have turned to creating life—not necessarily just microbes—to wipe out life where
other means have failed them."

For the next few seconds each of the six people thought
her or his own thoughts in silence. Then their ship interrupted
their meditations with a report.

Their main onboard computer was ready to confirm that
the material presented to it for analysis was almost certainly
from some kind of facility engaged in biological research.
But it was not prepared to deliver a quick estimate of the
berserker's probable purpose in working with such material.
Instead the computer suggested that the job should be given
to some larger computer, if the delay that would necessarily
involve was tolerable.

Domingo said to it harshly: "We'll do that as soon as we
have the chance; for now, keep working."

The computer acknowledged the order with a simple beep—
the captain did not care for unnecessary anthropomorphism in
any of his machines—and presumably kept on working.

Polly, speculating on what she had seen today, remarked:

"There may, of course, be other berserker space stations like this one somewhere."

"If the computer should ask me about that possibility, I'll tell it so."

But the computer was silent on that point. What it did ask for presently was more information, in particular more samples of various materials from the wreck.

"Such samples are difficult to obtain. What kind of answers can you give me without more data?"

"None reliable." The voice of the machine was very clear and quite inhuman.

"Keep working anyway." The captain looked round him at his crew. "Second watch, back to your stations. First watch, take two hours at ease."

After his crew had dispersed, Domingo stayed in the common room alone, considering. He felt that events so far had justified his instinct. His intuition, hunch or whatever you wanted to call it, fueled by his great hatred of Leviathan, had guided him correctly, at least up to a point. His intuitive judgment now appeared to be backed up by the calculations of the ship's computer. He had been led to something of great value. Now he was torn between wanting to return to the wreck and extract still more information from it and wanting also to hurry with the news of his discovery back to Base Four Twenty-five, where the information he already had gained might be used to forge a new weapon against Leviathan.

In a way, he was still as far as ever from coming to grips with his chief enemy. But now one of its allies was here before him, helpless. For the moment at least, he held a once-in-a-lifetime advantage, and such an advantage must not be wasted.

Finally Domingo decided to search the wreck some more. He could not shake the intuition that there was more to be gained from it; and whatever information might still survive aboard it was being steadily incinerated.

The *Pearl* was certainly not equipped to do much more

than she was already doing in the way of collecting and preserving materials, including some probably dangerous items. But she had the space and the equipment to do a little more. And there was much more to be seen and photographed aboard the enemy, in limited time. If only the six humans on the scene now could find and salvage what absolutely must be preserved . . .

Again Domingo called for volunteers. This time he wanted to bring four people, himself included, in the launch.

Iskander as usual was the first to raise his hand, a languid, minimal gesture. This time Wilma and Gujar, evidently feeling it was their duty to accept a proper share of the risks, both volunteered to come along. That was enough to make four searchers. Polly kept her hand down on this occasion and stayed with Simeon aboard the *Pearl*. Neither she nor Chakuchin made any pretense of being at all eager to join the boarding party; nor did Wilma appear surprised to see that her husband was staying behind.

The *Pearl* once more approached the wreck, to stand by at the same distance as on the previous effort. The launch, with the chosen four inside, cast off.

When the boarding party reached the near vicinity of the berserker, they once more measured the radiation flux and reported that it had now fallen off a little. Domingo paused at the lip of the wound to check the communications relay, which was still in place and still working. Again the launch was maneuvered inside the berserker and moored there, in the same place as before. This time Wilma stayed in the pilot's seat of the little vessel, ready to maneuver it close to any of the spacesuited searchers who might need assistance. The other three volunteers got out of the launch and separated, once more exploring individually. They reported that the rumbling and shuddering of the enemy's frame, so pronounced earlier, had largely subsided.

Polly, now in the pilot's seat aboard the *Pearl*, had just received another call from the ship's computer, which was protesting that it still lacked enough data for the problem it had been asked to solve. She had given the machine permission to reduce temporarily the amount of time it spent working on that problem. And now she was on her radio, listening intently to the conversation of the boarding party among themselves.

"I don't see anything more here than what you described," Gujar was reporting via his suit radio. "I don't—"

And that was the last that Polly heard. Communications had been broken off abruptly, dissolved in a sudden quavering whine of noise.

"What're you doing?" Simeon's figure, bulkier than ever in space armor, was unexpectedly looming at her side. He had come through the connecting tunnel from his own crew station. "What's going on—*Wilma!*" Even as he cried out his wife's name, the *Pearl* was already shooting forward.

"I'm getting the ship over there!" Polly shouted at him. "Get back to your station!"

His massive form hesitated.

"Move it!" she screamed at him.

Simeon lumbered away.

"Man our weapons!" she shouted after Chakuchin's retreating figure. Then she turned her full attention back to the controls and the radio. "Boards, can you read me? Wilma, what's going on?"

But as before, there came no answer from suit radios or the launch. Headlink tight on her forehead, Polly gunned the drive, urging the *Pearl* to the assistance of the boarders.

This was the first time, except for a couple of brief practice sessions, that she had flown this ship. She could only hope that her control was precise enough.

Domingo's first warning that something was gravely wrong came in the form of a stealthy movement that he happened to sight some forty meters away, clear on the other side of the ruined berserker. He thought the movement was too sharp and sudden to be that of any object merely adrift here in the effective absence of gravity; it looked rather like a furtive, purposeful dart.

A moment later, very near the spot where the motion had caught the captain's eye, he was able to recognize the shape of a berserker android. The thing was approximately the size of a human being, and when he increased the magnification in his faceplate optics it showed up plainly. Silhouetted against a white patch of nebula framed by the ravaged hull, the machine looked half human and half insect. For an instant the dark inhuman shape was there and motionless; then in the next instant it was not there, moving away again so quickly that it seemed to simply disappear.

Drawing a breath, trying not to make a gasp that the radio would pick up, Domingo uttered the coded message that had been worked out for this eventuality: "I think I'm beginning to see a pattern in this material here."

Chillingly, there was no immediate reply. There was only a faint whining nose in the captain's helmet, so faint that until this moment it had not impressed itself upon his hearing. Now that he heard it, he was certain of what it meant: the humans' radio communications had somehow been knocked out.

Knowing his fellow boarders might already be dead, Domingo drew breath and shouted into his transmitter: "Berserkers! Back to the launch!" He had already drawn his handgun, a small but powerful projectile weapon, from his belt holster. The thoughtsight that would have made his aim with the handgun well-nigh perfect, guiding projectiles to his point of vision, was still clipped to his belt, and for the moment he left it there. The connectors on his helmet into which the sight would have to fit were presently occupied by the spectroscopic lenses, light amplifiers and sensors that he had wanted to have in place while he was searching.

Domingo, drifting and nearly weightless, aimed his handgun as best he could by hand and eye and fired without benefit of thoughtsight. His aim was not bad, but far from perfect. In the quick serial flares made by the first burst of explosive projectiles, hitting home across the hull in airless silence, he could see the attacking berserker clearly limned, one of its multiple limbs vibrating, halfway torn off by a half-lucky shot. *Now it will know I'm here and kill me,* Domingo thought, but before his enemy could burn him out of existence he had time to fire again.

Again he thought that he did damage, and again the instantly effective return fire that he had expected from the android did not come. So the device he had just shot at might be only an unarmed mobile repair machine—unarmed except for the strength in its limbs and tools, the machine-power quite probably capable of tearing an armored suit apart along with the man inside.

Scrambling away in the opposite direction from his target, the captain got behind a bulkhead. Against a machine that had only its strength for a weapon, he might survive long enough to get his thoughtsight connected. Domingo continued to shout warnings into the unresponsive whining within his helmet as his feet thrust against broken machinery and structure to propel his body and his hands worked to get the weapon's fire-control system attached to his helmet. With fingers turned clumsy in their desperation, he tore off the special search gear he had been using, letting the disconnected chunks of hardware go drifting free.

Unexpectedly, the radio noise in his helmet changed, flowered into bursts of whining and singing that moved up and down the scale of audio frequencies. Maybe there was hope yet. The combat radio system built into the suits, technology borrowed from the Space Force, had detected jamming and was trying to fight through it, working to hold a signal pathway open.

Domingo's shouted warnings had brought no reply, and he could not assume that anyone had heard them. But the blasting flares of gunfire certainly ought to have served as an alarm, and so should the more subtle fact of the jamming itself. If only his crew had been quick enough to notice the jamming, and if any of them were still alive, to notice that the shooting had begun . . .

The captain was drifting in shadow now; his suit lights turned off, his hands still working to get his weapon ready for efficient action. Connecting his thoughtsight properly seemed to take forever. Before the device was ready, his eyes caught another flash of movement in another place across the hull, far from where he thought either of his shipmates ought to be. Perhaps it was the same machine he had seen before and fired at. Perhaps at least one more enemy device was activated, ready to join in an attack.

Domingo's hopes surged up suddenly as he saw, near the same spot, the flares of projectiles from other handguns like his own, bursting and glowing and dying away. A moment later, he caught a glimpse of two suited human figures, together now and still surviving, scrambling in the direction of the place where the launch was moored. But still nothing except noise was coming through on his radio.

Then something flared up brightly amid the wreckage where those last shots had struck, brighter by far than the explosive projectiles from the humans' sidearms. It was perhaps a delayed, secondary explosion caused by one of the humans' shots. The new light persisted long enough to reveal multiple movement by the enemy, a ruin almost swarming with their units. Some of the creeping machines Domingo saw were much smaller than humans, and individually these miniature units, probably repair or construction devices of some kind, looked ineffective. But they would all be equipped with potentially mangling tools of one kind or another. And it was evident that a berserker brain somewhere was still directing their activities.

The launch was abruptly in motion now, its mooring cast off. Domingo thanked all the gods that Wilma must have realized what was happening. And now there was fire from the launch, almost invisible beams of energy from its one real weapon. The beams probed neatly and precisely among the ruins, and small moving machines touched by that vague thin pencil flared up and vanished. Wilma, alone in the launch, had turned her attention from piloting and was cutting some of the enemy down.

The launch was hovering now in the middle of the hollow space inside the berserker, standing by to help the boarders, to pick them up. It ought to be easy, here in virtual weightlessness, for them to jump for it. The captain wouldn't be first to jump; he'd see his people on board first safely, if they were still alive; and before going to them he wanted to get the thoughtsight connected . . .

Of course, the launch. Of course, that was what the enemy was after.

The captain couldn't see the *Pearl* itself from where he drifted inside the carcass of his enemy. Nor could he guess what action Polly and Simeon might be taking. By now, if they were still alive, they must have realized that radio signals from inside the berserker were being jammed, and probably they could see the intermittent flares of fighting. If Simeon and Polly were to open up with the heavy weapons that the ship carried, the most likely effect would be the annihilation of everything that still remained of the wrecked berserker, along with the four people who were inside it and the launch that had brought them here.

So far, that fire from the *Pearl* had not lashed out.

Now the noise level in the captain's helmet radio suddenly dropped. Hoping that the built-in combat anti-jamming might now be able to force a signal through, Domingo shouted orders for the *Pearl* to stay clear of the wreck. He didn't know what additional weapons the enemy might still be able to bring into play, but if berserker units could seize the launch and then the *Pearl*, much more than this one skirmish would be lost.

Still no answer came to him from the *Pearl*. It was quite likely that the relay station had been knocked out.

Surely the people aboard his ship must realize by now that something was wrong. If only they didn't do anything that might endanger the ship, put it at risk of being boarded, taken over—

Domingo got confirmation that Polly and Simeon were at least aware of a problem. Now he could see the *Pearl* herself, hovering close outside the gap through which the launch had entered the berserker. But the radio jamming had come back, as effective as ever.

Still no more than half a minute had passed since the first alarm. Moving around within the wreck, still struggling to get the last connector of his thoughtsight properly attached, the captain could see that the relay communications station, on the lip of the berserker's wound, was gone. It had somehow been knocked out, quite possibly uprooted by a berserker android by main strength.

Then without warning a voice burst through the jamming into his helmet. Score one round at least for the Space Force technology; even the stereo effect worked.

The message was a shout of fresh alarm that turned the captain in another direction:

"They're trying to seize the launch!"

I know that, damn it, thought Domingo, and repeated an order that had earlier gone unacknowledged. "Wilma, keep it away!" The jamming came back, cutting him off in midsentence. But Wilma, whether she had heard him or not, kept on with what she was doing, maneuvering the launch close to an interior landing in a different spot from where it had been moored. Actually, Domingo realized, she was bringing it closer to where he himself had been a few seconds ago, as if she thought he needed to be picked up. She would be able to see, though perhaps only intermittently, where the people inside were. She was naturally trying to rescue them, get them out of this snakepit of swarming enemies. And she had stopped shooting for the moment. To fly the launch, determine where to go and at the same time work its weapon precisely was more than almost any individual would be able to manage properly.

The captain gave up trying to be last aboard and propelled

himself into a weightless dive to meet the approaching launch.
At the same time, with inhuman speed, berserkers went
jetting and lunging for the small craft as it appeared about to
touch down. Domingo's weapon blazed at them. His shots
were still hand-aimed, but lucky enough to reduce a couple
of small units to flying fragments. The recoil of his own fire
deflected him away from the oncoming vehicle, and he grabbed
at more wreckage to stop himself.

Why didn't they jump us the first time we came aboard? If
ever he had time to think again, he might be able to come up
with a sure answer for that one. Probably the enemy had
needed some time to mobilize its mobile units. Or else, on
the humans' previous visit, the malevolent computer planning
the attack had simply delayed its move too long, miscalculat-
ing the moment when the onslaught of its small machines
would be most likely to inflict maximum damage. Probably
the prime enemy objective from the start had been to seize
the launch.

At last, under the pressure of Domingo's fingers, the final
stubborn connector clicked into place; the thoughtsight was
installed on his helmet. He brought his weapon into efficient
operation now, locking aim and firing with fearful electronic
accuracy; one of the scurrying machines after another vanished in blurs of flying parts.

Now that his fire was seriously disrupting their coordinated
attack, he suddenly became the enemy's prime objective. He
saw a device that looked like a toolrack charging at him and
sent it spinning and reeling away, with a great hole blasted
through its middle. He got a new clip into his handgun barely
in time as an android charged him, hurling something that
clanged like a bullet off his armor. That machine, too, he
promptly devastated. To Domingo it seemed that he broadcast and focused destruction with the mere act of his will.
But there was only one more spare clip before his ammuni-
tion would be gone.

The return fire he had expected earlier struck at him now;
some kind of laser, he thought, but not quite powerful enough

to do the job. Domingo was left momentarily blinded, trying to tumble away. Even through his armor he could feel the searing heat.

The two other humans who had boarded the wreck with him had given up trying to hide. They were using their weapons steadily now, and more or less efficiently. As far as Domingo could tell, their efforts were no more than marginally effective. Domingo supposed that the others were having trouble getting their thoughtsights hooked up, too. Only the weapons on the launch itself, now briefly back in action again, were so far staving off disaster.

Iskander and Gujar jumped for the launch, propelling themselves easily in weightlessness, and one of them at least—Domingo couldn't see the suit markings to determine which—was clinging to it, gripping a small projection with one hand and firing a weapon with the other.

Wilma opened the hatch of the launch, responding to frantic gestures from one of the other boarders who was closely beset by machines.

The trouble was that as soon as the hatch was opened, the enemy went for it. It was naturally a double door, inner and outer, the EVA airlock.

The idea came to Domingo that the enemy were using the boarders as bait rather than going all out to kill them quickly, hoping to be able to lure the launch within easy reach to get it to open its entry hatch.

On the launch, Wilma could see her shipmates jumping around, exchanging fire with the enemy machines, in peril of being scraped off the launch and grappled by them.

The launch, unless she were to withdraw it from inside the berserker, remained within easy leaping distance of the surviving androids. And the humans' communications were still being successfully jammed.

Domingo went after the enemy machine that was closest to the launch. *Maybe one of the same kind that killed Maymyo*, he thought. He fired and fired at it, bathed it in explosions, but could not seem to do it any effective harm. It had some special, toughened armor. His small handgun projectiles were not enough.

It had no firing weapon of its own but was destroying things by main strength.

It somehow disabled the beam projector on the launch.

Now it wanted to get at the opening hatchway on the launch.

Domingo was there in time to somehow block its entry or to keep it from getting through the inner door of the EVA hatch.

The launch started to drift away, uncontrolled, when Wilma gave up her post at the controls to try to get the door closed again.

The thing was close in front of him, parts of it blurring with movement at invisible speed, a chopping machine into which he was about to be fed like sausage.

Domingo and the berserker both spun away from the launch. Wilma, trying to reach from inside to help, was drawn out with them, but either Gujar or Iskander lunged into the open airlock and got it closed again from the inside, just ahead of the reaching grapple of a machine.

Then he, Domingo, was wedged in a crevice somewhere and the berserker android was pounding at him, probing for him with a long metal beam. The weapon driven by those arms could mash him, armor and all, if it caught him solidly and repeatedly, wedged against an anvil as he was.

Domingo was not trying to get away any longer; he was as well-armed now for this fight as he was ever going to be, and he was fighting.

Domingo could feel himself being mangled. He spent his last conscious effort firing his weapon one more time, point-blank range against the damnable, the evil thing.

CHAPTER 10

There was a time, a long, long time, during which his awareness of his surroundings was no more than barely sufficient to convince him that he was not dead. Dead, slaughtered and gone to one of the legendary hells, one that had been re-created especially for him and repopulated with berserkers. Down there the damned machines were still killing Isabel and the children, and he still had to watch. Then, subtly, a divide was crossed down near the boundary of hell, and Domingo began to be sure that it was human beings and not only machines who had him in their care, though the gods of all space knew there were machines enough surrounding him. He allowed himself to be convinced that these contrivances were purely benevolent, or at least that was the intention of their programming. He had not become the berserkers' prisoner.

Lying there with his life no more than a thin bloody thread, he knew that he had survived some kind of a skirmish with the damned killers. But all the details of the event were vague. He had gone after them somewhere, and a fight had broken out—yes, inside their wrecked, spacegoing laboratory—and he had been terribly hurt, though now he was suffering no particular pain. Nothing else about what had happened was at all clear at the moment.

The thread of life was stronger now. The present, if not the past, was growing a little clearer. Domingo understood that he was lying flat in a bed, on his back most of the time, though once in a while he was gently flipped, for one reason or another. He realized too that there were people coming and going purposefully around him. As a rule the trusty caretaking machines stayed where they were. He had the feeling that the lenses and sensors of these machines were watching him with superhuman vigilance.

Sometimes Domingo thought that his left leg was no longer where it ought to be, that it was growing out of his body from somewhere other than his hip, sprouting grotesquely from his back or chest. And sometimes he thought that the leg was completely gone. Not that the mere absence of one limb was going to worry him especially. He was still breathing, and the berserkers did not have him. Those were the only two essential requirements of life that he could think of.

Given those two conditions, he would be able to build on them everything else he wanted. His wants were really simple, though they were not easy. Grimly, half blindly, half consciously, he started trying to make plans again. In time he could and would find the way to the appointed meeting that he was fated to have with Leviathan. That meeting would take place. He would create a way, a possibility, if none existed now.

More time, long days, passed before Domingo experienced an interval in which he was strong and lucid enough to ask questions.

His voice at first was no more than a crushed whisper. "What happened? Tell me. What did we bring back?"

That was the first thing Domingo asked about; and Polly

Suslova, wild-haired as usual and looking somewhat excited as she bent over him, was the first person he recognized and the first to whom he spoke coherently.

Polly's answer was given in soothing tones, in contrast to her appearance. The only trouble was that the answer was not, as he saw it, very much to the point: "You've been hurt, Niles. You'll be all right now, though." And suddenly she turned away, reacting as if she were terribly upset by something.

The second statement in her reply, he felt sure on interior evidence, was still problematical; as for the first statement, he had already figured that out for himself without help. With his memory slowly improving, he could recall something but not everything about the firefight inside the wreck and that last berserker android.

He had at last begun to hurt, and in a number of places. But the machines around him stared at him with their wise lenses, and listened continuously to his breathing and his heartbeat, and probed his veins and nerves, and kept the pain from ever getting too bad. He accepted the pain as a sign of his recovery.

The captain never had the least doubt that his recovery was desirable and necessary. Because he had to get well and strong before he could go after Leviathan again.

And still more time passed before Domingo was able to determine that the hospital in which he was recovering must be the military one on Base Four Twenty-five.

At about the same time as he understood where he was, Domingo comprehended also that Polly Suslova, more often than not, was still nearby. Like skillfully arranged background music, she had been with him for some time before he recognized her presence, before he was able to ask her those first questions. In fact, it now seemed to Domingo, once more able to think in terms of time and space, that Polly had been more or less in attendance on him ever since he had been wounded.

Even, if he thought about it, before that.

For a long time now, ever since the captain had started to regain consciousness, people had been pausing beside him and trying to tell him things, mostly reassuring platitudes about his medical condition. Facts were in short supply. But now, in a strengthening voice, he was able to ask more questions.

From Polly, from the medical people, from Iskander who came in often and from Gujar who came in once to visit him, Domingo learned, a little at a time, the details he was unable to remember of what had happened to him and the others who had been examining the wrecked berserker. He learned how, after the small commensal berserkers had struck him down, his crew had managed to crunch the enemy's attacking mobile units, down to the last machine. And how his crew had then got themselves and Domingo and the *Pearl* away from the scene of the battle. By the time they did that their captain had been totally unconscious, barely alive inside what was left of his space armor. They had needed power tools to get him out of the mangled armor, and he had made most of the trip back to base in suspended animation in the *Pearl*'s sick bay, surrounded by deep-frozen sample cases holding biological samples gathered from the wreck.

Now in the hospital, Domingo was pleased, he was even more elated than was reasonable, to learn that they had brought back what the Space Force analysts were calling a large amount of very valuable samples and recorded information. Iskander had even managed to bring along the demolished fragments of one of the berserker androids. When Polly saw how greatly this news delighted the captain, she went over it again, telling him in considerable detail how successful their effort had been and how Baza had insisted on salvaging parts of the vanquished enemy for later study.

When Domingo grew tired, Polly went away to let him rest after assuring him that she'd be back. He was glad to hear that she intended to return, but somehow he had been sure of it already.

Other human figures continued to come and go around him, all of them being professionally cheerful. Domingo slept again, this time with conscious confidence that he was going to wake up.

Next time he awoke, he was able to take a steadier notice of his surroundings. He observed that the base hospital was an alert and ready place, but not a very busy one. This hospital had almost certainly never been used to anything like full capacity, even for the casualties of war; and it was not being so used now. In the war against the berserkers there were plenty of human dead, but not that many wounded. And fortunately, wars like those on ancient Earth, of life pitted against life, were virtually unknown.

Again Domingo probed with questions at the people around him. This time he wanted to know if his crew had gone back to the wrecked berserker after the fight and gathered still more information. None of the hospital staff knew the answer to that one, or wanted to discuss it, and he had to be persistent. It seemed to him that the answer was important, bearing as it did on the reliability and dedication of the people in his crew.

The answer, unhappily, was no.

Domingo raged feebly at Iskander when he heard that. And raged again when he was told something he was later able to confirm for himself on the recordings: The main berserker, the damaged hulk, had not, even yet, been totally destroyed. The crew of the *Pearl*, once their captain was unconscious, had not stayed in the area even long enough to finish the helpless enemy off.

Iskander raised an eyebrow and accepted the rebuke tolerantly. "Sorry, Niles."

"Sorry. That doesn't help."

"It's done now. There's no reaction I can demonstrate that *will* help now, is there?"

No, there wasn't.

Gujar Sidoruk, making his second visit to Domingo in the hospital, assured him: "That piece of junk couldn't hurt anyone any longer, Niles. Even if some ship did stumble on it, and the chances against that are—''

Domingo made a disgusted noise. It was a surprisingly loud noise, considering his condition.

Iskander said soothingly: "It'll just lie there helpless, Niles, until its power fails eventually and it rots. No one's going to stumble onto it. Not there.''

The captain's voice was weak, but still it was hoarse and harsh. "There's life out there in the nebula. It'll go on killing that. It'll figure out some way to use whatever systems and power it has left, and it'll kill a little more at least.''

His visitors of the day looked at one another, a look that said the captain was still woozy from all that had happened to him. In the Milkpail there were cubic light-years of that kind of tenuous life around. It was scattered everywhere in the nebula. And aside from harvesting certain of its odd varieties and some useful byproducts, nobody gave a damn about it. Domingo certainly never had, before now. Berserkers killed that sort of life, of course, *en passant* when they encountered it—they were programmed to kill everything—but their main destructive interest was concentrated upon humanity. In the whole Galaxy so far, only intelligent life, synonymous with humanity in its several themes, appeared to offer any serious obstacle to the machines' achievement of their projected goal, the ultimate sterilization of the universe.

Gennadius, himself looking a little less grim than the last time the two had met, came to look in on the grim patient. The base commander reported, among other things, that the robot courier that had been dispatched to Four Twenty-five from the *Pearl* had never reached the base.

"To nobody's particular surprise," Domingo whispered.

"I suppose so.''

"Are you hunting Leviathan now?''

"We're doing what we can, Niles. We're doing what we can.''

Gennadius could also offer Domingo reassurance of a sort on one point. Following the *Pearl*'s return to the base, he,

Gennadius, had sent out a Space Force ship to look for the wrecked berserker. But after ten days the ship had come back to report the failure of the search. Again, a result not surprising to anyone who knew the difficulties of astrogation within the nebula.

Domingo now learned that two standard months had passed since he had been hurt. He had been unconscious or heavily sedated most of the time, while surgeons had begun the process of putting him back together.

Domingo wanted fresh news of Leviathan, but there was none. At least no one would tell him if there was.

He also kept coming back, in his thoughts, to the wrecked berserker. Iskander, the others in the crew said, had wanted to stay and finish the berserker off. But he just hadn't managed to give an order to that effect and make it stick.

The captain knew from experience that Baza was a daring fighter, cool and unshakable in a crisis. He had seen plenty of evidence also that the man hated berserkers, and he needed no one to tell him what to do. But he was simply not a very good leader, Domingo silently decided now. His chief mate and most faithful friend was unskilled at ordering or persuading others. Though Iskander had been second in command on the *Pearl* and had nominally taken over when Domingo was knocked out, the others had persuaded him that Domingo needed immediate care.

Well, all the gods and demigods of the far colonies knew that had been true. The captain had barely survived as it was.

Nevertheless Domingo crabbed more as his recovery in the hospital proceeded. He made silent, private plans for a reorganization of his crew. It wasn't easy. He wondered who might do a better job than Baza as his second-in-command. Domingo couldn't come up with a name.

But if they'd had their captain in suspended animation when they were ready to leave the wrecked berserker, it would have been all the same to him if they had stayed a little longer with the wreck. They'd had no excuse not to stay. They should have made another effort to wring the last bits of information out of the damned hulk, and then they should have made sure before they left that it was nothing but a cloud of expanding gas . . .

Another worry, about something the captain had assumed but never confirmed, now struck him forcibly.

He voiced the thought at once. "What about the *Pearl*? Is she all right?"

"In great shape. Hardly scratched. None of the little bastards ever got near her. She's been docked here ever since we brought you back."

Iskander, visiting again, asked almost timidly if he could take the ship out and use her, scouting.

Domingo probed him with his eyes. His eyes were among the few parts that had not been damaged. "Sure. But be careful. I'm going to need her soon." Domingo could see the people around him look at one another when he said that. To them—to some of them anyway—it must have sounded like a joke. Because, he supposed, he must look even worse off than he felt.

There was something else he had been meaning to ask about, if he could only remember what it was. Oh, yes. He inquired whether there had been any other casualties among his crew. There were certain crew members' faces he could not remember seeing among those of his visitors in the hospital.

Again glances were exchanged among the people standing around his bed before any of them said anything. The consensus appeared to be that he was now probably strong enough to be able to sustain the bad news, and so they told him. There had been one other casualty. Wilma Chanar had died in the grip of that last berserker android before it was demolished.

"That's too bad," whispered Domingo, realizing he was expected to whisper something. It was of course the first he had heard of Wilma's death, although if his thoughts in the hospital had turned that way at all he might have deduced the fact, or guessed it—that last fight was gradually becoming less of a blank to him. But he had not much feeling left for Wilma, dead or alive. Or for any of the others. He was still anesthetized by earlier and harder shocks. He knew regret at the news, but only numbly, and largely because Wilma was going to be hard to replace on the crew.

More time passed in the hospital. Day by day Domingo gradually improved, but it was obvious even to him that full recovery was still a long way off. His left leg was really gone, for one thing, almost to the hip. And that was far from being his only medical problem. He admitted, with his new habit of absorption in grim calculation, that his recovery, the first step toward revenge, was going to be even a bigger job than he had thought. At least while he worked at recovering, he could also make plans.

With growing competence to think about what he learned, he had to begin by seriously taking stock of his own body. Or what was left of it. Regaining anything like full normal function was going to take him even longer than he'd thought. The doctors told him that yes, they were going to have to fit him with a new left leg, some kind of artificial construction. Regrowth, the usual tactic employed when a limb was lost, didn't look promising in his current general condition, considering, as the doctors said, the overall neurological situation.

When Domingo heard of the plans to fit him with an artificial leg, an inspiration came to him at once. The more he thought about his idea, the more he grinned. Naturally the people who were around him every day, who hadn't seen him grinning at anything since his daughter perished, asked him what was up.

He inquired about the berserker android that had been brought back piecemeal from inside the ruined enemy. Yes, it was still here on the base. It had been studied, of course, but the technicians had found nothing really new about it.

Then he told the doctors and therapists that he wanted to

have one of the legs of the berserker android, or suitable portions of such a leg, adapted to his body.

They looked at each other and decided to come back and talk to the captain about it later. Some of them looked shocked, or taken aback, but actually one of the doctors was intrigued by the idea.

When Polly heard about it, she thought it was a little sick—maybe more than a little—and at her first opportunity she said as much to Domingo.

At first he only grinned at her. "Why not?"

"If you have to ask . . ."

His expression became more intent, almost hostile. "Why not? Why shouldn't I walk on one of their bones?" Then abruptly his weakness showed.

Polly felt guilty. "No reason, I suppose. You're entitled to do what you want." Then she changed the subject; she invited Domingo to come to her home on Yirrkala and stay there while he recuperated. "I'm going there for a while anyway," she announced, trying to sound as casual as possible. "I'm ready for a rest. I thought you might be, too."

Domingo thanked her, and agreed almost immediately. He could see that his quick acceptance surprised Polly somewhat. But he could see also that she was pleased. And he was exhausted. He had to save his strength for the arguments and fights that counted. He was a very long way from being ready to jump into a ship again and resume the hunt. He had to recuperate somewhere, before he could do anything else.

And he wanted to do as much of his convalescing as possible out from under the supervision of the Space Force. They wouldn't be likely to go along with certain of the preparations he intended to make for the next round of his battle.

The next time Polly came to visit him, Domingo asked her about Yirrkala and about her home and family there. He remembered casually talking to her about those things before—in what now seemed to have been an earlier life—but the situation could have changed. Her home on Yirrkala interested him now, because he wanted to make sure it would provide an environment that made for speedy convalescence. From all he could find out, it sounded acceptable. His own homeworld was gone, and he considered it unlikely that anyone was going to make him a better offer.

Presently Domingo was pronounced well enough for Polly to take him off to her own colony-home, and the two of them got on the first ship headed that way. Yirrkala was as well defended from berserkers as any place in the Milkpail, probably in the whole Sector. There Polly intended to nurse him back to the beginning of fitness; and she intended to do more than that, though she did not discuss all of her intentions with anyone.

Her private hope was to wean Domingo from the madness of revenge on clanking metal. She could tell that he was still gripped by that obsession, to a degree that was at best unhealthy. She thought the problem oughtn't to be hard to see for anyone who really looked at him or listened to him snarling at the ineptness of his crew. Maybe they had been inept; it was the *way* he snarled. Some kind of unhealthiness was festering.

But when she had tentatively mentioned the subject to the doctors, they told her that the patient was really doing quite well mentally, considering all he had been through. Psychotherapy, if indicated at all, could and should wait until later. Right now full physical recovery was the chief concern in the captain's case.

Domingo said to her, just once, as they were getting ready to leave for Yirrkala: "Thank you. For taking care of me like this."

She tried to make little of it. "All part of the job."

"It's not. I do thank you."

CHAPTER 11

Almost everyone who knew anything about the subject considered Yirrkala to be the most livable of all the Milkpail colonies. It was a somewhat bigger and slightly more Earth-like world than any of the nebula's other inhabited rocks, with enough natural gravity of its own to hold an atmosphere. The air enclosing its rugged surface had only to be augmented with oxygen, the mixture adjusted and not built up from scratch, to make it breathable, even at certain times and seasons comfortable. Surface temperatures could be mild on Yirrkala; genengineered fruits and flowers were commonly grown outdoors. And since the gravity had been artificially augmented, there were even sizable bodies of fresh water, on and just below the Yirrkalan surface.

Polly's homeworld was also considerably closer to Base Four Twenty-Five than were most of the other colonies. Therefore it was less susceptible—both in theory and historically—to berserker attack. Still the Yirrkalans, not content to rely on the Space Force, had never skimped on their ground defenses; and now even these already formidable installations were being hastily improved to counter the improvement recently evident in the berserkers' weaponry.

All in all, the place offered relative security, as much security as human existence in the Milkpail ever had, which was at best considerable. Domingo, disembarking on a robotic stretcher from the newly landed ship with Polly walking at his side, could see, beyond the glass walls of the port, a near horizon of pleasant hills, under a whitish sky mottled with many colors, predominantly blue. The captain's battered body was swathed in blankets as he came rolling off the ship, but the air he could feel on his face was almost comfortably warm. The distant white giant sun of this system was hidden in nebular clouds, but its light came filtering through the sky to make an indirect judgment upon this little world, touching all its surfaces with ghostly frost.

Vineyards and floral gardens covered most of the land that the newly arrived patient was able to see on his first look around outside the surface spaceport. In the direction where the horizon looked most distant there were ranks of the familiar screens and diffraction filters used as life-collection machinery, the same kinds of harvesting equipment that were common to most Milkpail worlds.

"Here come my people now," said Polly cheerfully.

Domingo looked down past his foot. Two figures that had to be Polly's sister and brother-in-law, Irina and Casper, were on hand, wrapped in coats of synthetic fur, to meet the travelers just outside the port. Irina resembled her husband more than she did Polly, being somewhat plump and with a placid air about her. She and Casper had with them Polly's two children, who immediately claimed most of their mother's attention.

The children were a boy and a girl, Ferdy and Agnes, about six and eight years old respectively, if Domingo remembered how to judge. He thought that neither of the kids looked much like their mother. Judging from the violence of the greeting they gave her, there was no doubt that they remembered who she was. Both children stared at Domingo with grave eyes, then looked away again, appearing to be impressed with their first sight of him on his robotic stretcher; he supposed they had heard some story of heroics. Their aunt and uncle were polite enough on being introduced, but not so much impressed.

He smiled at all of them as best he could and said hello, wanting to prepare for himself the smoothest possible environment in which to get on with the business of his recovery. The stretcher's wheels hissed faintly on the ramp bringing him down and away from the spaceport. Casper and Irina walking near him made friendly conversation, but still they seemed somewhat ill at ease.

They all rode in a private groundvan—a rented vehicle that could hold the stretcher—through streets lined with genengineered trees that made the scene look like pictures from old Earth. This was a bigger world than Shubra, but still most of humanity would have thought it very small. Polly's small house was out on the far edge of the settlement, but driving to it at moderate speed took much less than an hour. Most of the way they traveled through flower gardens and banks of life-collecting machines. The machines held up fine grids and nets to draw in the microscopic and near-microscopic organisms that came down out of the nebula, out of the sky.

The little two-story house, set in its own hectare of grounds, was somehow different from what Domingo had anticipated, though he could not have said just what he had been expecting. The little dwelling had been unoccupied for some time, they said, but Casper and Irina had been busy getting it ready for Polly's arrival and of course Domingo's, too.

Polly and her patient moved into the house at once, along with Polly's children. The appearance, Domingo realized, was that he had acquired an instant family. But there weren't any neighbors close enough to be misled by appearances.

His stretcher was guided into a small bedroom on the ground floor, next to Polly's room, as she explained. The kids' rooms were upstairs—Agnes and Ferd were evidently not used to a two-story house, and the mere idea of being upstairs was enough to enchant them.

Domingo rested on his stretcher in his new room and thought about berserkers, while other people took care of the moving in. Not that there was very much to be done.

On the day of his arrival on Yirrkala he was capable of dragging himself from stretcher to bed and back again, and of using his best hand to feed himself with only a minimum of human or robotic help, but that was about the extent of what he could manage. He had his room to himself at night— except for occasional look-in visits from Polly the nurse who slept next door—and from the start he often took his meals alone.

The first days of his stay passed uneventfully. The kids banged around in rooms nearby, upstairs and downstairs, or outside in their fur coats and caps, rollicking in the ever-ghostly light. Sometimes the young ones yelled, in anger at each other or just in celebration of life. They were on some kind of school holiday, Domingo gathered, and so around the house most of the time. Every once in a while their mother murmured them into temporary quietness, and when murmuring didn't work she took stronger measures to see that the patient wasn't disturbed unduly. But the patient assured her that the noises of life really didn't bother him.

He even understood why they didn't bother him. It was because life, as life, no longer meant anything to him, one way or the other. Domingo didn't bother to bring that insight to Polly's attention, but perhaps she sensed it anyway.

His appetite was no problem, not from the time that he was strong enough to chew. His teeth were still in good shape. He didn't much care what he ate, food was food, strengthening the body for its remaining purpose. On Yirrkala his devoted nurse saw to it that he got good food, and on Yirrkala he ate well from the start and grew in strength.

Faithfully the captain performed his prescribed exercises, some of them with the special robot that had been shipped to him for the purpose. The thing had arms and grips sticking out all over it, so it looked like an athlete melded with his own equipment. Some of the exercises he did with Polly, who took the opportunity to try to psychologize him and to find out how determined he still was to go after Leviathan. He was still determined. She was obviously much concerned about his welfare, his mental and emotional health. Too bad for her, Domingo thought in silence.

Casper and Irina lived at some little distance, or said they did, and so they came to visit only occasionally. On their visits they smiled at Domingo and chatted with him, but he could tell that in general they disapproved of his presence in Polly's house, and especially in Polly's life.

That was all right with him. He didn't say so, but he meant to be gone from both as soon as he possibly could.

Still, there were moments when Domingo was almost tempted to dream about what life might be like if it were possible for him to stay here with Polly and her family. Almost tempted, but not quite. To be nursed indefinitely. Something like that . . . the stillborn dream was pointless, it had no conclusion, and seemed unlikely ever to develop one. And even this faint inclination to dream of the impossible, such as it was, faded as his strength and mobility returned.

A standard month after Domingo's arrival on Yirrkala, his weight was already approaching normal again, allowing for the subtracted limb. The robotic stretcher had already been abandoned in favor of a semirobotic wheelchair, in which he could get around pretty much by himself. Both of his arms were working adequately now, but he was still a one-legged man—the prosthesis was going to be installed later, back at the base hospital.

The children, in free moments between sessions of play and the occasional jobs their mother thought up for them, had shown a continuing interest in various stages of his progress. He was still popular with Ferd and Agnes, and he wasn't sure just why. Neither of them spent that much time actually in his presence. Maybe that was the explanation.

Little Agnes once asked the captain if he had any kids of his own at home. He told her no, not any more he didn't, and at that point had provided some distraction and she had let it go at that.

Able to stand up at last, lurching and crutching his way across the room on one foot to get his first really good close look at himself in the mirror since his injury, Domingo was struck by how different his face appeared from the last time he could remember seeing it. He stared into the optical glass, wondering at himself. Not so much at the gross physical scars and alterations, though those were certainly great enough. The most noticeable of them in the mirror now, aside from the missing leg, was a twisty scar, not yet fully obliterated by the surgeon's art, that wound down one side of his jaw and neck and into his collar. The scar ended a little below that, fading indeterminately into his shoulder.

But he thought his face showed greater transformations than that, though the skin and flesh of it were pretty much back where they were supposed to be. Alterations deeper than that, greater even than the missing leg, had taken place, molding him into someone he did not understand.

He was still pondering when, beside his own face in the mirror, he caught a glimpse of Polly passing the open door-way of his room. The house was always kept quite warm, for his benefit, he supposed, and she was wearing almost nothing today as she moved about overseeing the machinery that did the housework. She looked just as she had when Domingo had first met her: compactly built, agile and shapely; an attractive young woman. Domingo was aware of her attractiveness, but only in an abstract way. She had no regular man, as far as he could tell, at least she never spoke of one. And she was drawn to Domingo. He knew that too, he could remember it as from an earlier life, and he could feel it now.

Sometimes it bothered him that he was making use of her and her feelings, that her investment in him was going to repay her nothing. Or at least he felt it ought to bother him.

But the feeling of vague guilt never lasted for long. Nor did he spend much time considering his failure to understand himself, to relate himself as he was now to the man he used to be. Actually he had little time to worry about those things, because they were basically unessential. Because there was something else that demanded almost all his thought and energy, something that he had to do.

Still—Polly and her children. They gave his mind a place to rest from planning, the only place it had. They provided something of a ready-made family, or the appearance of one, at least. But the sight of the little girl, especially, reminded Domingo painfully of his own daughters.

As for Polly herself . . . Domingo had not really thought at all about women, as women, since well before the berserker mangled his body. Not since what had happened on Shubra, in fact. His body was functional now, his physical strength was gradually returning, but he still had no urge to think of Polly, or anyone else, in that way.

Still looking into the mirror, Domingo found himself keeping a wary eye on the robot exercise machine that was waiting behind him. It was, or ought to be, a comical-looking device, with the gymnastic tools protruding from it everywhere. Polly made jokes about it sometimes, and he smiled to be sociable. But it had never struck him as amusing. It would be a while yet, he supposed, before he could feel at ease in the presence of any smart machine. That was one of the things he was going to have to train himself to do before he got back into his ship. His ship was a machine too, and he was going to have to use it.

Yes, in the mirror his face looked different.

The captain began to get out of the house on milder days, when real frost and dew were dissipated by the energy of the white glowing sky. Then one day the four of them, he and Polly and the two kids, took off on the Yirrkalan version of a summer outing. They went as far as getting into a boat, going for a cruise on one of the small outdoor bodies of open water. Domingo's wheelchair wore a flotation collar, just in case.

From the boat, cruising through the fantastic rock grottoes that edged the convoluted pond, they looked at a profusion of marvelous floating flowers. They stared at fighting flowers, plants that grappled with one another in slow motion and tried to drown one another's floating pads. They talked about what life was and speculated, half playfully, on what gods there really were. At least Polly speculated, and tried to get Domingo to do so, too. The children had a couple of ideas to contribute, but mainly they were obsessed with tossing pebbles.

Neither did the captain have much to say to advance the discussion. All Domingo could see when he looked for gods was a jagged wall of metal, trimmed here and there with blue flames. That and dirty fragments of a white dress.

There were genengineered fish, too, in this Yirrkalan pond, the biggest of them strange silvery harmless monsters, long as a man's arm, that went gliding about in the cold, almost murky depths. If you could really call these depths, two or three meters at the most.

The kids had somehow developed a scary legend of the deepest part of the pond, and they took turns relating it and elaborating on it. A big fish lived down there under a gloomy shelf of rock, a fish bigger than any of the others . . .

"And, and, you know what his name is, Uncle Niles?" Child-eyes growing wide with excitement. With fear, was more like it.

"I know. I know that, yes."

The answer didn't have a chance, because again there was a timely distraction from a sibling. No one in this world or any other wanted to hear any of his newly discovered final answers.

A little later, feeling sorry for his nurse and wanting to be reassuring, he said banally: "This is a nice world, Polly."

Impulsively though still quietly, she burst out: "Stay here. Stay with us." Then she looked as if she were afraid her words might scare him off.

All he could say was something noncommittal; then those words of his own sounded so bad he wished he could have them back, too. But they were gone.

An hour or so later, having regained the ability to chat inconsequentially—the children practically enforced that—they came back to the house. Berserkers were for the moment as close to being forgotten as they could be.

An unfamiliar groundcar was parked in front of the house, and a man was waiting in it. A bulky figure got out of the groundcar as Polly's vehicle pulled up. Gujar Sidoruk had come to Yirrkala for a visit and was waiting to see them—to see Domingo in particular.

At first Gujar didn't seem changed at all. "You're looking good, Niles. Real good."

"Considering."

"No, I mean it. Real good. Well, yeah, of course, considering everything."

Presently the two men were sitting in the house and talking; Polly's children demanded her immediate attention.

Gujar began telling the captain about the state of his, Gujar's, feelings. He was still grieving for Maymyo and for everyone else the machines had slaughtered. He still wanted to cry whenever he thought of her, and there were times when he did cry; and up until now he hadn't been able even to make an effort to resume some kind of normal life.

The bulky man looked half collapsed as he tried to talk about it. "I still think of her all the time."

Domingo said: "I do, too." He reflected that he himself didn't look collapsed at all, though a couple of months ago he had been half dead. Anyway, he'd just been told that he looked good, and he believed it. He added: "Is that what you came to tell me?"

Gujar said: "No. At first I didn't want to go back to Shubra. Because it would remind me too much of—everything. But now I think I am going back. I've been visiting there again, and . . . I think she'd want me to. I figured you'd be going on with your hunting, but I wanted to tell you that I can't.''

"I was counting on your help, Gujar. The thing that killed her is still out there. Killing more.''

Gujar got up from his chair and shuffled around, as if embarrassed. "The Space Force'll do a better job of hunting it than I can. I don't want to spend my life . . .''

Polly had got caught up on her mothering for the time being. She had come back into the room, and was listening sympathetically to this line of argument, or complaint, or whatever it was. But so far she was not saying anything. She'd never tried to argue Domingo out of his purpose, or even insisted on a long discussion of the subject with him. For which he was grateful.

Gujar went on: "There are plans for reconstruction on Shubra, Niles.''

"I suppose there are." That harsh voice of his was back at full strength now, sounding just as it had before he had been almost destroyed. Listening to it, Polly realized for the first time that these days Domingo sometimes sounded like a berserker himself. Not that she had ever heard one of them speak, but in stories when they spoke they usually sounded a lot like that.

"Heavier ground defenses of course, to start with." Gujar had overcome sorrow and was beginning to sound almost enthusiastic. "That goes without saying. I want to look over some of the new installations on this rock while I'm here.''

Domingo didn't say anything to that. He sat in the robotic wheelchair scowling, thinking with silent contempt of ground defenses and people who let such things occupy their minds.

His visitor kept trying to make him enthusiastic, too. "There's no shortage of people. I mean, new people ready to come in and settle . . .''

"I saw some of them once, back at the base.''

"Oh?''

"In fact, I gave them a little speech.''

"Oh?" Gujar didn't understand at all. He wouldn't have made an acceptable second-in-command . . . but he was going on talking anyway: "Sector says they have more than enough applicants. And Sector's willing to capitalize a new colony again. They have a big stake out here in the Milkpail now."

Domingo didn't doubt any of that. It was just that he could not help thinking of this young man before him as somehow being a traitor for feeling that it was already time to get back to normal. Maymyo was still dead, her killer gliding on its way through space just as before as if killing her had meant no more than wiping out another colony of nebular microlife.

Gujar stayed a little longer, then took his leave, heading back to Shubra.

"You don't need a nurse anymore," Polly said to Domingo that night, looking in on him before they retired in their separate rooms.

"That's true." *Nor do I need anyone else, either.* But he didn't want to announce that fact to her just yet.

CHAPTER 12

When the captain of the *Sirian Pearl* returned to the hospital at Base Four Twenty-five for his next checkup, the doctors there decided that the time was ripe for them to equip him with his new leg. The implanted graft could be permanently installed, berserker's metal bonded to human flesh and bone through carefully chosen interface materials.

Aboard ship heading for the base, Polly had thought privately about having another discussion with the doctors on the subject of Domingo's psychological state. But it was difficult to know what she ought to say to them. On Yirrkala her patient had said or done nothing extraordinary enough to provide evidence to back up her fears; there was very little new that she could tell the doctors. Yet neither had anything happened to diminish her concern. Nothing had really changed. What bothered her so much in Domingo's attitude and behavior, what made her still feel certain that some disaster was impending, would be very difficult to get across to anyone else.

In a two-hour operation at the base hospital, the new leg was attached successfully, to the delight of the captain. It still bothered Polly more than ever that something about having the berserker leg satisfied Domingo so intensely.

And Polly did speak once more to the psychiatrists, just before she and the captain were to leave the base again on their way to visit Shubra. She consulted them without telling him while he was somewhere else, busy trying out his new leg.

The psychological experts had just finished seeing the captain and chatting with him. And they had a brighter view than Polly did of the patient's progress.

"He's taking an interest in civic and business affairs on Shubra again, I understand, Ms. Suslova."

"He is? He hasn't really talked to me about that." That was about all she could say.

He could fool them more easily, she thought to herself; and they were, at bottom, less concerned.

Domingo still carried a cane, carved of Yirrkalan hothouse wood. But he was walking proudly, ably, almost naturally (the symbiosis would improve with time) on his new leg when he and Polly arrived on Shubra, where reconstruction was now under way in earnest. This wasn't a vacation trip for either of them; Polly still had some unfinished business on Shubra related to her former job, and Domingo still had legal rights and obligations here, where he was still a substantial landowner as well as the elected mayor.

The rehabilitation of his former homeworld was proceeding quite well so far without the mayor's involvement, or even his awareness, and it got little of his attention now. Domingo was really interested only in things that would facilitate his pursuit of Old Blue, and Polly knew it. He never did tell her the truth in so many words, not even when he left her to have business meetings, but he had really come back to Shubra only to sell off his property rights. With this in mind he postponed for a while his formal resignation of the mayor's

office; he thought that the hint of influence it gave him might
be useful.

The people who were resettling Shubra, the vast majority
of them strangers to Domingo and Polly, had already erected
a new assembly hall. It was a considerably bigger and better
facility than the old gathering-dome had been, a solid-looking
structure that conveyed an air of permanence, something to
show off to potential colonists. On entering this hall for the
first time, for the Festival of Dedication, Domingo was not
reminded of the old dome at all. The whole shape and design
were different, and there was less plant life in the new hall.
And here, in this substantial new crystal palace, the alert
lights were almost impossible to see. Until, the captain supposed, they were turned on; and no such demonstration was
scheduled for today.

Mounted on one wall inside the lobby, near one rounded,
ovoid interior corner of the building, not hidden but not very
conspicuous either, there was a metal plaque, a simple,
tasteful monument to all the people who had died here on
Shubra in the great disaster of a few standard months ago.
The captain didn't pause to read the listed names, but instead
walked into the auditorium and took a seat for himself at one
side near the rear. The place was starting to fill up, but there
were few faces in the crowd that he could recognize, and
fewer still showed any sign of recognizing him. There was
Henric Poinsot, who nodded back.

Music had already begun to play, but only irregularly and
at low volume. Musicians were evidently tuning up their
instruments and getting in some last-minute practice behind
the high, impressive cloth curtains at the front of the auditorium. The Festival of Dedication, proclaimed with the intention of having it as a yearly local holiday from now on, was
supposed to mark the end of the first phase of the rebuilding
of the settlement.

Mayor Domingo—today really the former mayor, because
political reorganization was under way as well—waved and

smiled at Polly when he saw her with the other performers, all of them wearing dancers' costumes, heading backstage. She smiled and waved back. She had been enthusiastic, for some reason, about getting into this performance, and he had promised her that he would be here at the Festival's opening to watch her dance.

The big room was filling up rapidly. By the time the show started the situation would be standing room only, more people in this one auditorium now than had lived on the planetoid in the old days. Someone was doing a good job of selling potential colonists on the place. Maybe they were just selling themselves. There were always a lot of people who were not deterred by danger if they thought that by facing it they had a chance to get ahead, to make something of their lives. Domingo had once thought in those terms—getting somewhere, getting ahead, building things, achieving. Owning a large share of a whole world, albeit a small one. It was certainly possible to grow wealthy here . . .

Domingo was attending this opening of the Festival partly because he had promised Polly that he would, and partly in hopes of running into people he wanted to meet, wealthy new property holders, who were otherwise difficult to see. He considered these people good prospects as purchasers of the final lots of his own remaining property. He could sell those off to someone else, but he wanted a good price. The next phase of his hunt, as he had planned it, was going to require a good deal of money. And there was no telling how long his hunt was going to last.

The musicians behind the curtains fell silent, and then within moments began again, this time in an organized way. The expensive curtains, all of old-fashioned cloth, parted slowly to reveal the new stage, superbly designed and surprisingly deep and wide. And there was Polly, looking very beautiful in a scanty silver costume, dancing among others. Watching, Domingo realized for the first time how good-looking she was, well above the average.

After he had been watching the show for a minute or two,

the captain began to realize something else. Her eyes flicked
in his direction, toward him and away again, whenever she
happened to face him in the dance. Even in this crowded
hall, Polly had taken the trouble to make sure she knew
where he was sitting. He understood now that basically her
dance was meant for him, as was almost everything she did
these days, apart from her two children.

Distraction in the form of a faint, familiar vibration in the
atmosphere diverted Domingo's attention from Polly and her
show. Inside the auditorium, with music playing, the thrum
was hard to hear, but Domingo's ears managed somehow to
pick it up. Turning to look out through one of the clear high
walls, the captain could see that a small ship was landing at
the new surface port not far away. As the craft came down,
he swiveled in his seat, keeping an eye on the silvery arrival
as long as possible. Maybe it brought news.

The ship was down now, and silent. Meanwhile of course
the show went on, the first dance over and a kind of comic
tableau being enacted. Polly was in this, too. The captain,
though still distracted by the thought of possible news, watched
the performance. She was a very good dancer for an amateur;
the whole show was a good one, with a couple of people up
front who must be professionals taking the chief parts.

Not many more minutes had passed when someone came
up behind Domingo and tapped him on the shoulder. A man
he knew slightly, from another colony, was crouching behind
him and whispered a message when the captain turned his
head: There were three people who had just arrived onworld
and who wanted to talk to him at once. "They insist that it
can't wait. I don't want to take you away from the show,
captain, but . . ."

The three, two women and a man Domingo had never seen
before, were standing in the rear of the hall, and with a
motion of his head Domingo beckoned them over. At the
same time he got up from his seat and moved toward an
alcove at the side of the crowded auditorium, meeting the
three visitors halfway.

They joined him in the alcove and promptly introduced themselves. All were high-powered experts, in technology or intelligence or both, from Sector Headquarters. To a person they were intensely interested in the samples and the information that the crew of the *Sirian Pearl* had brought back from that berserker biological factory, and in what that factory—they called it that—had been doing before it was destroyed. They wanted to know all the additional details about it that the captain could possibly tell them. The three stood there with Domingo in the alcove and kept him engaged in whispered conversation while the show went on.

At first he put off answering their questions, wanting to hear from them first whatever news they could tell him of Old Blue.

But the three let him know they didn't consider that subject of much importance. They were good at brushing aside questions, too; as eager to get information from Domingo as he was to obtain news from them, and just as insistent on getting their answers first.

The captain answered one question for them, to show good will. Then he waited to get a helpful answer in return.

Not having the information he asked for right at hand, apparently, they gave him what they had. They said Sector was almost completely convinced that a new biological weapon to be used against humanity was in the works, but that the people at headquarters were having a hard time even narrowing down the possibilities of what it was going to be.

All very interesting, but not what the captain really cared about. What else could they tell him?

When the two women experts went aside together for a few moments to confer, probably on how much they were allowed to tell Domingo, the male expert allowed himself to be distracted from business.

On the stage, to whirling music, the young women of the chorus line were now coming forward one at a time, to do individual turns. Polly's turn was on right now.

"Wow Who's she?"

"She's on my crew. Are you sure no more sightings have been recorded?"

"Sightings?"

"Of Leviathan." Domingo was trying to keep the edge of his impatience from showing in his voice.

"Leviathan. No. On your crew, hey?"

The two women rejoined the men, willing now to explain things to Domingo in a little more detail. The three visitors had brought with them the results of the computer work done at Sector Headquarters on the data gathered from the ruined berserker by the *Pearl*'s crew. That information now appeared to be of considerable importance.

"You said that before."

"The indications are that the berserker was probably working on cell development. Of certain types."

"I don't quite follow—"

"The development of large organisms, not microbes."

Domingo considered that, saw in it no direct relevance to his goal and filed it away. He continued to press the visitors for whatever information they might have on Leviathan, and at last extracted from them a promise to check with their ship's computer, as soon as they got back to their ship, to see if it had anything along that line.

By now the show, or the first phase of it anyway, was winding down. The curtains closed to enthusiastic applause. A soft spotlight picked out Domingo in his alcove, and he was called upon, as former mayor and war hero, to step forward and acknowledge a round of applause. The cheers were brief, and not overwhelming in their volume; war heroes were not that rare, and his performance, or nonperformance, as mayor lately had not won him any friends. Then the spotlight swung away; the newly chosen mayor was getting up to make a speech.

That was the moment when Polly, flushed from dancing, came swiftly and gracefully down the aisle, straight to Domingo. "Did you like it?" she panted lightly. Her silvery costume was clinging to her body, and she was sweating.

He stared at her, his mind still pondering the evolution of large life forms by the enemy. "What?" he asked, seeing her expectant look.

The look changed to something else. She drew herself up straight, saying nothing. He turned with a new question for the intelligence experts. When he turned back again a moment later, Polly was gone.

Soon after the Festival of Dedication, Domingo concluded his business on Shubra, selling off the last of his property rights for a satisfactory price. Part of the money and credit he obtained went to purchase munitions and more message couriers for the *Sirian Pearl*. The captain kept part of it for future needs. This time he meant to pay large crew bonuses.

When he saw Polly again the next day, she announced that she was not going to go with him this time. She was dropping off the crew.

He looked at her, she thought, as if she were someone he had met yesterday for the first time. He said: "All right. You're probably better off that way."

CHAPTER 13

The little machine that killed my lovely daughter was not the same one that mangled me. Almost certainly it was not even of exactly the same type.

The machine that killed her came from a different berserker—Old Blue. What destroyed her was a lander, an extension of Leviathan.

My encounter, my crippling, was almost accidental. Almost. But her killing was not. It was the arm, the fist of Leviathan that reached out for her and came after her and crushed her beautiful life to nothingness.

Leviathan . . .

Niles Domingo stood alone with his thoughts under the white Shubran sky. He was standing at the foot of a low cliff that was now almost an overhanging cliff because so much of its side had fallen in, filling in a cave.

That cave that no longer existed was the spot where his daughter Maymyo had died. At least the captain thought that this sterile, blasted area, flecked with ice and snow, was the

same spot where he had seen the charred flesh fragments and
the shredded wedding garments, the horrors that still seemed
to have nothing to do with her.

No connection with her. But the horrors had appeared and
had taken over the world, and she was gone.

In a few months the captain's old homeworld had progressed a long way from being a blasted ruin. Out here away
from the central settled area, the marks of the attack were
still everywhere to be seen. But the renewal of the atmosphere was almost completed, and here, too, people were
back. Hundreds of people, mostly contract workers, were
living in a temporary underground settlement. They were
hard at work using the hundred varieties of machines that
they had brought with them. They were decontaminating the
surface and the caves and rebuilding the underground ship
harbor. New and more powerful defenses had already been
installed.

The artificial gravity had been restored on Shubra months
ago, and the wind that had shrieked over Maymyo's freshly
murdered body had long since fallen; but there was the cliff.
There were the same low hills (Domingo thought they were
the same) rimming the theatrically near western horizon. And
there, to the east, was a long, declining, half-familiar slope
of clear land. Once there had been talk among the citizens of
Shubra of creating an outdoor park along that incline. But
the long slope was being terraced now by construction machinery, and even the hills to the west had had their profiles
altered. In almost every direction, people working with large
machines could be seen getting still more defensive emplace-
ments ready. Gouges and scars in the cliff and at its foot
showed the efforts that had been made to fill in the cratered
remnant of Maymyo's old cave.

Domingo's gaze dropped again to the ground at his feet.
His daughter's remains, along with those of her dead comrades, had been cremated months ago. Looking at the scraped
and frozen dirt where Maymyo had been destroyed brought

him no closer to her or to any of his vanished life. A metal shape still stood between, and he turned away.

The movement was quick and easy. His new leg was already working beautifully. Its cybernetics, which were naturally of human design and manufacture, were melding nicely into his nervous system. Like a fleshy organ, the new leg drew its power from the chemistry of his blood. Already the replacement was in some ways superior to his own original limb, stronger and untiring. When the leg was not covered by clothing, its appearance was stark and gray, hard and lifeless. He had observed that to some people the sight of it was shocking. An ordinary artificial limb would have had a much more nearly natural look, but it would still have been less than perfect. There were some ways, mostly sensory, in which any replacement would be inferior to the original. This leg that the doctors had given him was good enough for his purposes, and Domingo had his own reasons for preferring it. He was continually aware of the permanent difference between his new leg and his old—gleefully aware. It gave the captain a distinct pleasure to walk on an enemy's bone. There was of course nothing really left of the berserker technology except the structural metal, and that metal had been hollowed out and lengthened, padded and reformed into the same shape as his natural left leg.

As he was walking back toward his parked groundcar, Domingo saw another similar vehicle approaching from the north, the direction of the new temporary spaceport. The oncoming groundcar stopped beside his own, and a familiar broad-shouldered figure got out of it. Recognizing Iskander Baza, Domingo waved and walked a little faster. He was able to run now, if he tried, though the gait was still awkward and uncomfortable for him, and at the moment he didn't make the effort.

Baza, strolling to meet him, raised a casual hand. "Hi, Cap. You're looking good." In the middle distance, a hundred meters away, the digging machines went on scraping and groaning and grumbling.

The captain had to speak loudly to be heard. "You, too. What news?" He hadn't seen Baza in several months.

The other shrugged. "Nothing, really. I was hoping that you had some."

Domingo looked around at the eternal mottled whiteness of the sky. "About berserkers, next to nothing. On the medical situation, a little."

"Good news, I hope. Or is that too much to hope for?"

"Good enough." Domingo went on to explain that he had just received some encouraging words, via the regular message courier, from the doctors at Base Four Twenty-five. The results of the most recent medical tests were in, and they were pleased to tell him that he was now officially discharged, fit for any kind of physical activity he cared to try.

Domingo did not add that the doctors' message had also strongly recommended that he return to the base for psychological counseling on a regular basis, and that in fact an initial appointment had already been set up for him. The medics were planning to do his final plastic surgery, removing his neck scar, on the same visit. But the captain had no intention of keeping the appointment.

"That's good news." Baza always appeared to be uncomfortable when he had to say something optimistic or favorable about anything. He looked around, but made no comment on the significance of the site where he had found Domingo, if indeed he recognized and understood it. "Where's Polly?"

"She went back to Yirrkala." The parting scene with her had been quiet but thoroughly unpleasant for Domingo in several ways, and he had no wish to dwell on it.

"Oh. Just visiting there, or—?"

"She's off the crew now."

"Oh." Iskander looked quizzical, but it was not his habit to ask directly for explanations if the captain did not volunteer them. "And Gujar? He said he was going to look you up."

"He did. Back on Yirrkala. He's around here somewhere

now, I suppose, supervising some of the digging. But he's off the crew, too."

"Oh?"

"Yeah. Let's go over to the harbor and see if any armaments have come in."

In the hours and days that followed, looking around on Shubra for people he knew were capable in a spacecraft and who had the nerve he wanted, Domingo could find no one available and ready who matched his requirements except Iskander Baza. Poinsot was here but was absorbed in the rebuilding effort; Domingo hadn't even tried to get him back on the crew. There was no one else left of his own former company: Wilma was dead, her husband had gone away somewhere, Gujar and Polly quit. Anyway, as the captain told Baza—without telling him he was included in the evaluation—his old crew had been far from perfect.

The old Shubrans who remained here now were, like the newcomers, people determined to rebuild the colony; the restless as well as the discouraged among the survivors had already moved on to somewhere else.

People who were interested chiefly in rebuilding were not the ones Domingo wanted. He craved a full crew of six for the *Pearl*, but he wanted them to be the best space-combat people he could possibly get.

"It looks like we'll have to do our recruiting somewhere else, Ike."

"I think you're right, Cap . . . maybe there's one other possibility we could try first, before we go looking far afield."

"What's that?"

"Spence Benkovic. I've seen him work a ship, he's really good. Someone was telling me he's still up on his moon colony."

Domingo and Baza had turned in their rented ground vehicles and were walking the short distance back to the port, about to depart on the first leg of their recruiting journey to other worlds, when they heard their names being called behind them. Simeon Chakuchin had appeared back there, trotting to catch up and hailing them again.

They stopped and waited for him. "Where've you been?" Iskander asked, when Simeon had caught up.

The big young man only glanced at Iskander, then spoke to Domingo: "I just landed on Shubra an hour ago. I hear you're looking for crew, Niles. I want to sign on again." Simeon's face was thinner and at the same time puffier than when Domingo had seen him last, some months ago. Something had happened to him since then.

Domingo paused and thought before he answered. "You know what my plans are. It's not a trade voyage, and not harvesting. I'm going on a hunt, and I'll keep at it until it's finished. Until I see Leviathan's guts spread out somewhere in space, in the Milk or out of it."

"I know." Chakuchin had been nodding his agreement all along through Domingo's speech. "That's fine with me. I don't fit in anywhere any more, Niles, Ike. Since Wilma . . ."

Domingo was looking at him carefully. "You want to get back at the damned machines that killed her."

"I . . . yes."

Domingo looked at the younger man still more closely, into his eyes and at the puffy pallor of his face. "You're a good man, Simeon, once you make up your mind to be. But you've been on some kind of drug."

The other shook his head. "Not any more. After she died I had a real hard time for a while. But I'm off it now." Chakuchin blinked.

"Drugs won't go with me. Not on my crew. Leviathan will be all the drug we need. Got that?"

"Leviathan?"

"Old Blue. The damned berserker."

"Of course, I . . . Leviathan." The younger man repeated the word once more—thoughtfully, as if he were tasting it.

As if, thought Baza, watching with amusement, *he were trying his first dose.*

* * *

Chakuchin formally signed on the crew and was paid the first installment of his bonus. Then the three of them boarded the *Pearl* and lifted on the short hop up to the moon, intending to drop in on Benkovic's little settlement.

The moon was an angular body, shaped more like a badly made brick than like a ball. It was naturally a lot smaller even than Shubra. If the satellite had ever been given a name of its own, the local people had never got into the habit of using it. "The moon" was good enough, as Shubra possessed only the one satellite that was big enough to be noticeable at all.

The loss and restoration of artificial gravity on Shubra had not affected the satellite as drastically as some people had expected; artificial gravity varied more sharply than natural gravity with distance, and the change at the distance of the moon had been relatively small. The satellite was very nearly back in its old orbit now.

"I've lived on Shubra a good many years, and I've never been up here before," Domingo murmured as the *Pearl* approached the only obvious, dedicated landing place visible on the dark, angular chunk of rock. At the site below there were three transparent landing domes, two of them closed and already holding ships, the third dome open and apparently ready to receive visitors. A few small buildings nearby were connected to the dome complex by tunnels or tubes.

"I haven't been here before, either," Simeon murmured.

"I was once," said Baza. "Some time ago." He did not elaborate further.

Domingo had not bothered to radio ahead. As they drew closer to the moon's single small facility, they got a better look at the two ships that it already housed. One was the armed miniature speedbug that Spence called a battler—that was the craft he had been out in, scouting, on the day of Leviathan's assault. The other hangared ship was a slower, larger harvester, the kind of vessel generally used to reap shoals of microbial life from nebular clouds. The harvester looked new, as it no doubt was. Whatever ships had been berthed here during the attack must have been destroyed.

"Looks like somebody ought to be home. There are enough vehicles parked."

When Chakuchin transmitted a radio query, the equivalent of a polite knock at the door, the unoccupied dome flashed a signal of welcome for their ship, an automatic response.

The *Pearl* dipped closer. The port and the nearby house both looked new, as in fact did all the constructions here. No doubt they were new. Simeon could remember hearing that the berserker had left no more standing here on the moon than on the world below.

The dome port enclosed the visitors' ship, and then for their convenience created within itself, around their ship, a smaller bubble of force more easily refilled with air. Then the machinery signaled the three visitors that it was safe for them to get out of their craft.

They did so, and stood there on the floor of the dome looking about them uncertainly. There was no sign as yet of any human welcome. The hangar dome was sparsely furnished, a bare-bones kind of installation.

Then Simeon heard Iskander clear his throat and turned to look. A door had opened in the forcefield bubble, a door to one of the passageways, one that must connect with the small house nearby. A young woman had emerged from the open doorway to greet the three visitors. She was of average height, tending just a little to overweight. In the hot scented breeze blowing out of the tube passage, she stood there completely naked except for hothouse flowers of scarlet and purple twined in the glossy black hair that grew on her head and in three places on her body.

Simeon shuffled his feet in vague embarrassment, and looked at his companions; clothing was expected in almost every social situation. Iskander was grinning appreciatively at the apparition in the doorway, while Domingo also inspected her but looked somewhat worried.

Meanwhile the girl was smiling vaguely back at the three

men, but really it was almost as if she did not see them. She said nothing. The visiting men exchanged a second round of looks among themselves. For some time before the disaster, word had gone around on Shubra about the unconventional lifestyle that obtained at Benkovic's establishment. Some people had joked about a harem on the moon. Spence had even made overtures once to Maymyo, the mayor's daughter, suggestions that she come and spend a few days at his satellite colony, but she'd cut him off short.

The young woman continued to look rather vacantly at her three visitors. Or she might be gazing just over their heads. Drugs again? Domingo was already wondering. He thought the air blowing out from the house was perfumed, but maybe it was only flowers. His vague misgivings about Benkovic, whom he had met only in passing, were rapidly increasing; but according to all the testimony, there was no question that the man was good with a ship.

Their hostess, not in the least embarrassed by her lack of clothing, broke the silence at last to announce in a childish voice: "Spence isn't here right now." It was as if she had finally been able to overcome some inertia that had held her silent. "He's over on the other side."

The captain spoke up, businesslike and impatient. "Do you suppose he's coming back soon? Or would it be better if we hopped over there and looked for him?" The other side of the moon—assuming that was what she meant—might be all of ten kilometers away. "I'm Niles Domingo. This is Iskander Baza. And Simeon Chakuchin."

The young woman did not acknowledge the introductions or offer her own name in return. Her attitude did not appear to be one of deliberate rudeness any more than her nakedness seemed intended to arouse or shock. Rather it was as if she were not really interacting with the men at all. When she spoke again she might have been talking to herself. "I guess maybe he'll be back shortly."

"Has he guessed that we're here, d'you suppose?" Iskander asked.

"I'll give him a call," the young woman said, with the air of one struck by a sudden, brilliant thought. She turned slowly away, then walked quickly back into the passage. Her flowers, no longer fresh, swung droopily as she turned. Her figure under ordinary circumstances would not have drawn much attention.

She had left the door open behind her. The three men exchanged looks yet once more. Then, with Domingo leading, they followed their reluctant hostess through the tube and into the house.

In contrast to the landing dome, the dwelling had been profusely and wildly decorated. There were flowers, live and cut, everywhere. Shelves and walls held drawings framed and unframed, along with what Simeon supposed ought to be called found objects. But the place was none too clean. A housework robot stood propped at an angle in one corner of the room, the drivers on two corners of its base unable to reach the dusty floor. No one had expended the moment's effort necessary to set the machine upright.

The three visitors overtook their hostess in the first large room they came to amid heaps of garish pillows, more flowers and food containers, most of which were used and empty. Some of the furniture was reasonably conventional, and some of that was broken.

The dark-haired woman looked at them uncomfortably, murmured something that might have been "Wait here," and disappeared again through another doorway. Simeon supposed the odds were even as to whether she intended to come back or whether she was going to communicate with Spence.

The men looked at each other and sat down, rather uneasily. After about five minutes the three, still waiting, heard faint murmurings of machinery that were, to expert ears, suggestive of a ship's arrival. In a couple of minutes more, Spence Benkovic hurried into the room, to his visitors' relief.

Greetings were exchanged, and Benkovic offered drinks, though rather doubtfully, as if he wasn't sure what he had in stock. The offer was politely declined.

To Domingo, Benkovic seemed a bit nervous but gave no indication of being on drugs. The lean, dark-bearded man admitted readily enough, though, that he was running out of money. He'd got emergency relief funds, like other colonists, but the harvesting wasn't what it had been.

Benkovic seemed fascinated when he was told of Domingo's hunting plans and said he was ready to try something new, something that would provide him with a stake.

The captain could give assurances on that point. "I'm paying bonuses to all my crew." When he named a figure, Benkovic was impressed. He should have been. Domingo had owned a fair amount of prime property on Shubra.

"I hear you're good with a ship. But before I sign you on formally, I want to make sure of that for myself. We'll take a test flight in the *Pearl*."

"No problem."

"Good. How soon can you be ready?"

Benkovic sighed, as if he'd been waiting a long time for someone to ask him that. "Whenever you are."

The young woman, still nameless to the visitors and still naked, had followed Spence back into the room and curled herself up on a couch, as if withdrawing from the world. Now she made an inarticulate sort of sound that might have been meant as a question. She looked with a vaguely appealing expression from one man to another.

Spence Benkovic looked at her. "Oh yeah. Pussy here— she's no spacer."

"Too bad," Iskander murmured, acting sympathy.

Benkovic looked at him, then said to Domingo: "Something will have to be done about her."

"Before you can leave."

"Well . . . I'm afraid so, yeah."

"What'll have to be done?"

There was some discussion, in which Pussy—if that was really her name—chose to take no part. Benkovic pleaded her case. In the end the captain found it necessary to stake the young woman also, turning over enough money to allow her to get on a ship to another world of her choice. She'd come to Shubra after the disaster, Benkovic said, so didn't qualify for any kind of government relief. Fortunately Spence had no other companions on the moon at present.

Spence picked up some flowers, fresh-looking this time, as his visitors were saying good-bye. Simeon wondered confusedly if they were each going to get a small bouquet on parting. But the flowers were intended for something else.

As Benkovic was walking with his visitors back to their ship, taking a different tube this time, they passed a construction, an arrangement of odd materials, chunks of rock, components that had once been parts of furniture, other things harder to identify, that had been piled and fastened together into what looked like a monument of some kind. The structure was almost three meters high, and at the base proportionally broad. Either the tube had been widened here to accommodate it, or the builder of this thing had chosen this site as the place where it would easily fit.

Spence put down his flowers at the base of this construction, on a small pile of older, deader-looking flowers, and stood with folded hands, regarding the little structure silently.

The structure was so odd that Simeon kept looking at it until he figured out what it was. Indeed a monument, or a small shrine. There were two names, women's names as Simeon interpreted them, carved in large, precise letters on the front.

Iskander had to ask, at last. "You put this up, Spence?"

Their host looked at them with liquid eyes in which the pain showed all too plainly. "I set it up for my two friends who were here when the berserker came, who didn't make it." He paused, then turned slightly to face Domingo. "Want me to put your daughter's name on it too, Captain?" It sounded as if Spence thought that would really be an honor. He added: "It'll just take a little while."

"You'd better spend the time in getting ready," Domingo said.

*   *   *

The *Pearl*'s first stop away from Shubra was at Base Four Twenty-five, after a flight in which Domingo checked out Spence Benkovic's talents to his own satisfaction.

Later, the captain said: "You were right, Ike. He is good with a headlink on."

"Have I ever steered you wrong, Cap? Maybe you better not answer that."

When they reached the base, Domingo sought out Gennadius and talked with him briefly. Iskander listened in on the conversation—a wrangling about goals and priorities—which as far as he could tell got nowhere.

Then the *Pearl* was off again. Domingo had four on his crew now, counting himself, all of them people he considered good. But he really wanted six. And all the best people of the colonized planetoids were now working for Gennadius.

The captain decided it was going to be necessary to go out of the Milkpail to get the help he needed.

CHAPTER 14

After a few days of steady travel, the last hazy fringes of the Milkpail had fallen behind them. Now the *Pearl* could enter the c-plus mode of operation and began to move at real interstellar speeds. As the ship dropped into flightspace, the universe outside the hull virtually disappeared. Now no world in the modest portion of the Galaxy that had been explored by Earth-descended humans was more than a few weeks away.

It had been a long time, years, since Domingo had driven a ship in clear space, but doing so was a simple matter compared with piloting in the nebula. There was nothing to it, relatively speaking, in a ship as good as this one.

Captain Domingo allowed the autopilot to run all systems most of the way and devoted himself to pondering the mysteries of the enemy's biological research. He also called up and considered his most up-to-date model of the Milkpail's interior. In this model a superimposed spiderweb of black lines represented the pattern of all the known and deduced movements of Leviathan, going back as many years as humans in the nebula had been keeping records.

Nodding toward this holographic construction, the captain once remarked to Iskander Baza: "I asked Gennadius if he'd ever thought of doing anything like this."

"And?"

"He told me that of course his office kept records of berserker activity, and of course they tried to figure where the next outbreak might be. But the Space Force kept no specific records on Leviathan. They weren't interested, he told me, in individual machines."

"He said that?" Iskander, as so often, seemed amused at how unintentionally funny other people were.

"Words to that effect. You know, I suspect the berserkers keep better records about the Space Force than he does about them."

"They probably ignore the records of individual units also."

Domingo looked at his second-in-command solemnly, and solemnly shook his head. "Don't believe that, Ike. Don't believe it for a moment. Don't you think they want to know where this ship is?"

Iskander raised his eyebrows. "I hadn't really thought about it, Cap."

"Try thinking sometime. About that."

Simeon, overhearing, didn't want to think about it. To him it sounded like the edge of craziness. To berserkers, life was life, something to be stamped out, or tolerated temporarily in the case of the rare aberration called goodlife, people willing to serve and sometimes worship the damned machines. He'd heard of places where goodlife were a real factor in the war, but so far in the Milkpail it hadn't been that way.

As Simeon understood the situation regarding Old Blue, the damned machine had never been reported anywhere outside the nebula, and no one knew why. Maybe those outside people had encountered it from time to time, but to them it was just another berserker, as it was to the Space Force.

The more time Simeon spent with Captain Domingo, the more he became convinced that those people outside were wrong. He was more and more ready to follow Domingo, though where it was going to lead him he did not know.

The first leg of their extranebular recruiting flight wasn't a long one; the captain had no intention of heading clear across the Galaxy.

A day passed in the c-plus mode, and then the *Pearl* reemerged into normal space. Imaged in the forward detectors now, only a few hours ahead, was a Sol-like sun whose system included a world named Rohan, a planet that was said to be quite Earthlike. Not that any of the *Pearl*'s crew had ever been within a hundred parsecs of Earth.

It was Iskander's shift as pilot when the *Pearl* approached for a landing on Rohan's nightside. Like most other worlds, this one was wary of berserkers. Rohan wore a girdle of defensive satellites, and the military installations on the ground were visible even at night to the people on the ship as they drew closer. Not that the planet was all fortress. Here outside the nebula you could see anything, berserkers included, coming a long way off and could call up your own fleet, assuming you kept one handy. It was a safe bet that Rohan did.

The chief spaceport facility, the one Domingo wanted, was on the surface, open to the planet's natural atmosphere. The port clearance routine was no more tedious than most outside the Milkpail, and the captain soon had it out of the way. Disembarking from the ship onto an open ramp, standing in strong natural gravity and looking up at a real planet's sky, thrillingly like the sky under which he had been born, Simeon had his first chance in what seemed to him an enormous length of time to see clear stars again. This viewpoint also provided him with a good look at the Milkpail from the outside. As he came down the ramp on foot, the great nebula loomed just ahead of him, a sprawling blob of whiteness that covered a quarter of the visible sky; and he knew it would continue for a good distance below the horizon.

In interstellar space you almost always saw the stars and

nebulae at second or third hand, as images on one kind of instrument or another. But here there was not so much as a glass faceplate between the eyes and their sublime objects, only the kindly, almost invisible fog of a real, naturally habitable planet's atmosphere. To a child of clear space like Simeon, the psychic satisfaction provided by this view was enormous.

Simeon just stood there for a long moment, drinking in the openness of the sky. In a way, this view made the memory of all the time he had spent in the Milkpail unreal. It was almost as if out here, in this other, more natural world, Wilma might still be alive. Alive and laughing under a sunny blue sky, as on the day when he had first met her . . .

But now he saw the Milkpail with new eyes, imagined Leviathan lurking within it like a spider in its web.

Benkovic, standing beside him, nudged him with an elbow and said: "Let's move it, Sim. We've got things to do."

"Right." Simeon stood looking at the sky a moment longer, then moved on down the ramp.

Domingo had already walked on ahead, Iskander as usual at his side.

The four of them rode comfortable public transport into town. The city attached to the port was of modest size by the standards of most ED worlds, though it served as a center for all kinds of business connected with space affairs. Domingo's first recruiting effort on Rohan took place in that city that very evening, in a computerized employment bureau, a place where spacefarers were likely to appear when they were looking for jobs.

In the employment bureau the captain paid a modest fee for the privilege of posting an announcement on the electronic bulletin board: Three crew members wanted for a dangerous job; generous bonuses; experience in fighting berserkers was desirable, and so was experience in working a ship through thick nebula.

As soon as the announcement was paid for it became visible, in large letters on a wall, and the purchaser was assured that it was being reproduced on a thousand other walls around the city, and in a myriad other places around the planet as well. But the first few minutes of the ad's visibility brought no response. This wasn't one of the small-town worlds of the Milkpail here. Rohan was part of the mainstream of Galactic civilization, and there were a hundred other advertisements being carried on that bulletin board, many of them promising easier and safer money, maybe even one or two as likely to appeal to the adventurous.

Waiting for the notice to produce some results, the four men from the Milkpail walked to a nearby restaurant that Iskander said he had visited before. They dined well on food spiced with microbial nebular life, some of which had almost certainly been harvested by Milkpail colonists. Perhaps one of the four had himself harvested and sold it, in a more peaceful time.

Over dessert, Iskander said that he was well acquainted with this city and knew another place nearby where there ought to be a good chance of finding some capable crew people. Naturally not everyone who was qualified and available watched the advertisements all the time. When their meal was finished, the four of them took another little walk of a few blocks that moved them across a border between neighborhoods of the city and landed them in an environment considerably less reputable-looking.

Iskander's goal here was a certain place of entertainment. As he explained to his shipmates, this place catered to a special group of customers. Some people came here to take drugs, some to drink alcohol, some to talk philosophy or religion. There were some who did all three; and others, probably a majority, who were just there to watch the ones who did drug themselves, give speeches and heckle speakers, or sometimes all of the above. It was this majority group, according to Baza, that included a high proportion of able spacers.

Domingo had doubts about this theory from the start. And the captain, on first entering the great noisy room filled with people, smoke and roaring music, was quick to express his skepticism about being able to find anyone here who would be acceptable on his crew. But he acknowledged that a large proportion of the clientele appeared to be spacefarers; though it was true that no one could tell that about people with any degree of certainty just by looking at them.

To Simeon Chakuchin, moving on foot through the ways of this crowded city and entering the crowded tavern, the years he had spent in the Milkpail seemed progressively more unreal. This world was as different from any of the tiny planetoids inside the nebula as the view of the night sky here differed from the view from Shubra. There were probably more people in this one tavern right now than had lived on Shubra before it was wiped out. Within the nebula, a few dozen people lived on one small world, a few hundred on the next, up to a few thousand dwelling on the comparatively great metropolitan center of Yirrkala. And here, in this one city, were easily more than enough people to populate all of the Milkpail colonies several times over. Simeon thought about it: maybe a hundred times over; he felt he no longer had a good sense of proportion in such matters. At the moment there was nothing pleasing in the thought of great numbers of people. All he knew was that here the air-conditioning was fighting a losing battle to clean the air, and the noise, the roar of talk and music, was almost deafening.

There were certainly some spacefaring people in this crowded hangout, perhaps as many as could have been mustered from the population of Shubra at its height. There was a certain look, with certain habits of dress and mannerisms, by which they could usually be identified, though mistakes were certainly possible. On one of the walls a large electronic display showed, along with other offers, Domingo's help-wanted ad for crew. There were the big bonuses, but still the advertisement did not seem to be attracting a great deal of attention. In fact, none at all, as far as Simeon could tell.

Iskander suggested: "Maybe a little word-of-mouth advertising would help."

The captain agreed briskly. "Can't see how it can do any harm."

Domingo got up from the booth where the four of them had settled and walked over to the bar. He could still be sociable when he made the effort, as he did now. First Iskander and then Simeon followed him and played along. Benkovic remained in the booth.

It proved to be not at all hard to strike up conversations with people in here, except that the noise tended to drown out everything that was said. But none of the first group of people Domingo talked to sounded like they were much interested in his mission.

That group broke up. The captain muttered to Simeon, without trying to be quiet about it, that he wasn't sure he wanted to have any of these people on his crew, anyway.

Someone nearby in the crowd muttered something uncomplimentary in return.

Simeon swallowed a large part of what was left of his drink. He hoped he was going to be allowed to finish it in peace.

"Let the Space Force do the hunting. We'll take care of the home defense." That was another, even louder comment. Inside or outside the Milkpail, that attitude was pretty much the same. It was the way most people looked at the situation.

Another voice chimed in, from among the standees at the bar: "You people have any idea what you're getting into? What you're talking about when you say fighting berserkers? How big a fleet you got? You know anything about nebular astrogation? Or berserkers either?"

Iskander chuckled. "Why don't you tell us?"

"I know what they are," Domingo said. His voice wasn't any louder than before and probably few people heard him.

"Really?" commented one who did. Music began crashing even more noisily in the background.

The captain spoke up, loud enough to be heard now but still calmly enough. "I've spent most of my life in the Milkpail. And where we're going, my ship is as good as anything the Space Force has. Or anything they're about to bring in there."

No one argued that point against Domingo, though Simeon thought some of the bar patrons might have refrained only out of politeness. Some were really being polite. Or else they just weren't interested. Even the man who had made the most derisive remarks now appeared to be having second thoughts. It didn't matter, as far as Simeon could see. Probably there were some good potential crew present right now, but if so they weren't rushing forward to say that they wanted to join the captain on his hunt.

"That's my ad up on the board." The captain made the claim in a loud, arrogant voice.

No one disputed him on that, either.

"And I'm as good a captain as there is in the Milk." Domingo almost shouted. Now it was as if he were determined to be noticed, to provoke some intense reaction. He made a strange figure, standing before these heckling strangers on a leg formed from berserker metal, his face and neck still scarred from his last encounter with the perverted robots. Of course none of the strangers listening to him knew about the leg. And they probably thought the scar a mere romantic affectation. Few people had scars any more unless they wanted to.

Some of Domingo's hearers might have been ready to believe that he was as good a captain as he said he was. But that point didn't seem to matter to them either, really. Simeon, watching and listening to the arrogant appeal and to their reaction, got the impression that there was something about the captain that these people were quietly afraid of, and they were becoming increasingly aware of it, even though they could hardly know what it was. Simeon wasn't sure what it was, either, but he knew that it was there.

Simeon banged down his empty glass on the bar. Glancing back across the room, he noticed that Benkovic, still in the booth, had been joined by a young woman whose costume suggested that she might work here and was engrossed in conversation with her. No help likely from that source. Well, no help needed.

Emboldened by a drink of unaccustomed stiffness, Simeon raised his voice and started talking to the mistaken folk along the bar. He told them, or tried to tell them, because he felt a mad urge to tell them, how important the mission was that he and his three fellow Shubrans were engaged in. How Old Blue had to be something more than a misprogrammed piece of metal, because their tragedy would be so much less if it were only that. How their effort to destroy Leviathan led toward all manner of noble achievements. Even barflies like most of his present audience would be enabled to kick their dependence on alcohol and other drugs this way, starting life over by signing up to fight Leviathan. Signing up had certainly helped him.

A small but growing ring of people were falling silent, starting to pay attention to Simeon's harangue. With an effortlessness that surprised himself, he went on talking, pleased at his own fluency. Iskander was nodding and smiling encouragement. Simeon told his audience about the people who had died under the weapons of Leviathan, on Shubra and elsewhere in the Milk. He went into some detail about the terrible machines that killed, as if maybe these tavern-dwellers here on Rohan were the ones who just didn't know what berserkers were really like.

Simeon had intended to make it clear in his speech, make it clear calmly and politely and without overemphasis, about the personal losses that he and Domingo, at least, among the present crew of the *Sirian Pearl*, had suffered. But somehow he forgot to bring up that point. And now some among his listeners began to jeer. Who was he to tell them about berserkers? Some of Simeon's hearers laid loud claim to being real Space Force veterans. And they said that peasants from outlying colonies ought to know that berserkers existed outside the Milkpail, too.

At a key moment, Iskander slyly egged things on. Correctly picking out the ethnic background of one of the louder hecklers, he delivered a studied insult. A moment later he gracefully dodged a bottle thrown by the loudmouth.

In another moment, violence had become general, at least around the three Shubrans at the bar. It struck Simeon at once that brawls in big towns were just like those in small. He waded in, trying to help his captain, grabbed the nearest opponent and slammed a big fist into the man's face. The man staggered back but refused to fall. From the corner of his eye Simeon saw Benkovic, abandoning his new acquaint-ance, come erupting out of the booth to aid his shipmates.

A thrown bottle went past Simeon's head. Something else, fist or weapon, hit him hard beside his ear. Two men were wrestling with him, getting the better of him until someone pulled one of them away. Simeon and his remaining oppo-nent went down together, grappling.

Domingo was not personally disposed to fight with fellow humans, no matter what the provocation, unless they were clearly standing between him and his goal. But his valuable crew members were at risk now, and he went at the job of combat with methodical ferocity.

In the fight Domingo did well, bracing his back against the bar, getting the most out of his metal leg. Simeon saw it working like a piston.

And in the midst of the melee the fight broke off, died out, even more suddenly than it had started. A silence fell, or what seemed like silence by comparison. It was as if each and every combatant had suddenly become aware of some-thing important enough to distract him. Simeon, lifting his head from the job of trying to throttle an opponent into a more sociable attitude, didn't know what signal he was re-sponding to, but he had the feeling, more like the certainty, that the time had come to stop.

He got to his feet slowly, breathing heavily, letting his gasping opponent up.

No one was fighting any longer. And everyone in the room was looking in the same direction.

A Carmpan had entered the tavern through one of the street doors.

A stocky figure, certainly human by the standard of free will and intelligence, but just as certainly not descended from any life on Earth, was standing there alone just inside the door and looking at them all, with what expression it was impossible to say.

Every Earth-descended human knew what Carmpan looked like, though the Carmpan homeworlds were remote, and few ED had ever actually seen a human of that other theme. The figure standing now at the badly lighted threshold of the silent room was by Earth standards squat, blocky, almost mechanical-looking. For clothing it wore some simple drapery, belted loosely over gray skin that looked almost like metal. There was no hair worth mentioning. To read expression on that alien face was, for Simeon at least, an impossibility. But then the mere presence of the being here in a tavern on Rohan seemed incredible, though of course there was nothing logically impossible about it. Simeon, and the people around him, to judge by their expressions, had had no reason to think there was a Carmpan within parsecs of this world.

For centuries, almost every Earth-descended human in the Galaxy had known that the humans of the other theme called Carmpan were valuable allies in the war fought by ED humans against berserkers. That was true even though the specific contributions of those allies were hard to pin down. As far as any ED human knew, no Carmpan had ever actually fought, none had ever committed an act of violence, even against berserkers. No Carmpan designed or supplied weapons. And yet there were the authenticated stories of their sporadic telepathic achievements. And there were the occasional utterances, sometimes mystic, sometimes mathematical, that Earth-descended people called Prophecies of Probability.

"Captain Domingo?" The slit-like mouth scarcely moved, but the voice, deep and slightly harsh, was very clear and understandable, even in the farthest corners of the room. If the speaker had been behind a screen, you might have thought that voice was issuing from an Earth-descended throat. Only now did Simeon fully realize how quiet the room had grown. Even the music had stumbled to a halt.

Now there was movement again, alteration in the frozen tableau of suspended combat in the center of the room. Domingo stepped forward, separating himself from the people around him. He looked at the Carmpan—almost, Simeon thought, as if the captain had been expecting some such miracle.

Domingo answered: "Yes?"

The voice coming from the blocky figure continued to be almost eerily Earthlike, the tone and accent flawless in the common language. The Carmpan said: "I wish to sign on as a member of your crew. I am highly qualified in communications with the headlink. Or, indeed, sometimes without it. I am able also to operate the other systems of an ED ship with what I think you will agree is more than a fair degree of skill."

With that first sentence, the silence in the room had grown even more intense.

It was an unprecedented event; no Carmpan in history had ever signed up as crew on an ED-human voyage.

"I'll be glad to sign you on," Domingo said into the silence. A light trickle of blood was making its way unnoticed down one side of his face. A moment later the captain added calmly: "Provided you can demonstrate your competence."

"I can do so at your pleasure; I am pleased to be accepted. Have you any objection to concluding the formalities immediately?"

There was only a momentary pause. "No objection at all." The captain pulled a folder from his pocket. Paperwork was brought out. The Carmpan approached, booted feet shuffling in the silence, a sound vaguely suggesting clumsiness.

People made room at the bar, and someone even wiped an area clean. The Carmpan paused silently over the paper and then signed on. Simeon saw the gray fingers working a writing tool, lettering neatly and formally, even entering a legal name—Fourth Adventurer—on the crew roster. Later, people who knew as much about the Carmpan as ED humans ever did were to say that sounded like as good a Carmpan name as any.

Shortly the new crew of the *Sirian Pearl*, now five strong and almost complete to the captain's satisfaction, left the tavern together, passing a police vehicle that was arriving belatedly to stop the brawl.

Fourth Adventurer requested a stop at the spaceport hostel, and there, from a room in the wing for non-ED humanity where he—or she—was the sole tenant, picked up a modest amount of baggage. With this loaded on a small robot carrier, the four ED humans and their new recruit proceeded to the spaceport. Simeon noticed that the Carmpan's baggage included what looked like a well-tailored suit of space armor.

En route to the port, Domingo took the opportunity to explain to the Carmpan that food should be no problem on the *Pearl*. The ship's food synthesizer was an advanced model that would keep Carmpan and ED alike well nourished. Fourth Adventurer accepted this as if he had expected it all along.

Given the possibility of lingering trouble over the tavern fight, Domingo did not want to stay long on this world. But even before he could arrange clearance for departure, he had several calls from people wanting to sign on, to fill the one remaining position on his crew, assuming the Carmpan would be accepted. The word had spread quickly. But somehow none of these late ED applicants pleased the captain, and he said he was of a mind to turn them all down sight unseen.

"That is a wise decision, Captain," said the Carmpan unexpectedly. Everyone else looked at him, and he looked back.

* * *

Immediately after liftoff from Rohan, the Carmpan requested a general crew meeting in the common room. When Domingo heard what the purpose of the meeting was to be, he granted the request at once.

With the meeting assembled, the newest crew member assured his new shipmates that what they had doubtless heard about the telepathic capabilities of Carmpan was at least partially correct. But he solemnly pledged, here and now, to respect the mental privacy of his shipmates and gave them assurances that he had done so from the start.

Simeon wasn't quite sure whether to be relieved, impressed or doubtful.

"Fourth Adventurer?" Spence Benkovic, sounding confident as usual, approached with a question.

"Yes, Spence."

"For reasons of psychology, affecting the ED component of the crew, there's something some of us would like to get settled. Would you consider it impolite if we asked whether you are male or female?"

"You should tell whoever is curious on the subject that I am male. And for the duration of my service, you may disregard any special considerations of politeness where I am concerned."

Simeon thought that Benkovic looked vaguely disappointed.

Next day the *Pearl* departed Rohan. On the advice of the Carmpan, Domingo chose a course that seemed to lead nowhere in particular. En route, Fourth Adventurer easily passed the captain's tests of competence in controlling the systems of the ship by mindlink band. A few adjustments in the equipment were necessary to accommodate a non-ED brain, and with that out of the way everything went very smoothly.

But all the surprises were not over.

CHAPTER 15

No sooner had the Pearl departed from the Rohan system than Domingo's newest crew member called up the captain on intercom and suggested a different heading from the one just established.

Domingo's first reaction was to consult the holographic chart in front of him. The course he had just charted led directly toward the Milkpail, but now Fourth Adventurer wanted him to deviate from that by thirty degrees or so, heading into what amounted to an interstellar wasteland.

The captain, fully aware that most of the rest of his crew were probably listening in, shifted his gaze to the small, gray, enigmatic image on the intercom stage. "Why should I go that way, Fourth Adventurer?"

The Carmpan's voice was as firmly and convincingly ED as ever. "It will give you the best chance of recruiting the sixth crew member you desire to have."

"Aha. And who will this person be?"

"A very highly rated pilot."

That was the very skill that Domingo had been wishing for most strongly.

There was a pause, during which the captain studied his instruments some more. "You appear to be directing me into what we call the Gravelpile," he said at last. The formation known by that name was a dull, dark wisp of coarse interstellar matter, billions of kilometers long and deep, growing out like a dead or dying tail from one end of the Milkpail. Colonies were nonexistent in the Gravelpile, and suns almost so. Astrogation at any speed was difficult. Ships and people were almost entirely absent. Life of any kind was very rare, and so, therefore, were berserkers.

Fourth Adventurer's tiny image nodded. "That is true. That is where I am advising you to go."

Domingo was certain now that the entire crew was listening in. "Just what is this highly rated pilot doing there? He or she is aboard some kind of a ship, I presume?"

"That would seem logical, but I am not sure. It is hard for me to tell."

Simeon, watching the conversation through his own intercom station, thought that Domingo for once looked indecisive.

The captain demanded of Fourth Adventurer: "Is that all you can tell me?"

"It is all I can tell you at the moment that will be of help. You must understand that I am as reluctant to probe that pilot's mind as to probe yours."

"Ah. But you're certain he or she is there?"

"Indeed. And apparently alone."

Iskander broke in: "There must be a lot of good pilots' minds scattered here and there around the Galaxy. Is there some reason why we should go chasing after this one in particular?"

"The probabilities of success, in our mission of pursuit, are greater if we do."

Everyone had heard the legendary stories: how the Carmpan talents, telepathic and probabilistic, worked—at least sometimes. It was up to the captain to decide.

"All right," Domingo agreed, after a pause. He was thinking that it was no advantage to have special talents aboard if you were afraid to use them or trust them.

A voyage of several days brought the *Pearl* to the fringes of the Gravelpile, and here the Carmpan suggested—"ordered" was more like it, Iskander muttered—another course correction.

The second-in-command was not too happy. "What exactly are we supposed to find here, Fourth Adventurer?"

"A pilot alone . . . but I must report an unfavorable development."

Domingo spoke up sharply. "Let's have it, then."

"By now, captain, I am beginning to suspect that the pilot we are seeking is dying, or else in suspended animation. There is a quality of mind that I can only describe as fading."

"Great. Well, we've come this far. We'll push on."

The ship advanced, slowly, into the Gravelpile. From this point on, the average density of matter in the space around the ship was as high as in the Milkpail, making it necessary to travel in normal space, at relatively low speeds. The matter here tended to be concentrated in solid granules and larger chunks, but the overall effect was much the same.

In another hour, Fourth Adventurer suddenly recommended yet a third change of heading. The captain silently complied. No more was said.

Until about an hour after that, when the Carmpan called a halt. "Here," he said. "Somewhere nearby. Now you must take over the search. Captain, I am very tired. With your permission I am going to rest."

Spence Benkovic was muttering something uncharitable. But Domingo was looking at Fourth Adventurer with concern. "Permission granted."

"I shall be all right in a few hours. But now I must rest." And the Carmpan's intercom station went blank.

"Do that." Domingo sighed faintly, and looked around him on his instruments. His ship was practically at rest with reference to the nearby matter in space. "Iskander, Benkovic. Let's break out some seeking tools."

In a few more minutes the captain had his entire ED crew at work, examining space in the vicinity of the ship with various instruments. Still nothing that suggested the presence of any kind of pilot, good or bad, was showing anywhere on the detectors.

"Everyone keep looking. I'm starting a slow cruise in a search pattern."

To the professed surprise of some aboard, a few minutes of routine search effort did produce results. There was first a faint, distorted distress signal and then the image of what might well be a lifeboat, almost lost amid gravel at some forty thousand kilometers' range.

"I'm proceeding in that direction," Domingo announced. "I want everyone except Adventurer at stations."

The approach to the signal source was again routine, cautious and time-consuming. As the *Pearl* drew nearer, the object could be certainly identified as a common type of ED lifeboat. And as the investigating ship approached still closer to it, the small craft could be seen to be battered and scarred. It looked as if it had been through a war, as probably, thought Simeon, it had.

Probing at the object with a tight communications beam brought no response except a continuation of the distress signal, which was no doubt an automatic transmission.

Looking over the lifeboat from a distance of only a few hundred meters, it was impossible to guess whether it had been adrift in space for a day or for several hundred years.

"I say we wake the squarehead up"—this was Benkovic speaking—"and try to make sure he knows what he's doing. This thing could be some kind of a berserker booby-trap."

The captain dismissed that suspicion immediately. "Way out here? They wouldn't waste the effort. They'd go near a shipping lane somewhere to work that kind of a stunt. I want a couple of people to suit up and take a look at it."

"I guess you have a point there, Captain." And Spence, as if to make amends for arguing, was the first to volunteer.

Iskander for once did not volunteer; maybe, thought Simeon, the second-in-command disdained this job as too safe and easy.

Simeon decided that he himself was ready to get into a suit again. And shortly he was out in space with Benkovic. The Milkpail again dominated the sky, but here the great bright splash of it was barred and patched with blackness, the erratic patterns of the Gravelpile's intervening dark material. This really looked and felt like deep space, a hell of a long way from anywhere or anything, and if there was really a living pilot in the boat, she or he was going to have one miraculous rescue to tell the grandchildren about someday.

The two men reached the drifting lifeboat speedily and without incident. The main hatch on the small vessel opened normally, on the first effort, but there was no cycling of the airlock. The cabin atmosphere in the boat either had been lost, or else deliberately evacuated.

Benkovic went first in through the hatch, with Chakuchin hovering nearby outside. As with all lifeboats, there wasn't a great deal of interior room. But a moment later Spence was reaching out a gauntleted hand to beckon, and calling him on radio. "Take a look at this, Sim."

Simeon went in, just as Benkovic got the interior lights turned on. The boat appeared to be a standard, fairly recent model. There were two berths, as might be expected, convertible to suspended-animation couches.

And both of the SA beds were occupied. Simeon glanced in passing through the little window of the nearest. There was a dead man in it. One glance was enough; there would be no need to open this one to make sure.

But Spence was grinning beside the second berth. Simeon looked in there and beheld the countenance of a reasonably attractive young woman, eyes closed, as if she were in peaceful sleep. Readouts on the berth confirmed the immediate instinctive impression that she was alive.

Domingo's voice was in their suit radios, asking questions. Simeon answered. "Looks like one survivor, Captain. If she's still viable."

"Viable ain't the word for it." Benkovic was looking through the little window appreciatively.

Domingo was asking: "Anything about the setup look suspicious? If not, we might as well grapple the boat and bring her right aboard."

Nothing looked suspicious as far as the two investigators could tell. A few minutes later the lifeboat, entry hatch still open, was inside the *Pearl*'s ventral bay, and atmosphere was filling boat and bay alike.

Once atmosphere had been established, the men in the bay tried the standard revival cycle on the suspended-animation chamber. It worked. The watching men were soon rewarded with favorable readouts and signs of life. Their pilot-to-be—if indeed the young woman was going to fit that category—had undoubtedly started breathing. Iskander went to sickbay to get certain things ready in case they should be needed.

Presently the SA chamber opened. The young woman, dressed in a standard ship's coverall, immediately struggled to sit up in the *Pearl*'s artificial gravity. Spence and Simeon were at her side, offering physical support, and trying to be reassuring.

In a few seconds, with help, the object of their attentions was on her feet. The young woman was tall, and more than moderately attractive now that her long, strong body was fully alive again.

Presently Iskander and Spence were cycling with her into the ship proper. When they were through the lock, they walked her gently to sickbay between them.

"What time is it?" That was the first question she asked, the first coherent words she uttered, on waking up more or less completely. By this time she was seated in the sickbay of the *Pearl*, and could see she had an interested audience around her. Her speech and accent seemed to follow one of the more commonly heard patterns; she would not have sounded out of place at all on Rohan, though there was a trace of some earlier influence, an origin somewhere else.

Domingo, who had come along from his station to observe this phenomenon for himself, named the current standard year, and the month when the ship had left Rohan. Days and hours in deep space were always subject to correction for relativistic effects, despite the theoretical ability of c-plus travelers to avoid such effects entirely.

When she heard the numbers the young woman slumped, as if with relief. "That's good. It means I was only a few days in the boat. Don't know why the idea of a long sleep bothers me a whole lot, but it does. Not that I would miss anyone who's still alive in this century, particularly." She drew a deep breath and tossed back her full, flowing hair and looked around her. "I'm Branwen Galway. What's this? A trader?"

"I'm Niles Domingo. This is my ship, the *Sirian Pearl*, and we're hunting a berserker. What happened to you? Why were you in the boat? I don't suppose it was Old Blue that put you away?"

"It was a berserker—I didn't ask it if it had a name. My ship was the *Old Pueblo*, out of New Trinidad . . . did you say you're hunting a berserker? How big is your fleet? I've just been doing my damnedest to get away."

"No fleet. This one ship." The captain tersely recited the *Pearl*'s tonnage and her armaments. "So your ship was destroyed? But you don't know whether or not it was Leviathan that attacked you?"

Fully awake and aware now, Branwen Galway was looking at the captain with some curiosity. "No, sir. As I say, I didn't ask." She paused, evidently struck suddenly by a different thought. "The other berth on the lifeboat—there was someone in it too, wasn't there?"

"A man," said Simeon. "I'm afraid he's dead."

"Ah. That's no surprise." Branwen looked around at her audience. "He didn't mean that much to me, but I wondered

. . . I'm sure there wasn't enough left of our ship for you to find anything.''

"You're right about that." Domingo was smiling faintly; maybe the woman he had just rescued would be a pilot, maybe not. But at least she certainly did not seem to be the type who was going to cause a lot of unnecessary trouble.

Already she had abandoned the subject of her own past. "One ship, hey? Well, you've got guts. Why are you hunting a berserker?"

Everyone looked at Domingo. He said: "I'll tell you the story when you've had a chance to rest."

"That kind of a story, hey?"

The rest of the crew were in the process of introducing themselves more or less formally to the new arrival when Simeon suddenly saw Branwen's expression alter. She was looking past him at the doorway to the corridor outside sickbay, and Simeon knew before he turned what he was going to see.

Fourth Adventurer had appeared there, standing in the corridor. The Carmpan announced that he was rested now and ready to resume his full duties. Then he introduced himself to the newest arrival.

Branwen was suitably impressed at sight of the Carmpan, especially when she heard that his talents were responsible for her rescue; otherwise she could easily have drifted here for a million years.

Fourth Adventurer in turn looked at her for some time, and appeared satisfied with what he saw.

Domingo, indicating the woman, asked him: "Is this my pilot, Fourth Adventurer?"

"She is a very capable pilot, Captain. You must ask her whether she will be yours." And the Carmpan turned and moved away, still looking tired, almost shuffling, despite what he had just said about being rested.

Branwen was mildly bewildered. "What was that all about? I mean, I am a pilot, but how can he possibly judge how good?" Nobody tried to answer that.

Simeon noticed that Benkovic was already looking at the newest recruit with what appeared to be something more than medical concern. It was Spence who first reached to help her when she stood up again. "Feel dizzy?"

She pulled her arm away from his supporting hand, firmly but not making a big deal of it. "I'm coping, thanks. I notice I haven't got a lot of baggage with me. I could use a private berth somewhere, and a change of clothes. And then some food."

Provided with crew clothing including coveralls, some miscellaneous supplies and food, her residence established in the berth that had been reserved for the sixth crew member, Galway soon announced her readiness to join in a berserker hunt, as long as it was being properly planned and led. She said she would soon be ready to demonstrate her competence.

A little later, Simeon happened to encounter the Carmpan alone. Unable to keep from asking the question, Chakuchin demanded of Fourth Adventurer: "Why can't you do this kind of thing all the time? Rescue work, I mean?"

"There is a price that I and others must pay, whenever such help is given. You do not understand."

"No, I don't." Meeting those alien eyes, Simeon had the inescapable feeling that he was making a fool of himself. Lamely he added: "Anyway I'm glad you're helping now."

The Carmpan looked at him, unreadably, and turned away.

Fourth Adventurer resumed taking his regular turn on watch, but otherwise spent most of the next few days in his berth, more often than not out of touch with the rest of the crew.

Domingo had already reestablished his course in the direction of the Milkpail. At this distance the great glowing nebula already dominated the instruments in flightspace, and it was a looming presence in normal space as well.

Branwen Galway quickly made a complete recovery from her interval of suspended life.

From time to time, when asked, she related a few more

details of what had happened to her and her ship. But she
appeared to have put those events behind her now, and to be
reluctant to talk very much about them.

She was a tall woman, and now moved lithely about the
ship. With a woman aboard, the whole atmosphere on the
Pearl had changed. One part of the change was of course that
Domingo now considered his crew complete—as soon as
Branwen felt up to it, he had formally offered her the second
pilot's job, on condition of course that she demonstrate her
competence. She had a right to refuse the job, of course. But
as a mere rescued survivor, she had no right to demand that
the ship interrupt its own mission to take her where she might
want to go. Domingo said he could probably drop her at
some Milkpail world if she would prefer that to signing on.

Iskander, probing, indulging his perpetual itch to investigate and instigate, did ask her where she would want to go if
she had a choice. Branwen Galway responded with no more
than a shrug.

She was soon ready to demonstrate her competence to
Domingo's full satisfaction.

"Sorry I didn't bring any references with me, Captain. But
I can give you a demonstration." Branwen had already been
looking over the various onboard systems, and felt confident
of handling any of them. "What would you like to see?"

Domingo wanted to see a lot, and his newest recruit obliged.
He was well pleased with what he saw. There was no doubt
that his potential new crew member was good, very good, at
running any spacecraft system that could be operated from a
headlink. Considering the circumstances of her rescue, her
claim of combat experience was easy to accept. And when
the *Pearl* got into deep nebula again, Galway established her
ability to handle that. She gave the impression of being good
at a lot of other things besides.

Simeon thought that she was better looking than most of
her sex, certainly more attractive than the ones he knew who
had acquired hard-boiled reputations in space work. Not that
Branwen appeared to care whether any of the men aboard

thought she was good-looking or not. Simeon kept watching for Spence Benkovic to get his face slapped, but so far Spence, after that first gallant offer, was behaving in a very businesslike way. Playing hard to get, perhaps.

The crew member who most interested Branwen Galway appeared to be the Carmpan. Of course that enigmatic presence would intrigue anyone. Still none of the ED humans on the crew, thought Simeon, really had the faintest idea why Fourth Adventurer had offered to sign on. As far as Simeon knew, Domingo had never asked.

Next most interesting to the woman—perhaps first after the initial shock of the alien presence had somewhat worn off—was Domingo himself, who of all the ED men seemed to care the least about her sex.

She spent a fair amount of time, more than was necessary certainly, talking with the captain.

Domingo was soon ready to complete her formal signing on the crew. Iskander Baza seemed resigned to the fact, if not enthusiastic about it. Benkovic was as quietly pleased by this recruit as he had been quietly upset by the last one.

A little shakedown cruise now, the captain announced, and the ship and crew would be ready to face Leviathan.

CHAPTER 16

Branwen Galway and the Fourth Adventurer had both demonstrated their competence, to say the least. They were also alike in admitting to a relative lack of experience at operating a ship within a sizable thick nebula.

The captain was ready to agree that some nebular practice was in order for his two newest crew members before the time came for them to fight Leviathan. But he thought that difficulty would almost certainly take care of itself. Leviathan was unlikely to be waiting obligingly for the *Pearl* at the point where she reentered the Milkpail. The crew ought to have an adequate opportunity to gain experience within the nebula while they were trying to pick up the enemy's trail. Domingo wanted every member of his crew to be as highly skilled as possible at every job, and with that goal in mind, he tried to rotate assignments frequently.

Branwen had a question for the captain when their discussion came around again to the object of their mission: "Why do you so often say 'he' when you talk about this thing we're chasing?''

The two of them, both off watch, were alone in the common room at the moment. Domingo thought for a few seconds, running his fingers through his hair. Then he looked up at the tall young woman beside him. He asked heı: "Do you believe in any gods?''

Galway was standing, leaning on the console of the computer that was sometimes used to build ethereal models in this room—the captain had noticed that she often preferred to stand rather than sit.

She said: "Can't say that I do, Captain. Though there are times. Why?''

"If you believed in a goddess or a god, which pronoun would you use?''

She had to think that one over for a moment. "Are you telling me this damned machine you want to kill is your god?''

"That may be as close as I can come to it. But I was asking what you would do.''

Brawen considered him irreverently. "Well, at least you're not calling a berserker 'her.' ''

Once Domingo had got his ship back inside the Milkpail, he elected to begin his hunt in a direction that made it logical to select the world of Yirrkala as one of the first stops. Yirrkala, he explained to his new crew members, was one of the best places in the nebula to pick up the latest information.

As the *Pearl* approached Yirrkala, her crew observed that the populous planetoid was more heavily defended than ever, and it looked as if there were more settlers here than ever before. The mass flight from the Milkpail some people had predicted was evidently not materializing.

After landing, Domingo's first question to the local people, asked even before he got out of his ship, was of course for the latest news of Leviathan. The response was disappointing. Little news had developed in the days the *Pearl* had been gone from the nebula. No more attacks, only one more sighting, and that slightly doubtful. Neither particularly encouraging or discouraging, just another bit of information for the mosaic.

When he had seen that item entered in his computer's data banks, Domingo left the ship and walked down the familiar spaceport ramp. He went alone, saying only that there were a few more things he wanted to find out and that he would be back in an hour or two at most. His crew were meanwhile left with a few routine jobs and a little free time.

The captain was somewhat surprised to discover his own intentions when he realized what he was going to do next. He wanted to speak to Polly—exactly what he meant to say to her he wasn't sure, but the way they had parted just wasn't right. But his efforts to locate Polly Suslova met with failure. The local office known as Central Communications—the chief settlement on Yirrkala was trying to grow into a real city—pronounced her unavailable and would not elaborate on that reply.

A call to Irina and Casper earned the captain the information that Polly had left Yirrkala permanently. Her relatives told Domingo she had moved with her children to another world where she was now working at a new job.

"Another world?"

"That's right."

"Which one?"

There was a pause. "I'm not sure," Irina said.

Domingo was skeptical. But he didn't press any harder for the information.

Before the call was over, Polly's relatives also managed to drop a hint that Polly was much happier now that she was seeing a new man.

Walking rather slowly back toward his ship, Domingo found himself wondering if it were true. Suddenly a new thought struck him, and he began to wonder whether the new man could possibly be Gujar. Though why it should make any difference to him, even if it were so, was more than he could understand. Polly and Gujar were just people from his old crew, and naturally he wished both of them well.

It was certainly not as if he really needed Polly to fill a backup position on the crew, skilled though she was. Had that idea really been in the back of his mind? It would be foolishness. Six people were really the optimum number to have aboard. Practical experience confirmed it.

Things were all right the way they were. The pace of Domingo's walking speeded up.

While going through his routine of departure clearance at the port, he ran into an acquaintance who had actual information about Gujar. Sidoruk was again captaining a ship owned by someone else, but this time he was serving in the expanded Home Guard fleet that had been organized by Gennadius from among all the Milkpail colonies. No telling where Gujar and his ship were right now or where Gennadius was either, for that matter.

Captain Domingo's new crew hadn't really had a chance to get off his ship and stretch their legs before he was back among them. He quickly assembled them on board his ship again, took a quick look at his updated model and set out in the direction of the most recently reported sighting of Leviathan.

Two days had passed, and the *Pearl* had covered about half the distance to that spot when, as on their previous departure from a world, a call on intercom from his Carmpan crew member made the captain decide to change course sharply. But this time the call carried an unprecedented urgency.

Fourth Adventurer, in a strained voice, reported himself in telepathic agony. He said the cause was the destruction, currently in progress, of the population of yet one more small world colonized by ED humans, this one out on the edge of the nebula.

"Berserkers?"

"I am sure of it, though as you know I cannot perceive them directly."

"Of course, berserkers. What else would it be? *But is it Leviathan?*"

"I cannot tell that, Captain." Nor could the Carmpan see, or the other crew members deduce from his report, the name of the afflicted planetoid. But the direction and the approximate distance of it were determinable: *that* way, for a couple of days' hard traveling.

The ship had traversed less than half the estimated distance when Fourth Adventurer reported that the attack, the agony, was over now.

"How did it end? You mean—"

"I perceive only that it has ended. But the application of logic to that fact produces no reassurance."

Domingo held his course steady in the same direction.

Aboard the *Pearl* a conversation was in progress, concerning what was reliably known of the actual fighting strength of Leviathan, and how the *Pearl*'s armament compared with what the enemy was known to have.

A computer model, this one an image that Simeon had rarely seen before, was on display. The holographic model showed the size and structure of Leviathan, based on what had been recorded and reported from all known sightings, and what had been deduced and estimated from that.

On the little holostage the jagged shape of the model rotated slowly. A symbolic presentation of the *Pearl* on the same scale showed all too clearly how much smaller the human ship was than its potential opponent.

The comparison was sobering, but everyone on the *Pearl*'s crew was able to look at such matters with a professional eye, and there appeared to be good prospects for victory. No one had any doubts that Domingo's objective was to win, and that they had reasonable expectations of achieving that objective. No one, the captain least of all, wanted to make a futile effort that would serve only to give the enemy another triumph.

During these tactical discussions Domingo emphasized that

there were advantages in being relatively small. One was the capability of moving faster within the nebula. Another point was that the shields of the human ship had a more compact area to defend—a much easier job than trying to cover the whole sprawling surface of a planet or planetoid, or even the area of a machine the size of Leviathan.

The armament of the *Sirian Pearl* did not include a c-plus cannon, but she did mount some of the latest missiles capable of driving themselves effectively faster than light, by skipping in and out of normal space in very nearly the same way as a projectile from such a gun. The ship also carried beam projectors modified for nebular work, with new focusing modulation that ought to be able to eat through such shields as Leviathan was known to possess.

This discussion in the common room was interrupted by a call to battle stations, delivered by the crew member manning the forward detectors. The detectors had offered a sudden indication of what looked like a whole berserker fleet, cruising the eternal mists out there at no very great distance ahead of the *Pearl*.

Everyone aboard the ship scrambled to get to his or her combat position. Even before Domingo had any chance to think about tactics, it became apparent that there was no chance to retreat. Evidently the *Pearl* had been sighted too, by whatever or whoever was ahead. That shadowy fleet up there was reacting, turning toward the single ship. The range was already so short that it would be hopeless for the *Pearl* to attempt flight.

"Weapons ready. We're going to—"

The IFF transponder chirped, bringing a spontaneous and general gasp of relief from the crew, or at least from four of its five ED human members.

The captain was the only one whose manner betrayed no relief; if anything he sounded exasperated. "It's the Space Force."

"Well, damn it all anyway." Iskander's intercom tone

managed to make his annoyance almost convincing. "If we'd been trying to find them, we never could have done it."

Domingo was quick to open communications with the approaching ships. The Space Force responded, sending clipped jargon with their usual tightbeamed caution. The pulses of transmitted talk came through only blurrily at first. Then as the distance lessened, with the *Pearl* and the Space Force fleet speeding through the nebula on gradually converging courses, a real conversation could get started.

Soon the image of Gennadius, seated on the bridge of his combat ship, had come into being on the several small individual holostages the crew members of the *Pearl* were watching.

Even padded and armored as he was, obviously on red alert for combat, the commander looked more haggard, more cadaverously thin than ever. His voice was suspicious, almost hostile. "What the hell are you doing out here, Domingo?"

"I think you know what I'm doing. I just hope you're doing the same thing, and suddenly I find I have a new reason to hope so. Is this really where your big computer says Old Blue ought to be?"

"Nothing my computer says has been doing me much good lately. So I'm trying some guessing, as I suppose you are. All right, I admit I'm after Leviathan."

Domingo stared for a moment at the commander's little image. Then, in a sharply changed voice, the captain of the *Pearl* demanded: "He's hit another colony, hasn't he? Which one is it this time?"

" 'He?' " The commander sounded mystified. Then he gave up quibbling. "All right. It's hit another colony." Gennadius named the latest victim. Simeon tried to place its location on his mental map. Yes, it was presumably the same world whose suffering, detected by the Carmpan, had brought the *Pearl* moving in this direction.

"And you guessed his route of departure might lead him along this way."

"Something like that." Gennadius appeared to take counsel with himself and came to a decision. "Look, Domingo. My theory is that some berserkers, the one you call Leviathan probably among them, have a repair and refitting base somewhere around here in the nebula, maybe in a dark-star system. I'm looking for it now, but my chance of finding it would be better if I were able to call in more ships."

"Then call them in."

"It's not that simple. If I call ships here, I have to take them away from somewhere else. Most probably from guard duty near some colony, and I don't want to do that. I'll make you a deal. Take the *Pearl* and stand guard duty at da Gama, and I'll call two of my ships in from that area to help out here with the search. It would give us a considerably better chance of finding what we're looking for. If I can catch Leviathan with my battle group, I'll bring you back a blue light. Or any other part of its anatomy you want."

"No deal," said Domingo instantly.

"I didn't think so." Gennadius was angry, though not surprised. "All right, then, let me repeat my first question. What the hell are you doing out here? If you know something, I want to know it, too. What have you seen? Or found out?"

"I've seen nothing out of the ordinary. I've been extrapolating Leviathan's earlier movements—as you must have been doing also."

The commander snorted. "With your little shipboard computer? You've been damned lucky, then."

The captain nodded, smiling lightly. "You might say that a certain amount of luck has come my way."

Gennadius had his fleet deployed in a far-flung formation for maximum sweep, Simeon observed. He supposed that for that reason it was not amazingly odd that the encounter with the *Pearl* had occurred, given that the two commanders were following the same basic plan of search.

The Space Force commander once more demanded to know what other sightings the *Pearl* had recently made.

"None at all," Domingo repeated at once. "What about yourself?"

"We picked up something about two hours ago—movement of some kind at spacecraft speeds. At extreme range, and we weren't able to close on it. I'm still not sure if it was berserker movement or not—but out here, nothing else is likely to . . . what in all the hells is *that*?"

Checking his indicators, Simeon realized that Fourth Adventurer had just turned his intercom station on two-way as if intending to join in the radio conversation. Now for the first time Gennadius was able to get a good look at all of the six crew members on Domingo's ship—including the one whose presence represented a unique event in the history of Earth-descended spacefaring.

"Just one of my crew." Domingo sounded distracted; his thoughts as usual were still on berserkers.

"One of your crew. Just one of your bloody crew. Iskander, what's going on over there?" For a moment the Carmpan's presence appeared to outrage Gennadius more than anything else that had happened yet.

"Things are just as you see them, sir." Baza sounded sweetly reasonable. "If I may, I would suggest a more diplomatic attitude toward our ally of the Carmpan theme."

"I . . . should have known better than to ask," Gennadius muttered, almost inaudibly. Then he roused himself, or tried to rouse himself, to his diplomatic duty. "Absolutely." He started to address himself to the Carmpan. "Let me assure you, sir, or—" He was getting nowhere. "Domingo. Domingo, I warn you, if you're doing anything to get us in trouble with—with—"

Fourth Adventurer spoke at last. He introduced himself calmly and assured the commander that there were no difficulties in prospect involving intertheme diplomacy. He, Fourth Adventurer, was present on this mission by his own free choice as an individual, and his presence would be more likely to alleviate diplomatic trouble than to cause it.

Gennadius briefly tried to grapple with that but gave up.

He had too much else to think about. "I, I don't understand that, sir."

"You need not worry about it now, Commander."

There was a pause. "You do claim diplomatic status, then?" Gennadius at last inquired. The image of his face was growing clearer as the hurtling ships approached each other.

"I have made no such claim as yet, and at present I do not intend to do so. But I would be within my rights, and I reserve the right to do so in the future. Matters of vast importance are almost certainly at stake here, Commander, more important than getting rid of a berserker."

Suddenly Fourth Adventurer's shipmates were staring at him too, as if they had never seen him before this moment.

"Ah." Gennadius obviously couldn't make any sense at all out of what he had just heard. Everyone was waiting for him to try. "Ah—Fourth Adventurer—matters of vast importance?"

"Yes, Commander."

"Such as what?"

"I said 'almost certainly at stake,' Commander. If and when the proper word is 'certainly,' you will be informed."

"Ah. Good. Well, in the meantime I have a job to perform. We all do."

The commander and the captain talked a little longer.

Gennadius pragmatically welcomed the presence of Domingo's ship as adding to the total strength available in the region; but at the same time the commander was fearful that Domingo's fanaticism was going to raise more problems. Certainly it was keeping Domingo and his ship from being as useful as the commander would have liked.

In the privacy of his own mind, Gennadius decided that he was going to try not to think about the presence of the Carmpan and what it might mean.

"Captain, I don't suppose it would do any good to order you to take your ship and stand Home Guard duty near da Gama. Or to go home."

"I don't suppose it would. I've told you again and again what I'm doing. My plans haven't changed."

The commander heaved a long sigh. "All right." In an easier voice he added: "Looks like we've got some dirty weather coming up ahead. Going to run for it?"

"I'm not that much worried about a squall."

CHAPTER 17

The detectors on all the ships now showed a nebular storm ahead and coming on. The storms arose from a combination of magnetic and gravitational forces; in them the matter composing the eternal clouds was compressed beyond any density it normally attained. The masses of it were ringed and shot through like Earthly thunderstorms with electrical discharges—though each storm was considerably bigger than the Earth itself—and glistened with iridescent rainbows. The onrushing disturbances were now only minutes away.

If a colony lay in a storm's path, the inhabitants took shelter in shielded underground rooms or perhaps in reliable ships that could outrun electronic weather. Sleets of atomic and subatomic particles, knotting and lashing fields of magnetic and other forces, would disrupt human movement and communications, wipe out food crops in the nebula and on planetary surfaces and almost certainly inflict some human casualties. It was fortunate that storms of great size were rare.

This was not one of the larger ones. The squall, as Domingo had called it, struck the ships.

Screens and holostages went blank as the nuclear-magnetic lash tore up communications between ships and impeded forward progress. The energies of the miniature tempest extended outside normal space, confusing astrogation systems and temporarily negating drives, robbing them of their normal hold in the mathematical reality of flightspace.

The people on Domingo's ship had a glimpse of the Space Force ships scattering before their own instruments roared with white noise, cutting off the world. And then the *Pearl* was swept away.

The intercom was still working perfectly, but the Carmpan's unit remained blank even after repeated efforts to call him. When Branwen and Iskander went to Fourth Adventurer's berth to investigate, they found him tossing in his acceleration couch as if he were spacesick or feverish.

Bending over the supine, blocky figure, Branwen shook him gently by a corner of his gray garment. But Fourth Adventurer was unable or unwilling to respond to that stimulus or to the first anxious questions from his visitors.

The woman turned uncertainly to Baza. "Can a Carmpan have a fever?" she asked. "He feels warm."

"I don't know." For once not amused, Iskander flicked the intercom. "Anyone on board claim to be an expert in Carmpan biology?"

No one did, apparently. Nor did anyone want to suggest what sort of first aid or medical treatment, if any, to attempt. The decision fell to Domingo by default, and by his orders a policy of watchful waiting was adopted.

Hardly had this been decided when to everyone's relief Fourth Adventurer roused himself enough to announce that he had not really been taken ill. He was, he said, only suffering from the strain of having made telepathic contact with strange forms of life in the raw, seething nebula outside. The native life forms here were also endangered by the storm when it engulfed them and suffered pain, and their distress communicated itself to the Carmpan's mind.

Simeon didn't understand. "I thought you were able to tune things out."

"Ordinarily. But just now I dare not."

There was silence on the intercom, but Simeon thought most of the crew were probably listening. He asked the Carmpan: "You knew all along there was life out there in the nebula, didn't you? Of course, everyone knows that."

The feeble answer was more a gesture than a sound. It conveyed no meaning to Simeon.

"I'd say it would be a good idea to keep your mind away from it if it makes you sick."

Fourth Adventurer managed to get out intelligible words. "I repeat, that is not possible at present. Matters are not that easy."

Branwen took up a point in which everyone was interested. "You said you could, ah, keep your mind away from ours."

"And I have done so, be assured. But in the case of the life outside, my duty is to probe."

"The 'matters of vast importance' you mentioned to Gennadius?"

"That is it."

Beyond that it was hard to get the Carmpan to say anything on the subject at all.

After some hours the storm began to weaken. It no longer represented any threat at all to the survival of the ship, but the weather was still too nasty to allow much headway or any determination of position.

With the ship no longer endangered, Domingo relieved three of his people from duty and sent them to rest. They were all tired, but none of them rested easily.

Spence Benkovic didn't try to rest at all. Instead he came looking for Branwen Galway, wanting to talk to her, wanting to do more than that; it was almost the first time since this

attractive woman had come aboard that he allowed himself to
show an open interest in her.

When Spence appeared at her door, trying to get himself
invited in, Branwen had somewhat mixed feelings about his
renewed attentions. Mainly she was repelled by them. Branwen
found Benkovic acceptable as a casual acquaintance, even—so
far, at least—as a shipmate. But as soon as she tried to think
of him as a potential lover, something about him changed. Or
something in the way she saw him changed, which amounted
to the same thing. Well, naturally, the altered role would
make a difference in how you thought of anyone, but . . .

It was hard to explain, even to herself. But she was more
certain than ever that Benkovic was not a potential lover, not
for her.

Galway did have to give Spence credit for being good-
looking. He could be entertaining, too, she had discovered,
when he made the effort. Maybe, after all . . . but no.

He wasn't inclined to take no for an answer. And so she
closed the door of her berth on him, after first politely and
then not so politely declining to let him in.

To Branwen's surprise, he was still there, in the short
corridor, when she came out a few minutes later. She had to
maneuver past him in the narrow crew tunnel. There was
momentary physical contact, which he tried to turn to some
advantage. When he was again rejected, he passed it off
lightly as a joke.

Benkovic's eyes glowed after her when she had passed
him; she could feel them without looking back. They were
attractive eyes, she had to admit, and he knew how to use
them. She thought he would have liked to try a more determined grab at her, but knew better than to try that kind of
thing with her, and on this ship.

She was now the only female available. Well, the possibility of having to adjust his sex life should have occurred to
him before he signed on for a long mission.

One ED female on the crew, four ED males. She wondered if the Carmpan ever worried about his sex life, or lack

thereof. That aspect of things didn't matter to his theme much, if all the stories one heard were true. Maybe she would ask Fourth Adventurer sometime.

Meanwhile she had a much less theoretical problem to contend with: what to do about Spence Benkovic. Experience suggested strongly that in this situation she would be better off being a sexless crew member, just one of the fellows, as long as that role was playable. Unfortunately that no longer seemed to be a possibility. The trouble, one of the troubles, was that no one knew how long this voyage was likely to go on before Domingo was willing to call, if not a halt, at least a pause somewhere for some R and R.

One way to keep Spence at a distance, possibly a good one, would be to take up with someone else. Domingo might well have been her first choice, but she understood by now that he just wasn't available, even if she did not yet understand exactly why. Because he was captain for one thing, probably. But she had the feeling there was more to it than that.

Iskander . . . no. She'd rather not. Though from the way Baza looked at her sometimes, Branwen thought that he too might be interested.

That left Simeon. Who had been, she thought, in some way her first choice all along.

Branwen went knocking at Chakuchin's door.

Conveniently, Simeon too was off watch at the moment. He was pleasantly surprised to see her.

She got the conversation off to an easy start by asking Sim whether he had anything to drink available.

Simeon, having asked her in, started to explain that the only stimulant he needed now was Leviathan. But the words sounded so ridiculous now that he never finished saying them.

Instead he came out with: "I hate to be alone in weather like this."

Inside, she let the door of the tiny space sigh closed behind her. "You don't have to be alone, Sim. Not all the time, anyway."

Soon the two of them were sitting close together—there was no other way to sit in one of these berth-cabins—with privacy dialed on both the door and the intercom. Only genuine emergency messages ought to be able to get through. Branwen had left her own berth closed up in the same way; supposedly the curious wouldn't know if she were in there or somewhere else aboard.

For the time being, berserkers were forgotten and so was the captain. And so, for Branwen, were her worries about Spence Benkovic.

A little later, Simeon was saying, rather sleepily: "We never did find anything to drink."

Galway murmured something and stretched lazily against the cushions of Simeon's berth. Her standard shipboard coverall had been totally discarded, and his was currently being worn in a decidedly informal configuration. Drink was not really prominent in her thoughts at the moment. She muttered a few words to that effect.

"I know, I don't need one either, but I thought . . ." Then Simeon's words trailed off in astonishment at the expression on his companion's face.

Branwen was gazing past his shoulder. Her eyes were wide, and her lips made a sound, something totally different from any that he had heard her utter yet.

He twisted his head around just in time to see it, too. *Something* had just come into the little cylindrical room where they were lying as if to look at them, and in the second or two that Simeon was frozen, looking at it, it appeared to go out through the solid wall and come back in again. The intruder was not ED, or Carmpan, or berserker; it hardly looked like a solid physical body at all. More like a heatwave in the air, or a curl of smoke, but there was too much purpose in the way it moved.

A moment later the man and the woman were both grabbing for the single hand-weapon that was readily available.

What confronted them appeared to Simeon as a physically tenuous, amorphous thing or being, resembling nothing so much as a photographic negative. Before he could make a guess at what the image in the photograph was supposed to show, the thing drifted out of the room again, right through the tightly closed door.

Simeon, whose hand had happened to close on the handgun first, was pointing the weapon after the apparition, on the verge of babbling. He pointed again, helplessly.

"I saw it, too, I saw it, too!" Branwen was already on the intercom, trying to raise help.

Iskander Baza was the next crew member to encounter the intruder. He came across it in one of the small tunnels that served the compact ship as corridors. Without hesitation Baza drew the small hand weapon he liked to carry at all times and fired. The gun was a short-range beam-projector of a type that he considered unlikely to do any serious damage to the essential equipment within the ship. Iskander's shot hit—whatever it was—but the beam appeared to have no effect except to make the apparition withdraw.

By now all the crew members, with the possible exception of the lethargic Carmpan, were alerted to the fact that some kind of emergency was in progress. Everyone not at battle stations was scrambling to get there. But for the moment no one saw anything else strange aboard the *Pearl*.

Space in the proximity of the ship was a different matter. There were suddenly a swarm of spacegoing vehicles nearby; or else they were constructions or congregations of hitherto unknown life forms; or else they were things that no ED human had ever seen or even imagined before. Whatever they were, they were suddenly detectable around the ship in considerable numbers by the people who were on watch.

A fight began, because the people on the *Pearl* considered themselves under attack.

The *Pearl*'s heavy weapons thundered out, striking at flickering, evolving, changing nothingness.

CHAPTER 18

Even in those first few seconds of alarm and scrambling desperation aboard the *Pearl*, it was already obvious that none of the blasting, melting, disintegrating weapons usually employed in space combat were at all effective against these mysterious encroaching shapes.

Domingo had been in his combat chair at the start of the crisis and was still there. Even with all his instrumentation before him, his first indication of trouble was the alarm on the intercom, the voices of his crew announcing the presence of an intruder on the ship. Such was the subtlety of the invader and of its fellows just outside the hull.

Whatever the things were out there, they were very difficult to see, hard to detect on any of the instruments that the captain presently had in use.

A gabble of speech grew steadily on the intercom.

"They're not ships, I tell you—"

"I can see that. They're not berserkers, either."

"Not any kind of berserker I ever heard about."

"Not like any . . . not like any *thing* I've ever seen."

Before they could push each other completely into panic, Domingo roared for silence, then made specific demands on specific people for readings, reports, information. In moments the incipient panic had subsided. The coordinated use of instruments even began to bring in some useful data.

Within a matter of seconds after the first alarm, using a helpful observation or two passed along by other crew members, Domingo had managed to adjust his instruments so as to be able to get a better look at the things, whatever they were, that had his ship surrounded. What he beheld were bizarre entities of varying and almost indeterminate size and shape. There were dozens of them swarming, flitting by his ship at ranges varying from only a few meters out to several score kilometers and at speeds that ought to mean ship or machine and not any kind of self-propelled life form. But somehow, as he studied them, the impression that these were life forms gradually dominated. Seemingly they were able to avoid the centers of the blasts from the *Pearl*'s armament while passing unharmed through the outer regions of the explosions, even through zones where steel would have been vaporized. The forms, whatever they were, appeared to be altering themselves from moment to moment, changing their very structure somehow, so beam weapons that would have chewed up a berserker's shields passed through them harmlessly.

It was almost, the captain thought, as if these things surrounding him and his ship could at will become no more than illusions.

The time elapsed since Branwen and Simeon had sounded the first alarm was still less than a full minute.

Domingo shouted to his crew: "Cease fire. We're not doing any good. Cease firing!"

The barrage of pulsing beams and flying projectiles ceased, almost instantly. Inside the ship the difference to the ears was minimal, but the alteration in the inward energies of space briefly left an empty feeling in the bones.

The fusillade had achieved nothing but a waste of energy—which would be easy enough to replace—and of certain types of missiles, which would not. The things outside, whatever they were, did not seem to have been injured in the slightest by being shot at, and certainly they had not been driven away. On the bright side, the six humans in their ship were also unharmed. That in itself was enough to convince Domingo that the entities outside the ship were not berserkers and probably were not enemies at all. If the swarming of the wraithlike things around the ship had been meant as an attack, it had to be considered a failure, though at least one of the things had penetrated the hull itself.

But still, a moment after the captain had called a ceasefire, he came near countermanding the order.

His crew were already shouting new alarms at him; unnecessarily, for he could see for himself what was happening now that the *Pearl*'s guns had quieted. The view outside the ship was changing, becoming vaguely obscured in strips and patches. It was as if translucent nets were being spread around the *Pearl*.

"I think they're trying to tie us up, Chief," Iskander drawled.

To Domingo, the entities outside—units, creatures, beings, whatever they were—appeared to be trying to grapple the *Pearl* with forcefield weapons. So far, very little power was evident in these weapons, which as far as the captain could tell were indistinguishable from extensions of the creatures' own bodies; but they appeared to be able, as before, to penetrate the ship's defensive shields.

Fourth Adventurer's voice came suddenly on intercom. The tones of weariness and illness had vanished from it, but the words were unsteady with unprecedented excitement: "It is not an attempt to tie you up. It is a probing for information. Act, Captain, act. Respond, lest you be taken for something inanimate."

Act? And do what? Suppressing a sharp retort, Domingo instead answered his own question for himself.

On Domingo's orders, crisply and precisely issued, the *Pearl* put out her own forcefield weapons in several strengths and varieties, trying to disengage the grip of the enemy's fields. His crew was trained in the tactics of grappling and ramming with such devices.

Clipping out more orders, Domingo assigned each member of his crew a different section of his ship's hull to defend. They all went to work in intense silence, manipulating the *Pearl*'s defensive fields, trying to find a way of repelling the intrusion. Now and then a few terse words were exchanged; for the most part the intercom was silent.

The shadowy tools of the outsiders were now opposed by a variety of fields generated from the *Pearl*. The result after the first moments of struggle was a tangled snarl that still held the human ship delicately enmeshed. Domingo was confident that even an easy application of his ship's drive would break the *Pearl* free; but for the time being he withheld that stroke. He was coming more and more to the opinion that his crew and the outsiders were not so much locked together in a struggle as engaged in a mutual groping for information.

Confused grappling ensued and was protracted over a period of several minutes. Domingo, reading his ship's instruments from his own station and sifting the fragmentary reports from his crew as best he could, decided there was now at least a strong possibility that the aliens—it was now definite in his own mind that living things opposed him—were also trying to withdraw from the tangle of interlocking forces but found themselves unable to do so, either. Perhaps they too had forces in reserve.

The next report from Fourth Adventurer confirmed definitely that what surrounded the ship were indeed living minds and bodies. "I now have established mental contact with them. It is difficult. Only intermittent communication has been achieved as yet, but it may be the minimum we need."

"They're living, then."

"Indeed they are."

"They must be aggregations, swarms, almost like the ones we sometimes harvest. But—"

"Yes, Captain. They are in many ways like those other nebular life forms, and related to them through evolution. But these around our ship are more than that. Much more." Fourth Adventurer said that much and fell silent.

"Can we communicate with them? On an intelligent level, I mean?"

"I shall try now, and report again."

The *Pearl*, and the entities around her with which she struggled, were not only bound together but isolated, lost, in swirling nebula. There was still no sign of the Space Force fleet.

"There's not as many of them around us as there were," Branwen reported, almost calmly. Some of the mysterious aliens had evidently departed—or dissipated—or died. She thought that their numbers around the *Pearl* had been greater at the start of the confrontation than they were now, though Domingo thought it was still hard to guess whether there were now twenty of them or a hundred.

Whether the entities might simultaneously be conducting a similar struggle with the Space Force somewhere in the nebula nearby was more than anyone on board the *Pearl* was able to determine.

Anyone, at least, but Fourth Adventurer. In response to a question from Domingo, the Carmpan now announced that he thought that any such confrontation between the entities and the Space Force was unlikely; his own presence on the *Pearl* was tending to draw the nebular things here.

"Your presence? Why?"

"They sense my mind, as I sense theirs."

Benkovic's voice, sounding shaken, came over the intercom: "What are they, then? What are they? These things aren't berserkers!"

Domingo spoke almost soothingly. "All right, we already know that much. They seem about as far from being berserkers as they can get. Fourth Adventurer says he's sure they're

alive, and I have to agree. But what level of intelligence are
they, and what do they want?''

The Carmpan at last was able to announce some success in
trying to determine that. He was, he said, still managing to
maintain a limited telepathic contact with the aliens. ''They
are of human intelligence. And at the moment the main thing
they want is to know what we are; or more precisely, to
understand our ship. They sense the continual close presence
of my mind and wish to know why it is so bound in heavy
matter.''

There was a pause. ''You're saying they're—a human
theme?''

''Indeed, yes. My hope in joining your crew was to welcome a new theme to the brotherhood of the Taj.''

There was silence momentarily on intercom, people looking at one another's imaged faces. *The brotherhood of the
what?* Simeon wondered silently.

When no one else said anything, Fourth Adventurer resumed: ''I am also endeavoring to explain to them your
natures, as the controllers of this ship, but it is difficult.
Ships in general are a great mystery to them, as are berserker
machines. As, indeed, is telepathy. They communicate among
themselves on a purely physical level, as do you and I.''

''A new human theme.'' It was a hushed whisper in
Branwen Galway's voice. Others were murmuring, too. Such
a discovery had happened perhaps half a dozen times in the
whole previous history of Earth-descended exploration.

''Indeed,'' Fourth Adventurer repeated patiently, ''a theme
of humanity whose existence has heretofore been completely
unknown to humans of your theme, and only guessed at by
my fellow Carmpan and myself. The reason is that only very
recently have the people of this new theme become a thinking
species. They are the reason for my presence here, for my
application to become a member of this crew. Another ship
might have brought me to them, but only your ship, Captain,
was ready and equipped at the right time and place to have a
chance of giving them the help they need. More than words

and good wishes will be required to clear their pathway to the Taj.''

Someone asked: ''To the what?''

But the captain, impatient, interrupted before the question could be answered.

Domingo said: ''Great, great. Meanwhile we seem to have a problem. Two problems, at least.''

''You refer to our physical entanglement with the life forms around us, and to our social relations with them. I believe both problems can be solved.''

''Can you tell them that we wish them well? That we are alive, as much as they are, that . . . you know what we want to tell them.''

''I believe I do, Captain. On that general level. Allow me a few more moments of silence.''

Silence fell on intercom again. Simeon, watching his instruments, observed that the entanglement of forcefields persisted; it seemed almost to have taken on a life of its own by now.

The Carmpan was back on intercom presently. ''War is almost an alien concept to them.''

''Then, damn it, tell them we're not looking for a fight, either. Not with them.''

''They say they thought our ship was an odd type of dead-metal killer.''

''If that means what I think it means . . .''

''I am sure that it does.''

At least neither side was trying to escalate the struggle. In fact it now seemed that the encounter had been turned away from being a fight at all, though what it had become was still uncertain. The contending fields of force still rested tautly against one another, maintaining a quivering, fluctuating balance, the fields generated within the ship more powerful, those from outside more penetrating and elusive.

The *Pearl* drifted, enfolded in enigmas, her crew waiting intently at their stations.

Benkovic came on a private intercom channel to voice his own suspicion to Domingo.

"Captain? A private word?"

"Go ahead."

"I don't know if we ought to buy any of this, Captain. Except that these things can still come aboard our ship when they feel like it. Looks like we can be sure of that much."

"What're you telling me, Spence? That our Carmpan's lying to me?"

"Nossir, I don't know that. Maybe he wouldn't lie, but he could be wrong. Getting fooled somehow."

"Well. Anything else?"

"Maybe so. Maybe one thing more. I told you I saw something strange in the nebula near Shubra the day Leviathan was there. Other people have seen strange things out in the gas near other colonies, the colonies that have been hit. It could have been the same characters we've got flitting around us now. They could be goodlife, acting as berserker scouts of some kind. I don't know what to tell you to do, except— watch out."

"I assure you, I am watching."

Immediately after Benkovic switched off the intercom, the Carmpan came on another channel with another report.

"My sense of the situation, Captain Domingo, is that some of the nebular creatures are still suspicious of us. This heavy, metallic ship in some ways strongly resembles a berserker machine; and that resemblance suggests to the people we have just encountered that we are really allies of the berserkers."

It was almost, the captain thought, as if Fourth Adventurer had been aware of Benkovic's warning to Domingo, despite the closed intercom channel.

The Carmpan was speaking again. "They are unhappy that this ship is making an effort to trap them with fields, as the dead-metal killers sometimes do."

"Trap them? Only after we got the impression that they were making an effort against us—as you know."

"I have already conveyed that thought, Captain."

"What do you think, Adventurer? Can they be trusted? To a reasonable extent, I mean?"

"It is my belief that they are speaking the truth to me. That I am wrong is very unlikely, though not impossible."

"All right. That's all I can expect. Good. Next question is, can we reach some arrangement with them so we can all get our fields untangled? Tell them we'll pull our horns in if they will."

"I will try to talk with them again, and emphasize that that is our wish."

The ship drifted. Minutes passed.

Then Fourth Adventurer was back, reporting. Communication with the beings outside the ship proceeded slowly, but it seemed now that at least something was being accomplished.

Domingo asked his translator: "What do they call themselves?"

"It is . . . there are no useful words. Refer to them by what name you like, and I will try to manage a translation." Fourth Adventurer paused, then added: "They wish to find out what you know about berserkers."

"We'll be glad to exchange information on that subject. Very glad. Be sure you tell them that."

Iskander now came on intercom to add his caution to Benkovic's. Baza too still halfway suspected the aliens of being either goodlife or some creation of the berserkers. He recalled all the biological experimentation by the enemy that they had discovered.

Domingo listened, admitting the possibility but unconvinced. The captain knew intellectually that goodlife existed, perhaps in every theme of humanity. But he had never encountered it, and it would be hard for him to believe that any living thing in front of him had really chosen an existence as the berserkers' servant.

Iskander Baza had a question for Fourth Adventurer: "You say their species just—came into existence recently? How recent is recent?"

"For all I can tell, as short a period as one of your own
lifetimes. It is hard to say."

"No offense, Adventurer, but that sounds incredible. I
mean, how can you *think* if your brain is the equivalent of a
hard vacuum? In that short time they've developed a—a
language? How long are their individual lives?"

"You would not find it so incredible if your own knowledge of the Galaxy was greater."

"Huh." Even Iskander seemed unable to come up with a
clever response to that.

"But I admit my estimate of their evolutionary speed may
not be accurate. What I can see of their time frame is only
their own perception of it. As it exists in their minds. I find it
hard to translate from that to your frames of time, or to mine.
I guess, and estimate."

Simeon was thinking that the aliens were certainly weird
by Earth-descended standards. He supposed that it worked
both ways. To us the aliens were mirror-image, photographic-
negative, transparent, *nebulous* beings. To them, thought
Simeon, we are—what? Voices from a hurtling lump of
metal, very doubtfully alive at all?

It was a weird picture, the ship with himself and the others
in it, seen from outside that way. He wondered if some of it
at least was spillover from the laboring Carmpan mind nearby.

Now that the situation appeared to have quieted down, at
least temporarily, Simeon would have liked to duck back to
his berth and finish dressing. But there would be no getting
away from battle stations just now.

There was another brief flurry of alarm. One or more of
the nebular beings had come aboard ship again, uninvited.
Domingo saw one of the things directly this time, a gray
transparent presence moving between him and the instruments a meter from his face. A moderate heat wave in the air
would have been substantial by comparison. But the creature
was gone again before he could do more than start to react.

The crew continued to experiment with their field generators. Certain fields slowed or deflected the movements of the

aliens, while others appeared to cause them discomfort. And yet other types of field created a barrier that the beings could penetrate only with the greatest difficulty if at all. To enclose the whole ship in that kind of barrier, though, might be beyond the capabilities of the present equipment.

Meanwhile the creatures, basically undeterred, continued to investigate the ship.

"Adventurer, tell them to stop coming aboard. It causes problems for us."

"I will ask them. I suggest that it is not advisable to order them to stop."

"That's fine, if they're amenable to being asked. If not, I'll have to find some way to make it a statement instead of a request."

Whatever method Fourth Adventurer used appeared to be effective. The visitors departed shortly.

The ED component of the *Pearl*'s crew began to speculate on what it might mean that these creatures—*Nebulons* was a name for them that seemed to spring up out of nowhere—were in fact a much younger race than the human race of Earth, had much more recently undergone the step of speciation that brought them into intelligence.

Domingo had only a limited interest in the subject. He did not forget that, despite Fourth Adventurer's opinion, there was no certain evidence that the suspicions of Iskander and Spence were wrong; these Nebulons might, for all anyone on board the *Pearl* could tell, be creations of the berserkers, intended somehow to spell doom for ED humanity.

Others were aware of the possibility, too. "How could berserkers create a life form so complex? We can't do that, and we're supposed to know more biology than the damned machines do."

Through the Carmpan, some of the aliens once more put forward their own suspicions that it was the solid, incredibly massive ED people who were allied with the berserkers; in their view, they said, the two types of entity had so much in common, it was hard to believe anything else. But yet the

two forms, berserker and human ship, could be distinguished
from each other—ED vessels almost always contained life,
the dead-metal killers very rarely so.

Another distinguishing factor was the fact that the human
ships did not always and routinely kill as they passed through
the shoals and drifts of nebular life; some of the aliens took
that as evidence that these objects were not necessarily allied
with their enemies. Sometimes the ships killed, harvesting or
sampling. But the intelligent nebular-theme humans also killed,
ingesting concentrations of energy, patterns, complexity from
the lower forms, often the same types that the ships and
colonies also harvested.

By now the minutes since the first encounter with the
aliens had lengthened into an hour. It felt to Simeon like the
longest hour he had ever lived through, except perhaps the
hour of the fight in which Wilma had been killed.

By now it had become plain, through steady observation of
the aliens, that these nebular-theme humans possessed a faster
means of travel through the nebula than either ED humans or
berserker machines had ever been able to attain.

Fourth Adventurer, on this point, offered the observation
that the nebular-theme creatures were able to detect the thin-
vacuum or hard-vacuum interstices in nebular turbulence.
The obvious point was commented on: the same ability, or
some variation of it, allowed them to get into a spaceship's
hull without opening a hatch or making a noticeable hole.

Through the Carmpan, the creatures acknowledged that
they could use this ability to get at berserkers, too, if the
berserkers could be taken unawares and were moving slowly.
But the enemy was aware of the Nebulons' existence now,
and such attacks were no longer a practical possibility.

"Cap, if they can knock out a berserker somehow, they
can knock out this ship."

Domingo remained calm. "I see that, Ike. Go on, Fourth
Adventurer."

The dead-metal killers, after losing a unit or two and
coming close to losing others, had not only developed effec-

tive repelling countermeasures and barrier fields but killing fields as well. But those worked only at short ranges, and the berserkers still had trouble hunting and killing the nebular people.

"They admit to us that a killing field exists. Seems a little naïve."

Benkovic snorted. "Maybe it's meant to seem that way."

The discovery of another intelligent species, another theme of Galactic humanity; it had to be one of the rarest events in history. Everyone aboard the ship was shaken by it, even in the midst of other problems. Almost everyone. Domingo had taken it in stride. He did not even appear to find it particularly interesting, except as it might affect his chances of hunting down Leviathan. Not until now had Simeon fully appreciated the intensity of the captain's monomania.

The captain demanded to know more from the nebular creatures, all that any of them knew about berserkers. And he was even more interested in the apparent fact that these people might be able to help him find Leviathan.

"Ask them if they know one of the dead-metal killers in particular. Ask them if they know Old Blue."

The Fourth Adventurer somehow determined that they did.

They had a special name for Old Blue too, which Fourth Adventurer translated as best he could into the language he shared with the ED humans: Dead-Metal-That-Bears-The-Radiance-Of-Death.

CHAPTER 19

Fourth Adventurer said: "There is one among our guides whose mind is more clearly open to me than the others. It is with that one I hold most of my communication."

The captain grunted. It was a satisfied sort of sound. "I thought that might be the case. What do you call this one? Or what name should we use, for him, or her?"

"I can tell you nothing meaningful about the names of Nebulons. But I find a definite suggestion of femininity in that person's mind."

Simeon, listening in, wondered how a Carmpan would judge that quality in a human of a theme never before encountered.

Domingo asked: "This one is some sort of leader among them, then?"

Fourth Adventurer answered thoughtfully. "Though I am sure there are leaders among them, I am not sure that she is one of them."

The captain nodded. It would not have made much sense—or

at least Domingo thought it would not—to apply such terms as *leader* or *follower* to Fourth Adventurer, either. From the centuries of knowing—or rather failing to know—the Carmpan, the more thoughtful among Earth-descended folk had learned not to project their own psychology onto other themes.

Fourth Adventurer continued: "Let us agree to call their spokesperson *Speaker*, at least among ourselves. If she is not really a leader, even loosely speaking, she is in close touch with those who are."

"Do you suppose," Simeon asked after a brief silence, "they might be starting to make up names for us, too?"

"Probably none we'd want to hear," said Branwen. No one else aboard ship was ready to offer an opinion.

The Carmpan might have refrained from answering because his mind was busy on another channel. He said to Domingo: "I have asked more questions of those who surround us on the subject of Leviathan. Unfortunately they seem to have no knowledge that will be immediately helpful to us in our search."

Domingo softly profaned the gods of little rocks in space and those of distant galaxies.

"But wait . . . they now have more to tell me. Ah. You will be more pleased by this, Captain."

With that, Fourth Adventurer fell silent. After he had remained quiet for some time, evidently in mental communion with the ethereal beings around the ship, he announced that he had an offer to relay to Domingo.

There was something, evidently another berserker project of some kind, that was bothering the Nebulons particularly. If Domingo and the beings with him inside the weighty metal could help the Nebulons eliminate this extremely objectionable thing, whatever it was, Speaker and those with her would be eternally grateful. "At least," Fourth Adventurer concluded, "I believe that to be the sense of what they are endeavoring to communicate."

"Another *project*, did you say? Does that mean a fighting machine? A base?"

"The thought as it comes to me from them is vague, Captain. They do not understand what this project is, except that it is harmful to them."

"But where is this thing? What is it like? Can't you be a little more explicit?"

"I regret that I cannot. It is in just the form of such a vague concept that the message comes to me."

Still the captain was quick to make up his mind. "Very well. We will help them if we can. Tell them I accept—provisionally. Can you tell them that?"

"We shall see."

"If it is something I can help them with, I'll do so. Provided they then do what they can to help me do what I want. I need allies, Adventurer. I need, I want, all the help that I can get. You don't necessarily have to tell them all of that."

"I believe I understand your position, Captain. Let me try to convey it."

The translator was silent for a while, and then announced: "They confer among themselves now, Captain. I think they will be ready soon to lead us on. To this 'berserker project,' whatever it may be."

"And how far away from here is this—never mind. I know, you can't tell."

"That is correct."

Spence Benkovic spoke up suddenly. "Maybe we ought to confer among ourselves too, while we have the chance. Before we just follow them somewhere."

"Confer about what?" Domingo asked him sharply.

"I know I signed on to go hunting, Captain. Okay, I'll go. But something new and very important has come up since then. I mean just finding these—these people, or whatever they are. That's changed things. We're playing a whole new game. We can't just ignore that, and go on about our business as if it hadn't happened."

"The business of this voyage is what I say it is, Benkovic. But let me hear what you suggest."

"I suggest that we have to do something right away to tell the Space Force, tell people in general. Great gods and little berserkers, we're not talking like just finding another planetoid here. This has—has *meaning*. I mean, a whole unknown theme of humanity, native to the space within the nebula."

Domingo was not impressed by that argument. "Just how do you propose to reveal the wonderful news? There's no way of knowing where Gennadius and his fleet are now. We'd have to go all the way back to Four Twenty-five. And I've just undertaken to help these people, not run out on them."

Benkovic muttered something but was unable to come up with an effective answer.

Simeon thought suddenly: Spence wants out of this trip now. He wants the ship to go immediately to a world somewhere where he can get off, even if it means breaking a contract and having to give back money. Why now, all of a sudden? Why, Benkovic could take anything, except that there was only one good-looking woman on board and she went for someone else, if it was only for a day or for an hour.

Domingo meanwhile was proceeding with his argument: "If the prospects for finding Gennadius aren't good, then what chance have we of finding our way back here, once we leave, and linking up again with these people we've discovered? How big a range of territory do they occupy, Fourth Adventurer?"

"I have no means of knowing that as yet." The Carmpan shook his head, an ED gesture he had adopted, consciously or unconsciously, from the start of the voyage.

"We've been led here," said the captain. Simeon wasn't sure if the older man was referring to the Carmpan's advice, or just what. "I'm not about to simply walk away at this point."

"We could drop a courier," Branwen suggested. The *Pearl* had begun this hunt with two robot message couriers tucked away in storage.

The captain appeared to consider that suggestion carefully. "I don't think so. We might well need both of our couriers later." Domingo sounded as if he were still reluctant to bring the Space Force in on his hunt at all.

"Our guides announce that they are now ready to lead us, Captain," came the voice of Fourth Adventurer. "To show us the project of dead metal. That phrase is as close as I can translate what they are thinking. But their readiness, and even their impatience, are manifest to me."

Iskander asked suddenly: "How about their trustworthiness?"

"As I said before, I do not think that they are lying to me. To judge beyond that would involve an estimate of what their thoughts will be in a future situation. I regret I cannot do it. Their minds are too new to me, too alien. Their reliability, as you would perceive it, I cannot judge."

"Ah," said Baza. "Maybe they're more like us than I thought."

"They can't be a whole lot more impatient than I am," Domingo said. "I want to find out about this berserker project. Tell them to lead on."

"I shall."

For a few seconds nothing happened, or at least no change occurred that was perceptible to the ED crew. Then suddenly the space immediately around the ship was clear in every direction of the mysterious forms. The beings who had been swarming in the close vicinity of the *Pearl* had moved away.

"But where?" the captain muttered, pressing his headlink to his forehead, conjuring up new electronic visions with his instruments to augment those already on the stages and screens before him. "Ah. There they go."

Domingo took thought purposefully, easing the *Pearl* forward. A voyage through the nebula under the guidance of the nebular-theme humans had begun.

Three of the *Pearl*'s crew were posted on a regular watch, three others officially relieved. Simeon had a chance to get back to his berth and finish dressing.

In another hour the voyage had settled into a routine. The routine was to persist for several days with little change.

Gradually, with the storm out of the way, the people on the *Pearl* were able to work out at least a tentative idea of their general position inside the Milkpail. The guides remained always in sight, and always clustered now in one direction. From that position they kept darting ahead, as if reluctant to believe that the heavy ship really could not keep up with them and wanting to urge it on to greater efforts.

The Nebulons doubtless observed, as did the humans inside the ship, the pinging of nebular molecules and larger particles against the leading shields that plowed an open pathway for the advancing hull. The Carmpan proclaimed his inability to tell what the Spacedwellers made of the sight.

Apparently the Nebulons, or Spacedwellers—that was another name that had popped up as if out of nowhere and had quickly been adopted among the *Pearl*'s crew as an alternate title for their guides—employed a means of propulsion similar to that of advanced spacedrives. Branwen and Simeon theorized that this necessarily involved tapping into the fabric of spacetime itself, riding a flow of natural forces rather than burning fuel. But given the Spacedwellers' lack of hardware, they must be managing their tinkering on a microbiological scale.

Despite Fourth Adventurer's repeated testimony regarding their chronic impatience, the guides paused at fairly frequent intervals. During these breaks they could be observed among shoals of the common microlife, evidently feeding; Fourth Adventurer gave his opinion that they were probably resting as well.

"Speaker asks me how, if my companions and myself are really living things here inside this metal shell, we can remain here without ever coming out to eat. I have explained as best I can that our usual food is as heavy and solid as we are. But I am not at all sure that she believes me."

Aboard the *Pearl*, other members of the crew, Galway

and Baza in particular, speculated on the course of evolution that might have produced such creatures as the ones flitting around them.

Benkovic also began a round of speculation among the ED crew about the reproductive systems of their guides. There seemed to be more of the creatures now, in the group leading the ship, than there had been only a little while ago. Of course the most likely explanation, in ED terms, would be simply that more of the beings had joined the group as the journey progressed; but none had been observed to actually approach the group or enter it.

The routine of the journey had persisted for several days before Fourth Adventurer announced that he thought their trip would shortly be coming to an end. He said the thoughts of several of the guides gave him the strong impression that a destination was near at hand.

Branwen, piloting now, called in: "We're approaching a system, Captain. I don't think it's on the charts."

Rousing himself from dreams of Isabel to bitter wakefulness, Domingo looked at his detectors and presently saw that there was a white sun ahead. Evidently the star was only a small one, bordering on the white-dwarf classification.

"I'll bet right now," said Iskander, "that it's not on the charts."

The surmise proved accurate; the spectrum of the modest sun ahead could not immediately be identified with that of any known to exist within the nebula. But it was no real surprise to anyone; the Milkpail contained more than one star that had never made it to the charts.

The nuclear fire of the star ahead grew clearer and clearer through thinning mists of matter. At the same time the pace of the journey slowed down until the *Pearl*'s guides and the ship herself had almost stopped.

The star ahead was not part of a binary or more complex system. Still it had no lack of dependent family. The *Pearl* was drifting on the edge of a spherical domain a billion kilometers across in which the small white star was dominant and from which the star's radiation pressure had cleared out most of the tenuous nebular material. This in itself was no surprise. About half of all the Milkpail stars, though generally not the ones with colonized planetoids, were surrounded by similar cleared spheres of space.

But this star had in orbit around it more bodies of measurable size than did most suns in the nebula. Within that gigantic rough sphere of cleared space at least two belts of minor planetoids were rotating, most likely representing the debris of more than one shattered planet. Those protoworlds must have been sizable, much larger than the usual colonized planetoid, when they were whole. And one small belt of this sun's present crop of planetoids was in retrograde motion, prompting speculation among the ED crew that two counter-revolving planets might once have existed here and then collided. Comparatively minor collisions would necessarily be frequent in the system as they observed it now. It could hardly be very durable, on the scale of astronomical time, but then no solar system within the Milkpail was long-lived in terms of stellar chronology.

The Nebulons still had not completely halted their advance. They continued to creep on, moving ahead of the ship toward the sun but ever more slowly. To Simeon the slackening pace of their forward progress irresistibly suggested increasing caution.

The small swarm of Spacedwellers and the ED ship following them were now almost at the very edge of the cleared space.

The Carmpan, confirming Simeon's instinctive thought, now reported hesitancy and a measure of disagreement in their guides' ranks.

"Ask them to stop, Adventurer," Domingo ordered. "I think we need a conference with them before we go on any farther."

The message was passed along somehow. The slowly advancing swarm halted, and presently the drifting ship caught up with it.

Through the Carmpan's mediation, the Nebulons communicated that the berserker project was here in this system, on one of the larger orbiting rocks. It was a planetoid well within the cleared space, away from the larger belts and fairly close to the sun. On that small orbiting body, the dead-metal-killers had established *something*. If the ED people wanted to know what that something was in terms they could understand, it appeared that they would have to go and see for themselves. Extreme danger lurked there, at least for Spacedwellers.

"If it's permanently built into a rock, it must be some kind of a bloody base." Domingo's voice fairly quivered with excitement. Branwen could almost hear him thinking that he might now have Leviathan's secret repair and maintenance base within his grasp.

The ED humans aboard the *Pearl*, having been told through translation the precise location of the berserker base, now did their best to observe it from this relatively distant vantage point. They had no immediate success, but Domingo decided to spend a few hours in surveying the whole system as thoroughly as possible from this position.

The initial lack of success in spotting a base did not necessarily mean that their guides were lying or mistaken about the location of the berserker project. Any base in the system was probably camouflaged to some extent, and almost certainly dug into rock. Traffic in and out ought to be observable, but it might be infrequent. Certainly no machines or recent trails were now observable from where the *Pearl* now drifted almost passively, electronic senses busy.

Domingo at the controls eased his ship gradually and steadily closer to the sun and closer to the inner orbit of the planetoid on which the base presumably lay hidden. The captain was working to keep the *Pearl* concealed as well as possible behind an intrusive wisp of electrically active particles, a tendril of nebular material that here wound its way into the sphere of space otherwise swept mostly clear by the radiation pressure of the small white sun.

The vast swirl of particles offered the ship some concealment, but it also made it difficult for the people aboard to see much of anything. After intensive and repeated efforts, instruments did confirm the apparent presence on one of the inner planetoids of some kind of base. And here and there along the perimeter of the cleared sphere, among the outer belts of planetoids, the relic trails of ships—or more likely of machines—oozed faint radio whispers.

Iskander had a suggestion. "Let's take out the launch. It's a lot smaller, and we ought to be able to get closer to the sun in it without really showing ourselves."

The Nebulons, Fourth Adventurer reported, were duly surprised when the doors of the ship's ventral bay opened, and the launch appeared.

Domingo decided to drive the launch himself, and he chose Branwen and Simeon to come with him.

The launch, with the captain at the controls, moved through thin concealment yet closer to the sun and got in among the outer orbital belts of the system, formations containing dust and fragments large enough to resist radiation pressure. In a belt with a density of one rock larger than one gram's mass per hundred cubic kilometers, the little craft drifted for an hour, with everyone aboard busy making observations. From this vantage point it was possible to get a somewhat better look at the planetoid where the berserker facility supposedly had been established.

Now observation confirmed the Nebulons' claims more definitely. There was a base of some kind there, all right.

It did not appear to be a large facility or suitable for the construction or repair of large fighting machines. Certainly it was not swarming with mobile spacegoing units of any kind. There was no certain connection between this facility and Old Blue. But on the other hand, such a connection might exist, and it was impossible to say that Leviathan never came here.

After their hour spent in data gathering, the people aboard

the launch decided that they had seen enough. They eased
their little craft out of its long orbit around the sun and back
to where it was possible to signal the larger ship with little
fear of detection. This effort, conducted cautiously, con-
sumed another hour.

The people aboard the *Pearl* maneuvered her a little closer,
and the ship picked up the launch.

At a meeting to analyze the images that had been obtained,
some people thought that a certain structural similarity was
indicated between this lab and the previously visited wreck.
When the *Pearl*'s larger telescopes were focused now, they
provided some confirming evidence for this idea.

The most obvious difference between this facility and the
wreck was that this one showed no signs at all of combat
damage. At this distance no weapons could be observed, but
there was no doubt that the base would, at a minimum, have
something with which to defend itself.

Why had the enemy chosen to establish a base here? It was
certainly an out-of-the-way place, unlikely to be discovered
by ED humanity. And someone aboard ship propounded a
hard-to-follow theory that it might confer some advantage to
a researcher in biology to operate in this kind of space,
cleared by radiation pressure.

The debate was abruptly interrupted by a minor alarm.
Instruments had just picked up a small burst of activity at or
very near the biolab—if that was indeed its function—
suggesting that the facility there might just have launched a
missile, or alternatively sent out a robot courier of its own.
Whatever it was had not been aimed at the *Pearl*. The base
might well have decided to get off a message to its mechanical allies, wherever they were, reporting that it seemed to
have been discovered by the human enemy and now faced a
probable attack.

The Nebulons, through the Carmpan, confirmed that something of the kind had happened: a small dead-metal unit had
just departed the planetoid at high speed.

The courier, if such it had been, had already left the system, evidently having tunneled off into the nebula on the far side of the cleared volume.

There appeared to be no time to waste. Domingo, with the help of Fourth Adventurer, made plans with the Nebulons as best he could. Then the captain hurriedly briefed his crew and prepared to take the *Pearl* in to the assault. The idea was to pacify the lab, to render it inactive if possible, without destroying it completely.

CHAPTER 20

Domingo was nothing if not decisive, and the time he spent in planning the attack was held to an absolute minimum. Simeon reflected that this had the advantage of not allowing anyone much time in which to become frightened; but in Simeon's case that did not help. He had already discovered that he could be terrified in no time at all.

The captain was trying his best to synchronize his ship's coming effort with one to be made by the Nebulons, and after the hasty plan was made, he had to wait for a signal from his translator. When word arrived through Fourth Adventurer that the Spacedwellers were moving to the attack, the *Pearl*, everyone aboard at battle stations with mental fingers on mental triggers, came hurtling out of what its crew hoped had been concealment toward the enemy installation.

The Spacedwellers were now about to fling their insubstantial bodies against whatever field barriers the berserker would be able to put up. Whatever fears the Nebulons had of approaching the berserker installation, they had managed to put aside in the hope of achieving a victory.

Defensive fire from the base opened up almost at once when the *Pearl* broke cover, long before light could have borne the image of the moving ship in across the hundreds of millions of kilometers intervening between her and the base. The enemy had to be aiming and launching on subspace clues.

At least the barrage was not as heavy as might have been expected from a berserker base. The shields of the ship held up, though the hull rang with sound induced by the drumming of plasma wavefronts upon its outer surface, and the crew had something of the experience of being in an echoing metal room or barrel pounded on the outside by titanic hammers. Simeon had never before been under fire of anything like this intensity. He gritted his teeth and held on and did his job.

When the captain had the range he wanted, he calmly gave the order to return fire. Missiles were launched first, that their arrival on target might be simultaneous with the energies of the swifter destructive beams.

The first look at the results came long seconds later, when lagging light brought back to the ship the images of impact. The heavy fire from the ship had not immediately broken through the berserker station's defensive fields. But it had succeeded in disrupting those barriers, so they were no longer able to hold the onrushing Nebulons at bay.

The Carmpan relayed the Spacedwellers' telepathic shout of triumph.

The insubstantial swarm of Nebulons still could not be seen from the *Pearl*. But Fourth Adventurer reported them surging in through solid rock and metal, entering the facility. Once inside, as Fourth Adventurer reported, the Spacedwellers moved at once to disable the main destructor charges, whose probable locations Domingo had been able to guess successfully.

As the ship continued to close rapidly with its opponent,

the Carmpan had another bit of news for his shipmates, this one unexpected.

"Captain, I am informed only now by Speaker that one of our allies' people has been held a prisoner at this base for some lengthy though indeterminate time. Naturally enough, to rescue this prisoner is one of our guides' chief objectives in making this attack."

"Naturally. And they didn't bother to tell us . . ." Domingo, intent on the tactical decisions he was going to have to make within another minute or two, sounded beyond surprise. "How the hell can even a berserker hold one of those things a prisoner? I'd like to know the trick."

"It is a matter of creating special forcefields. No doubt you will be able to discover how to generate such fields, if you survive this fight."

Simeon, holding his breath, thought that the chance of his personal survival was looking up. The berserker base, trying to fight off a Nebulon invasion, could not simultaneously cope very well with the superior firepower of the ship.

Domingo chose weapons, issued firing orders and observed results.

The berserker installation still fought back, but ever more feebly. After another exchange or two against Domingo's missiles and beam weapons, the enemy defenses were obviously crumbling, and the *Pearl* moved in closer still.

There were a few seconds of relative calm in which Fourth Adventurer issued a further report on Nebulon affairs. The prisoner had just been freed, but while in captivity had been the subject of horrible experiments, and the Carmpan had the impression that she or he might now be close to death, madness or both.

Soon after that the Carmpan was able to report that the main destructor charges on the installation had been effectively disabled.

Now the *Pearl* moved even closer to the enemy.

Presently the berserker's last defensive shields had been wiped out of space. Two more hits by beam-projector pulses on weapon clusters along its perimeter and the last of its return fire stuttered to a halt. At the moment the weapons of Domingo's ship looked powerfully impressive.

Domingo called a cease-fire. A few moments later, with his ship gradually approaching the ruin below, the captain announced that he planned to board the enemy to look for information, clues to the location of Leviathan. He asked for one or two volunteers to accompany him.

No immediate answer came, at least not audibly. Simeon found himself having to repress hysterical laughter.

Iskander and Branwen finally volunteered to come along. There was something so utterly new and mad about this enterprise that the woman felt herself unable to resist it; and if she were going to learn any secrets about Domingo, this seemed like the most likely way to go about it.

Domingo decided that now, facing a defeated enemy, was a good time to practice fast-boarding techniques.

The *Pearl* rushed closer to the target planetoid, pulling back only at the last moment from a final ramming impact against the rock and metal of the enemy.

The launch, carrying the three boarders, came flying out of the ventral bay almost like a stone from a sling. The idea was to minimize the time of the little ship's exposure in space to enemy fire. But this turned out to be a practice run; nothing struck at the launch. It appeared that this particular enemy had nothing left with which to strike.

The three invaders left the launch. The little craft, running on autopilot, hovered near the planetoid's surface. Lugging heavy weapons and explosives, the three quickly got themselves down to the surface, which was still glowing with the heat of their own bombardment.

Protected by their armor, they quickly approached and crossed the broken outer ramparts of the enemy installation. Moving in, they blasted open doors and burned great holes through bulkheads. They were determined to leave themselves a clear and unblockable line of retreat as they forced their way in to the mysteries below.

The berserker had been unable to destroy itself or its central computing units or even to kill its prisoner, but some of the commensal machines of the base were still active. The small maintenance machines, lacking in weapons, speed and tactics, tried to carry out harassing attacks but were blasted out of the way with relative ease.

The insubstantial bodies of the Nebulon attacking party, presumably including the rescued prisoner, came fluttering and wavering around the boarding party, then passed on, up and out to freedom.

"Good-bye, perhaps forever," Iskander muttered, waving an arm toward the Nebulons, struggling to be funny. But the attitude no longer seemed to come naturally to him. He was giving a feeble imitation of his usual self.

This station was not as big, or the underground portion of it as elaborate, as the boarders had somehow been expecting. There were no large docks in sight. Certainly this could never have served as a major repair or construction base even for small fighting machines, let alone the huge killers of Leviathan's class.

What appeared to be biological research gear, much of it intact or almost so, came into the boarders' view as soon as they had penetrated underground. And here, as on the enemy unit they had previously boarded, the invading humans discovered a collection of complex field generators. These devices no doubt had served to create the prison walls and bars within which the Nebulon had been confined for study and experimentation.

Finally, a small chamber containing what had to be the central brain of the base was uncovered. "Some interesting-looking data banks here, Cap." After that effort Iskander ceased to probe or even to talk. It was as if he had run out of energy.

For this expedition Domingo had equipped himself with hand-held gear that was supposed to be able to read most berserker data storage systems. A good portion of his wealth had gone to buy it. He clamped cables onto the memory units he could reach and connected the device to his headlink. He stood taking readings with intense concentration while his two crew members stood guard beside him.

"This unit . . ." the captain said finally and paused. A few moments later he spoke again. "What's been going on at this facility . . . the machines here have been trying to determine what would be the most effective, the most deadly anti-ED human life form that could possibly be created."

The others waited, listening.

Domingo said: "The suggestion seems to be that this life form would be an ED human itself."

Back aboard the *Pearl*, Simeon was saying: "Get them on the radio."

"Right. The message?" Spence Benkovic sounded weary to the verge of collapse.

"If you have to send it in the clear to get through, do it. Tell them our deep detectors have picked up a shape at a range of two hundred million kilometers. Like a jagged birdcage with a skull in it. There's even a hint of blue flames. Leviathan is here."

CHAPTER 21

When the message from the *Pearl* came in, Branwen moved as fast as she could. But from the first step, Domingo was already ahead of her in the mad scramble to regain the launch, and Iskander was right at her side.

As she passed the memory units that Domingo had begun to disassemble, she hastily grabbed up some of the components he had been testing. Domingo, who a moment ago had been fascinated by the same bits of hardware, had dropped them instantly the moment word came that Old Blue was now actually on the scene, within his reach.

Iskander too ignored everything else when he heard that. Branwen caught a brief glimpse of Baza's face inside his helmet and was struck by the strange look he was wearing, wooden and almost lifeless.

Half a dozen of the small memory units were under Branwen's left arm as she leaped and ran, shoving pieces of berserker aside, following the captain.

The captain did not turn back or even look behind him to

see if his two crew members were still with him. It occurred to Branwen that Domingo was actually ready to leave them here if they could not keep up with him in his rush to get back to his ship and come to grips with his archenemy.

The three humans, moving with practiced speed in low gravity, went bounding and plunging back through the passageway they had blasted open.

They were within meters of regaining the surface when a slab of rock the size of a spaceship came slowly toppling toward them—perhaps the battered berserker brain that ran the base had been able to organize one last attempt upon their lives. But in the low gravity the humans easily avoided the falling mass. Metal and rock jumped and shuddered beneath their feet as it came down.

Moments later all three were in the clear. Branwen, burdened with her collection of possibly priceless hardware, had trouble keeping up with the two men now, although she considered herself as skillful as anyone at getting around in space armor. Iskander, having raced ahead of her, turned back once, wordlessly, to see that she was not falling hopelessly behind. Domingo did not turn back at all.

The three of them were running and bounding now across the planetoid's surface, still radiant with heat. The eerie landscape of the rocky mass surrounded them, marked with long shadows and the stark white light of the small but nearby sun. The sky beyond the sun was mottled white with distant clouds of nebula and devoid of any other stars.

Now one artificial star had come into being overhead and was brightening quickly. The autopilot had been randomly maneuvering the launch, and now in response to Domingo's radio command it was bringing the little vessel quickly down to the boarding party.

There was another movement nearby, this one of almost invisible entities skimming across the planetoid's airless rocky surface. Branwen had expected that the former prisoner and the original Nebulon rescue party would be long gone by now. But two shimmering shapes, coming almost within reach of the three running, suited humans, appeared as evidence that their new allies had not entirely abandoned the field. She wondered if one of the formless flickerings might be Speaker. Without the Carmpan on hand, there was no way to tell.

The Spacedwellers moved near the three who ran, as if to keep their heavy partners company. The almost immaterial presences, fading in and out of visibility, were reassuring even though the creatures were unable to communicate more directly.

The launch was down now, the autopilot opening a hatch as it skimmed the planetoid's surface just ahead of the three who ran across it. As the ED humans hurled themselves into the vessel, Branwen muttered a private vow that she would seek, as soon as possible, another means of communicating with the Spacedwellers; it was not good to be totally dependent on the Carmpan for all messages, and it was all too easy to foresee times when such dependence might be downright fatal.

Once the boarders were sealed into the launch, good radio contact with the *Pearl* was once more available. Now they could hear Benkovic, back on the ship, still wondering aloud if the Nebulons were somehow responsible for the arrival of Leviathan.

"If I believed that," Domingo announced, "I'd see they got a reward. I hope you're moving the ship our way?"

"Yes, sir. About twenty seconds to pickup."

Meanwhile Domingo, his headlink firmly on, was driving the launch as fast as possible to rejoin the *Pearl*.

Branwen, after clamping herself into a combat chair and hooking up her headlink, was trying to catch a glimpse of the famous blue glow through the cleared viewports of the launch. But Leviathan was still too far away to be directly visible in whole or part.

Fortunately for Domingo and those with him, the *Pearl* had already been maneuvered in quite close to the planetoid.

And with Benkovic at the helm she now came speeding in even closer to pick up the launch carrying the boarders.

Leviathan was already opening up with ranging fire, probing at the *Pearl*'s defensive shields. Before the pickup could be made, the launch rocked as it was struck by the wavefront of a weapons blast, a surge of particles and electromagnetic waves. In comparison to this, the just-conquered base had been firing popguns. The intensity was such that Branwen could feel the impact of the near miss in her bones, even in her combat chair and in the absence of atmosphere to help transmit a shock.

The Carmpan was murmuring something hopeful on the radio, in the intervals between the brisk comments of the two pilots of the swiftly approaching vehicles. Just at the awkward moment of retrieval of the launch, as Branwen understood Fourth Adventurer's commentary, the Nebulons would be busy creating a valuable distraction. They feinted an attack on Leviathan, which provided enough of a diversion to enable the ED humans to get back aboard their ship.

Branwen was the first out of the launch into the ship's ventral bay, and from there went scrambling immediately toward her battle station. There seemed to be no good place to put down the memory units she had brought along, and so she kept them with her.

Domingo arrived at his own combat station just in time to take over the helm from Spence before the real in-earnest action started.

As the captain made the headlink connection to his helmet, the ship was already in swift motion, and the space around her flamed with combat. Leviathan's weapons were very much heavier than those the berserker station had used to defend itself, and, according to all early indications, they were also better aimed and synchronized.

Now the whole ED human component of the crew were crouching at their stations, doing their best to draw upon the energies of spacetime, channeling power approaching that of

suns. Mindlink networking shared out pictures of the interlocking systems in operation among the human minds; operating this ship meant, among other things, playing an intricate
game as a member of a skilled team.

The Carmpan reported that the Nebulons were now ready
to make another effort at attacking. Word had spread somehow among their people of the new allies who rode within a
heavy metal casing and effectively fought the dead-metal
killers; reinforcements were pouring in to the swarm of
Spacedwellers, and Speaker reported new hope among them
of being able to overcome what they considered their ancient
enemy.

"And mine, too. Mine first of all. But I'll take all the help
that I can get."

The *Pearl* withstood the enemy's first ranging fire and the
jolts of even heavier weapons that followed almost immediately. But Branwen had the gut feeling that the defenses were
not holding with any great margin of safety; she could tell
because just now sustaining them was her assignment. She
heard and saw and felt the weapons of the human ship struck
back, without as yet doing any observable damage.

The *Pearl* had now become a swiftly moving, evasive
target. Domingo was maneuvering his ship away from the
sun but not yet directly toward his enemy. For a period of
minutes he took the *Pearl* dancing in and out of the maze of
planetoids and dust rings. Clever enemy missiles pursued her
on her twisting course, and she dodged them, but her object
was not to get away. The captain was stalking Old Blue now,
even as the great berserker was stalking him.

Again, on the captain's order, the *Pearl* struck back. This
time with full power.

When the haze of ionization spread around Old Blue by the
latest bombardment had partially cleared, it could be seen
that the enemy too remained essentially undamaged. Against
this tough opponent, the new missiles, the new beams, were
not performing as well as had been hoped and expected.

It was at moments like this that Branwen Galway felt most

intensely alive; they were what kept her coming back into space.

But now there ensued a brief lull in the actual fighting. Evasive action continued. Briefly the instruments on the humans' ship lost track of Leviathan.

Had the enemy fled the system? No, now the bizarre birdcage shape, licked with blue fire, was back again. Domingo made a sound of relief and satisfaction. Once more the humans' computers worked to lock Old Blue in their sights.

"It's playing 'possum," Simeon said. "Wants us to come after it. It's afraid we'll get away otherwise. If it just chases us we might be too small and fast for it to catch."

"It's not afraid of anything," said Benkovic.

Neither was the captain, evidently. Domingo was sliding toward his enemy again, having got the angle of approach he wanted, one that would allow him to maneuver his ship in and out of relative concealment.

The dead shape of a battered planetoid now loomed up close to the *Pearl*, coming between the combatants and cutting off their direct view of each other. Which way to dodge around the obstacle?

Just when everyone aboard Domingo's ship was most intent on which way the captain would turn next, distraction came. Another shape was showing on the remote detectors, that of a machine or ship coming through the clouds at the edge of the cleared space, almost behind the *Pearl* as she faced her known enemy. Did it mean berserker reinforcements?

That possibility hadn't really occurred to Branwen until now. She knew that Leviathan, due to some trick of programming or randomly selected tactics, generally fought alone as a solitary rogue rather than attacking in concert with other death machines.

The range was too great for the IFF transponder to be useful, but a closer look at the ominous new shape proved it to be that of a Space Force ship.

The captain muttered grimly: "Gennadius. For once he's on hand when I can use him. With his whole fleet, I hope."

Eagerly the *Pearl*'s instruments probed the nebula in the area surrounding the new arrival. But there was no fleet to be seen there, only the one ship. A steadier look confirmed that it was indeed Gennadius's cruiser.

Where was Leviathan now? Still out of line-of-sight . . .

Gennadius had good detectors too, and was already trying to establish tightbeam communications. Some of the beam from the Space Force cruiser managed to get through this space still ringing with weaponry.

In an encoded message the commander promised aid to the embattled *Pearl*. Gennadius assured her captain and crew that he too was skilled at trailing and tracking. He had had no success in reassembling his scattered fleet or even in making contact with any of its other components. Instead, after the storm had passed, Gennadius had followed the one trail that he had been able to find, and that trail had led him here to the *Sirian Pearl*. And to the enemy.

Simeon found himself breathing more easily. Now, with two first-class fighting ships and three themes of humanity working together, Leviathan's enemies appeared to have a good chance of winning in this particular fight. He could sense how morale aboard the *Pearl*, which had been numbed and wavering, went up slightly.

After another half-garbled three-way conference call, including Speaker, straining electronic communications to the limit and calling upon the Carmpan's mental ability, the two ships closed on the foe from opposite sides as the Nebulons simultaneously began an infiltration of the defensive fields of Old Blue.

"Here we go." Captain Domingo said it unnecessarily.

Simeon, before focusing the total abilities of his mind on tactics and fire control, took a last look at the intercom image of Branwen. If he had been expecting to get a look from her in return, he was disappointed. She was already concentrating utterly on her instruments.

Old Blue maneuvered as if it were trying to shake free of

the double attack but failed to do so. Fighting ships screamed toward the death machine from two sides. But did they have it trapped, or did it have them? The *Pearl*'s shields were taking hits at a rate that made Simeon wonder if the enemy might have received reinforcement, too. But evidently not. Leviathan must have been keeping some of its heavy weaponry in reserve through the first exchanges of blows, probably trying to get its smaller opponent to come closer or to put too much reliance on its shields.

The *Pearl* shuddered, diving into an inferno, being blasted helplessly away from her intended course. The sound and vibration inside the hull were overwhelming. How much of this could any shields withstand? Or any human crew? The great damned berserker was stronger than Domingo had predicted or expected; it was stronger than both human ships together. It seemed plain now that if the *Pearl* had been alone when it faced the full charge of Leviathan, the human ship would have been lost.

But Domingo's crew still functioned, and his ship hit back, hard.

The Space Force ship was somewhere—yes, there—still surviving, still fighting.

The battle raged.

Branwen Galway's job now, through her mindlink, was to try to keep the shields functioning, summoning up and channeling power into them.

Simeon Chakuchin's mind hurled missiles, on the captain's order or sometimes at his own discretion. There had been nearly a hundred heavy missiles aboard when the fight started, but they were going fast.

Spence was aiming and pulsing beams, and the Carmpan was handling his own special brand of communications. Domingo drove his ship, while Iskander functioned as general flight engineer, ready to handle damage control or fill in for another crew member as needed.

For just a moment, as he sent an outgoing salvo of missiles passing through the *Pearl*'s shields, Simeon thought he could touch Branwen's mind directly; but the impression slipped away before it could distract him seriously. He got on with the job on which both their lives and more depended.

The dodging and maneuvering in and out among the complex belts of the planetoids, the exchanges of unimaginable violence between ships and machine, went on. Had minutes or hours passed since the fight began? Time had disappeared. For Domingo's mentally and physically battered crew, no other world but this existed.

Simeon could believe that he had always lived in this world of combat, than which there was no other; and yet it was an unreal universe, stretching beyond the door of death, filled with vivid mental visions in which imagination beckoned through the mindlink to disaster. This world tottered at every second on the brink of annihilation. The mind tried to fight free of it and could not, and drifted at the entrance to the harbor of insanity.

Pyrotechnics had completely taken over the space around the ship.

Dozens of the small rocky bodies populating this space were struck accidentally by heavy weapons and blew up, shattered or turned into fiery blobs, lighting up the dustclouds nearby like so many miniature suns. Domingo, issuing precise orders, blasted some small planetoids, creating screens of covering plasma behind which he stalked his enemy.

The speeds of the ships and machine engaged made the thinly scattered material of this space appear on instruments like a dense cloud of rocks and gravel. Collision with a particle of more than microscopic size could mean the end. Human nerves and senses, woefully too slow to compete in this game directly, entrusted the ship's computer with course calculation, a fraction of a second at a time.

Violence shocked Simeon out of a near-hypnotic mental state. Death's bony fingers brushed him hard before they slipped away. For a moment he thought that the fight was lost, and he was dead. Alarms were sounding everywhere. When he could think again he knew that the *Pearl* had taken an internal shockwave. It most probably had been induced deliberately by the berserker, with simultaneous weapon detonations at the opposite ends of the ship's defensive shields. The shock had been almost completely damped by the defenses, but still the interior impact was beyond anything that the crew had endured yet.

The captain was calling around the intercom, station by station. Everyone except Galway answered.

Benkovic's voice came, saying he was on his way to help her. It was necessary for someone to get her headlink disconnected quickly, as a dazed, half-conscious mind hooked into the system could well mean disaster. Simeon was immobilized for the moment by his job, still throwing a pattern of missiles. There were now no more than forty remaining in his magazines.

Domingo steered his ship into concealment within an orbital belt of dust, and again the fight was temporarily broken off.

Through a fog of pain and bewilderment, Branwen saw Benkovic come into her combat station. She heard him say something about helping her to her berth.

He disconnected her headlink and assisted her through the short tunnel. As he put her down in her berth, she briefly lost consciousness again.

When awareness returned, her helmet had been taken off, her armor opened. She could feel Benkovic's hand inside her clothing, first on her breast, then moving down her ribs, her belly . . . his hand was bare but he was still wearing his combat helmet, and it was difficult to see his face . . . she groaned something, and fought herself free.

His suited figure crouched, getting still closer to her. His uncovered hands reached out. His helmet's airspeaker made his voice more mechanical than human. "I'm trying to help you. Don't be crazy." Then, more softly: "Doesn't it turn you on, babe? Doesn't all this turn you on?"

She rolled away from him and got to her knees. She didn't

try to argue. "Out. Out," was all she said. Her hand came up with a gun.

Spence looked at the weapon and said nothing. He was in armor that might save him, but his hands were exposed. Still she could not really see his face.

"Out," she repeated.

Without saying anything more, he turned away and left her.

She closed the door after him and mechanically dialed for privacy. She was near collapse. *Later,* she thought. *Later I'll report that, or I might just settle it myself. Right now we have this battle to fight . . .*

In quiet waiting, the ship was doing a passive imitation of a planetoid. Now the crew could see and feel the eternal emptiness of space again, the thinness of the distribution of matter even here inside a dustbelt. In seconds the fury of the battle had vanished totally.

No one doubted that it was going to burst over them again or had time to contemplate the universe. The ship had suffered damage, but so far nothing was critical. Iskander through his mindlink was doing what he could to patch it up.

Simeon got permission to leave his station momentarily to check on Branwen; Spence's report on her condition had been brief and uninformative. Simeon found her semiconscious, and would have taken her to sickbay but at that moment Domingo ordered him sharply to get back to his station. On his way out of her berth he picked up some of the samples of material and information that she had brought from the most recently searched berserker installation.

A quick look at the samples, when Simeon was back in his own station, suggested that they would provide more evidence concerning the berserkers' research and development efforts in the field of biology.

But there was no time now for anything like a thorough scientific analysis.

*   *   *

The enemy was in sight again, and Gennadius was on the radio. The two captains managed to act in concert once more.

The great berserker, being pursued relentlessly, taking a merciless pounding from two sides, bedeviled continually by the Nebulons who still swarmed after it, continued to strike back with fury.

The battle seesawed back and forth.

But then at last the berserker turned tail and fled.

Domingo, despite the damage to his ship and the desperate condition of his crew, despite depleted stocks of missiles and red warning signals everywhere, immediately gave chase to Leviathan, vowing that his ancient enemy would not escape him now.

Fourth Adventurer, somehow still able to withstand the killing strain of what he was doing, taking part in combat, fatalistically accepted the result of what he had already done as a matter of free choice: "I have signed on."

Gennadius, wholly caught up at last in the spirit of the chase, overrode the warnings of his own second-in-command about his damaged ship and chased the enemy too, and recklessly. The alternative would have been to fall back in guard position at some nearby colony. His ship was now in better condition than Domingo's, and the commander took the lead in the pursuit.

The speed of both ships was perilously high as they hounded their quarry among the innumerable tiny planetoids and through the fringes of the encroaching wisps of nebula, and then departed the system, still in hot pursuit.

The berserker was not dead yet. It turned at bay, and the fury of the battle came back, worse than before. Simeon heard strange cries on intercom, and he found himself closing his eyes and praying, to a God of the Galaxies someone had taught him to adore in childhood.

Someone else on the crew—Simeon could not identify the tortured voice—had cracked now and was pleading with the captain. Whoever it was shrieked and babbled, but Domingo would not slow down. Eventually the human screaming ceased.

But not the noise of the alarms. Those mechanical voices screamed on, and there was no doubt that the ship was continuously sustaining damage, as it went tearing its way through clouds of gas molecules and microscopic particles.

The shields were maintained somehow and the headlong pursuit went on. It could not be endured for another moment, but yet it was endured. The timeless minutes passed, with people and machinery still somehow taking the strain.

The enemy fled again.

The unnamed sun, and the space that sun had cleared for itself within the nebula, were now astern, the white light shifting red with its recessional velocity. Abruptly, at an insanely dangerous speed, dense clouds of nebula once more enfolded the quarry and the hunters alike.

An outer belt of planetoids that until now had been concealed in nebular clouds now loomed ahead, appearing as a bombardment of rocks hurtling past the ship and at it, out of fog and darkness.

There was a startling flare on the *Pearl*'s detectors, seen by everyone on board. All heard a last burst of garbled communication, ending in a radioed scream.

Simeon grasped the fact a second later. Gennadius's ship was gone. Either it had hit a sizable rock or had been ambushed by Leviathan and totally destroyed.

Domingo, not delaying for an instant his headlong charge after the enemy, ordered the firing of most or all of his remaining missiles. Simeon obeyed. At this speed the captain himself dared not divert an instant's attention from his piloting.

"Captain, I have what looks like a lifeboat on the detectors. Might be Gennadius, some of his people."

Domingo said: "We can't stop."

His ship did not waver for a second from its course, straight after Leviathan. He had the helm and no one could stop him. Or no one dared to try.

CHAPTER 22

Domingo, dragging his crew along with him by the power of his will, hurled his ship after Leviathan without pause, keeping the pressure on.

Simeon had gone beyond weariness, beyond fear. Now he was being caught up, hypnotized, in the fascination of the chase. Vaguely he was aware that Branwen, Spence and even Iskander were reaching or passing the limits of their endurance. Fourth Adventurer was a special case. It was hard to know what was going on with the Carmpan, but for now he appeared to be enduring successfully, if grimly.

Again the battered berserker plunged into the billows of the Milkpail. It displayed surprising speed in its flight: in a human such behavior would have been called reckless or even suicidal daring. There was no doubt that a machine of Leviathan's size had to be taking considerable additional damage from the inevitable particle collisions at such speed. The generators sustaining its forcefield shields must be near failure, and its armor ablating away. The machine was running a serious risk of sudden and total destruction at any moment.

Yet the blazing trail left by the enemy persisted, did not reach a cataclysmic end. Its luck, if machines had luck, was holding.

The captain followed it at high speed, accepting an equal risk. Such a track would have been practically impossible for any pilot to lose, given the will to hold the course. The turbulent wake of the berserker increased the danger for the following ship, the probability of microcollisions. Domingo was forced to avoid the enemy's wake as much as possible, thereby losing a little ground.

"You've got it all calculated out, Skullface. All the odds to the last decimal. But you haven't figured me into your odds yet. You haven't figured me in well enough. I'm coming to get you." Domingo was muttering to himself, but the others aboard his ship could hear him.

Again the *Pearl* shot into the nebula, right after her escaping foe, at a speed that neither the ship or the machine would be likely to tolerate for long. Not in these clouds. The clamor of onboard alarms resumed.

The drive of the *Pearl* had been weakened by combat damage. Despite Domingo's maniacal determination, Old Blue might well have escaped cleanly, except for the efforts of the Nebulons.

The Spacedwellers had no trouble keeping up with the fleeing berserker, but whenever they tried to attack it its fields stung them and brushed them away. Fourth Adventurer reported several fatalities among the nebular-theme humans from these encounters. But still their speeding formation kept the dead-metal killer in sight, and through the mind of Fourth Adventurer they continuously relayed the enemy's position to Domingo. When the machine abruptly changed course in an apparent effort to loop back and try for another ambush, the pursuing *Pearl* was able to change course also, almost instantly, gaining some distance on its quarry in the process.

Now the berserker would be aware, if it had not been before, that the Nebulons were somehow able to report whatever they observed to their allies in the ship, virtually instantaneously.

"It's going to get away." Those words were the first from Iskander in some time.

Domingo's voice sounded no different now than it had on the day after Shubra. "It's not trying to get away. We can follow that wake and he knows it. He's risking a pileup to try to get somewhere."

The only question was, was Leviathan trying to reach allies, or a final kamikaze target?

The chase continued, pressed by Domingo with fanatical intensity. Timeless minutes stretched into eternal hours. Punishing jolts came through the artificial gravity as the *Pearl* dodged rocks at thousands of kilometers per second.

Simeon, looking about him in the moments when his mind refused a total concentration on his job, was amazed that everyone on the crew could still be alive. That anyone could be. The ship and all her systems were a shambles. Backup systems labored, with nothing to replace them when they went. He could see in all the indicators before him what a beating the *Pearl* had taken.

She ought to be limping away, cruising slowly, doing her best to make port somewhere before one of the impending catastrophic breakdowns happened and finished her off. Instead she hurtled on at the best speed her captain could whip out of her, pursuing the thing that had not quite destroyed her yet . . .

They had built her well, those people at the Austeel yards. But how well could anyone build a ship?

Simeon clung to the thought that Old Blue was now heavily damaged also. It had to be. But there was no reason to think the berserker had lost its capability of inflicting ruin on any attacker that caught up to it.

Only one man was trying to do so.

Only utter grim determination, to carry the hunt on to the

death, had a chance now of overtaking the berserker. Only obsession, only suicidal madness, had any chance of outlasting a rogue computer's will.

With all Domingo's efforts and those he could still wring from his crew, it remained impossible to close the gap between pursuer and pursued.

Galway now called the captain on a private channel and reported herself fit to resume her duties.

He glared at her impersonally, a man trying to estimate how long one of his few remaining tools would last before it broke. "You're not going to fold up in the middle of a fight?"

Her image tossed its head. "*I'm* fit for duty. I don't know about Benkovic."

"Benkovic? What's that supposed to mean? What's wrong with him?"

Tersely she supplied the captain with the facts, a recital of what had happened in her berth when Benkovic had been alone with her. "If he tries to paw me again," Branwen concluded, "he's going to have plenty wrong with him. Like a new belly-button. Battle or no battle."

The captain only continued to stare at her, digesting bad news about another tool. She could see that he had no capacity left in him any more for shock or surprise, let alone sympathy.

At last he said: "You take over fire control for a while, Galway. Simeon needs a break. I've got to keep one good person going, and right now he's the best I've got. We're pushing on."

"Yes, sir." She was not surprised at Domingo's reaction. No time or energy could be spared now for anything but the chase. Anyone on the battered crew who could still function had to function. Branwen understood that Domingo had no real interest in crew conflicts or even in serious breaches of discipline, except as they might endanger his mission. She understood that he was not now going to pursue the matter of what exactly Benkovic might have done to her or might stand accused of doing. If they all lived, which they were not going to do, something might be done about it. She might very well take care of it herself. But right now her head still ached, and she could hardly think.

The captain broke the intercom connection and concentrated fully on the chase. Still, the knowledge of Branwen's complaint had registered on some level with him.

Domingo himself no longer cared where the chase was taking him and his ship. But Simeon found himself trying to calculate or estimate the present position of the *Pearl*. Curiously, his mind felt clear and active now. He had passed beyond the first stages of exhaustion, and now it was as if his mind, like the ship herself, could tap the wells of the universe for power to keep going. It would be a help to know what kind of nebular material lay near ahead, and what the chances might be of enlisting some aid in the chase.

According to the best calculations that Simeon could make, the speeding enemy ahead was now rapidly approaching the location of the colonized planetoid da Gama.

When Simeon had checked this conclusion as well as he could, he got on the intercom to the captain. Domingo, when pressed, agreed to let him launch a courier now, trying to recruit more Space Force help.

Simeon took thought, and the courier was gone.

The defenses of da Gama were springing automatically to life. Alarms sounded across the planetoid, in every place that humans were. The early warning detectors of local Ground Defense had picked up the charging berserker at extreme range. Leviathan was coming on in an all-out kamikaze charge, and if the machine maintained its present course and speed, no more than an hour would elapse before it arrived.

The mayor of da Gama, arriving at the control center of Ground Defense, was further informed that, if this were indeed a suicidal ramming attack, the ground defenses unaided were probably not going to be able to stop the onrushing berserker.

She sat down slowly. "What can we do?" she asked.

At the moment, no one had an answer for her.

The tactic of dangerously rapid flight had served the berserker well on several previous occasions in its long career when it had been pursued by superior forces. Not, of course, that Leviathan knew fear. It considered its own survival not of the highest priority, but still important. If it were destroyed it would no longer be able to carry out the program that was of highest priority, at the core of its existence: the effort to destroy all life.

Not that escape was any longer Leviathan's prime objective. Too many of the badlife missiles had achieved nearly direct hits. The cumulative damage was severe and would be fatal in a few hours at the most. Beyond the next hour or two, the destruction of life was a task that would have to be left to its fellow machines.

The human ship behind it had moved a little closer.

Again the thing that humans called Leviathan slightly increased its speed, getting the most it could from the drive units that were still functioning, ignoring accumulating minor damage, accepting the risks involved.

All human commanders in the past had turned back and given up the chase when faced with such risks.

But whatever unit of badlife commanded this currently pursuing ship did not turn back.

At the present rate of closure, it was still hours from overtaking the berserker.

What could be done to destroy the maximum amount of life in another hour or two?

What was the most profitable target that could be reached in another hour, or a little longer?

The central computer aboard Leviathan had already searched all of its still-functional memory units for information on the nearest colonies. It had observed that one of the larger colonies in the Milkpail was within range.

The people aboard the speeding *Pearl* had now come to realize what the speeding berserker's plan must be. As nearly as they were able to read the situation, only one Home Defense ship was anywhere close to being in the right position to try to defend da Gama from this mad charge.

Whoever commanded this lone Home Defense ship, visible on the *Pearl*'s remote detectors, obviously grasped the situation too. She or he had changed course and was coming out hell-for-leather to try to intercept Leviathan's attack.

"Slow him down," Domingo urged the other ship. His voice was a soft mumble. "Just slow him down."

There was no way by which the people on the Home Defense ship could hear the captain's urging, and they were too far out of position anyway to try to engage Leviathan in a running fight. All the Home Guard ship could do was to try to hurl itself directly in the enemy's way—and that was what it did.

That tactical maneuver was accomplished, with what great effort others could only guess. Simeon, with his eyes closed, could still see what his headlink brought him, dim flares light-minutes distant. In a matter of seconds the bravely aggressive ship was brutally wiped out of the way by the onrushing monster's remaining firepower. Belatedly Simeon realized how small that human ship must have been, how hopelessly outclassed by its opponent.

The people who were still functioning aboard the pursuing *Pearl* now scanned desperately through every quarter of nearby space; but nowhere in the area could they see other Home Guard or Space Force ships that might be able to arrive on the scene in time to help.

It was beginning to look to Simeon as if da Gama was doomed. He tried to remember what its ground defenses were like. Not all that great, as he recalled. Not only were thousands of tons of metal coming at it with more speed than a meteorite, but Leviathan had just demonstrated the power of its remaining weapons. And there was also its c-plus drive, which could become a terrible weapon indeed when a berserker machine or a human ship went suicidal.

Domingo cursed and groaned. He wanted to thwart Leviathan, achieve its destruction on his own terms, not allow it to run up a final score, a final personal insult to him, as it died. He offered to sell his soul for a c-plus cannon and three or four cartridges.

Simeon reflected that a near-miss of the enemy now with such a weapon might well wipe out all life on da Gama as the planetoid's gravitational well sucked in the massive leaden slug, traveling effectively faster than a photon. But the captain would not have been unduly worried about that possibility. In any case the question was academic. No power was bidding that much hardware for Domingo's soul.

The captain's muttering went on. "Someone stop it. Someone delay it. Hold it up just a little, and I'll ram this vessel down its bloody throat."

"We'd wreck ourselves for sure, trying that trick. I don't know if we'd be able to wreck—that." Simeon recalled the model showing how structural members stuck out around the body of the enemy like an exoskeleton of ribs—or the bars confining a caged skull. He wondered what that framework was made of and how much of it was left.

Suddenly Domingo went on radio, trying to reach the enemy, shouting now. "I'm back here, Skullface, behind you. I'm the one you want. Turn back and get me, here. Turn back for me and I'll come aboard you."

Something in Simeon's imagination was fascinated by the mad plan. But Old Blue did not respond. "We're going to have to catch it, Captain, somehow."

Now Domingo sounded almost rational again. "Maybe we can catapult the launch ahead . . . it's a much smaller cross-section, we can get it moving faster without piling up. Ike, are you suited up?" The only good reason not to be in combat armor at this stage would be if you were tending your wounds.

Ike's first answer on the intercom made no sense. The words were hard to make out, but they sounded like a snatch of song.

The captain tried again. "Ike, are you suited and ready?"

"Be there in a minute, Cap."

Baza could be seen on intercom, coming through the padded tunnel for a face-to-face confrontation with his captain. Iskander, startlingly, was not wearing his helmet, and his face, even in the tiny image visible to Simeon and Branwen, was no longer that of a sane man. It was as if all the strain had been removed; actually Simeon thought Iskander's countenance showed a very great relief, as if it had somehow been revealed to him that in a little while, very soon, he was going to be free of this unendurable situation at last. In one way or another.

His first words as he met the captain were: "I mean, Cap, a joke's a joke, but you're on the verge of carrying it too far." And Baza laughed, something he rarely did for all his jesting, and began pulling off what he was still wearing of his combat armor.

At first Domingo persisted in trying to get his second-in-command into the launch. But quickly even the captain realized he had to give up on that. "Get back to your station."

His former second-in-command ignored the order. "I thought it—didn't matter. To me. What happened, now or later. Thought it was all a big joke. But I can't take this. Can't take going after it again, see, Cap? I—" Another chunk of the protective suit came off and was cast aside.

"Get back to your station. Or to sickbay. This is the last time I'm telling you."

"I don't care, Cap. I was . . . I was supposed to be the one who kept you going. Or watched you crack. But I . . ."

Domingo shot him. It was a beam-projector weapon that

the captain used, and Simeon could only think, or hope, it
had been set to stun and not to kill.

In the next moment Domingo had shoved the fallen body
out of his way, and turned his full attention back to his
fleeing enemy. No time to drag the man to the sickbay, there
was piloting to do.

The chase went on.

The next voice that came over Domingo's radio was that of
Gujar Sidoruk, now commanding the Home Defense ship
next closest to da Gama, and visible now on the *Pearl*'s
detectors. Domingo acknowledged the call without surprise.
The two captains were soon doing what they could to coordi-
nate their efforts.

Gujar was quickly provided with an outline of what had
been learned so far about the Nebulons.

He commented that with such allies, berserkers could now
be cleaned out of the Milkpail entirely.

Probably. Eventually. But that didn't help the immediate
crisis. The Nebulons were already doing all they could, as
Fourth Adventurer still reported feebly from time to time.
Gujar was simply too far away to be able to intercept Leviathan before it hit the planetoid.

Da Gama's Ground Defense weapons opened up abruptly
on Old Blue at long range. The berserker fired back. Communication between the two ships became very difficult, what
with all the ionization and other noise spreading out between
them, and no one wasted words trying to tell Domingo
that Polly was on Gujar's ship.

Aboard Gujar's ship, Polly and Gujar talked after the
communication with the *Pearl* was broken off.

Polly knew now that the ship pursuing Leviathan was
Domingo's and that he was at the helm. But her thoughts
were frozen on her two children, who were both on the
imperiled colony of da Gama. Gujar was getting there as fast
as he could. But not rapidly enough.

Gujar was also thinking about Polly. But he was very well aware that she was really concerned with certain other people much more than with him.

The Carmpan, who had been huddled at his station for a long time, rarely speaking, now had a new communication for his ED shipmates. The berserkers had for some time been concentrating on attacking those colonies the Spacedwellers had approached, trying to examine the ED humans' way of life. The death machines had wrongly assumed that the two kinds of intelligent life forms were already cooperating in some way against berserkers. Therefore the berserkers had targeted their attacks with a view to breaking up or frustrating the cooperation.

"Thank you, Adventurer," Simeon said when the report was over. Domingo said nothing.

Old Blue's weapons, from medium range, leveled the inadequate ground batteries on the surface of the planetoid ahead. It dropped intelligent proximity mines to blast at the *Pearl* when the pursuing ship drew near. And it used its own remaining missiles to pound at Gujar's craft.

Simeon hurled the last of his missiles, hoarded until now. More near-misses that must have inflicted more damage. But Leviathan plowed on.

The world of da Gama was coming closer and closer, now only a few minutes distant.

This close to da Gama's sun the density of the nebular medium interfered even more seriously with the progress of the huge machine. Its drive was evidently failing as well. Now it was rapidly losing speed, despite all that its battered engines could do.

Ferdy and Agnes, along with a thousand other people, were in a shelter, down about as deep as anyone could get on a small planetoid, with kilometers of rock above their heads. Drastic measures were being taken to conserve power, and only a few distant emergency lights relieved the darkness. The game the two children had been trying to play was halted when the lights went out.

They both wished aloud for their mother, and both assured each other that they knew she couldn't be there but that she was going to be all right in her ship.

Then the artificial gravity let go. The two children and the people around them had no warning before it happened. But the authorities came on the loudspeakers promptly and managed to prevent panic at least for the moment.

Leviathan, trailing blue flames, still came on toward da Gama at a rate measured in kilometers per second. But the ground defenses were making their final inspired effort to slow the hurtling mass of death. A countersurge of inverse gravitational force was generated and focused, burning out all the generators and doing other damage everywhere across the surface; but not nearly as much damage as an undampened impact would have done.

One strange and unexpected result was observed, a scattering away from the enemy of what looked on instruments like a swarm of harvestable nebular life. But that made no sense and had no bearing on the immediate threat, and the technician who made the observation said nothing about it until later.

The Nebulons, caught at a crucial moment by the surge of contending gravitational fields in space, had to retreat from the conflict. They were stunned and scattered, and until now their great dead-metal foe had managed to keep its most vital organs shielded from their attacks.

The berserker, stopped almost completely by the unexpected countersurge of force, came crashing down on the surface of the planetoid. At the last moment, forced to change its plans, it used what was left of its own drive to brake its forward progress. It had lost so much momentum that a mere crash would no longer do the damage that it wanted. Now, having been slowed so much despite itself, it wanted to arrive on the surface with some dangerous hardware left intact.

Its final impact with the surface took place at a very modest velocity. Nothing was vaporized in the impact, and even the subsurface shelters nearby were not collapsed.

But the humans huddled in the control center of Ground Defense and those in the watching ships understood the situation and held their breath collectively, waiting for the c-plus blast that did not come.

To fire at the enemy now with heavy weapons might trigger the berserker's c-plus drive into detonation, so that was ruled out. Not that Ground Defense had any heavy weapons available that could fire at an object on the ground.

Domingo had none left, either. He might not have used them if they were available. He had decided—or he understood now that it was his destiny—to go aboard one more berserker before he died.

CHAPTER 23

Domingo, on the point of jumping into the launch alone, held back at the last moment, forcing himself to calculate carefully. It was possible that he would need all the support his ship was still capable of giving him. He had to make sure that the most effective person available was left at the helm.

Iskander—no. Dead, or still unable to function. Domingo hadn't seen the man since Simeon had dragged him away, but Baza could hardly be in shape to command. He would have to trust his ship to someone else.

The captain, standing in the ventral bay outside the launch, quickly patched into the intercom. "Fourth Adventurer? You are to assume command of this ship in my absence. This is an order."

"I must respectfully refuse, Captain."

Domingo was taken aback. "An order, I said."

"I understand, Captain, and still refuse. You do not know what you are ordering."

In that voice Domingo could hear stubbornness equal to his

own. He was sure that threats would do no good, nor would shooting Fourth Adventurer bring about the desired result. Besides, if the Carmpan was that sure, he was probably right.

Branwen, then; but no, she was still suffering from her concussion-like injury.

Spence? No, another use for him had just suggested itself to the captain. And if the captain had a choice, he didn't particularly want to leave Branwen and Spence Benkovic effectively alone together. Not after hearing the story the woman had related to him.

It would be Simeon then. He was, Domingo judged, in the best shape of anyone aboard.

It required only a moment on intercom to leave Simeon Chakuchin in command of the *Pearl*.

Domingo's next call was to Spence. Benkovic, like everyone else, was haggard and on the verge of cracking. But when ordered by the captain to come along on yet one more boarding, Spence did no more than give his leader a strange look before acknowledging the order without protest. A minute later Benkovic, suited and ready, appeared in the ventral bay.

Domingo's plan called for the launch with the two boarders on it to be slung on ahead of the *Pearl* by a maneuver of the larger ship. Chakuchin, now at the *Pearl*'s helm, would manage that as best he could, with what help Galway could give him.

Leviathan, though crashed and grounded, was not yet totally subdued. Or at least Domingo would not have been willing to believe for a second that the machine had been effectively defeated. But the captain's first good look at his fallen archenemy through the clear windows of the launch brought home to him with striking force how close he now was, or ought to be, to final victory. The great mass of the berserker was sprawled on rock, physically broken. Like a flung starfish, still more like a shattered skull, the huge machine lay bent over what had once been a small rocky hill.

Though the central part of the hull was still intact, it seemed clearly impossible that the vast ruined bulk could ever move again under its own power. The huge ribs of the projecting exoskeleton were bent and fractured, and even as Domingo watched, what remained of Leviathan's defensive forcefields were sputtering and dissolving in a faint rainbow whose dominant hue was still essentially blue.

There were no signs that human habitation had ever existed in the immediate vicinity of the downed giant, but in the distance, dropping back over the near horizon of the planetoid as the launch hurtled closer, were roads, harvesting towers and buildings, most of them now at least partially destroyed.

"Looks dead. Damned dead," said Benkovic, meaning the berserker.

"It's not. Not yet. I know."

Benkovic said nothing.

The voice of Elena Mossuril, the mayor of da Gama, came into the launch through a radio relay requesting Captain Domingo to respond.

The captain ignored the first two calls before answering the third out of irritation. "Niles Domingo here. I'm busy."

A brief pause. Then the voice on the radio resumed. "I'm sure you are, Captain Domingo. I must talk to you, though. This is the mayor, Elena Mossuril, and I want you to tell me what you're doing. Coded transmission and tightbeam, please."

"Talk to my acting second. Simeon, take over this conversation." And the captain concentrated again on his ship. But he listened in to what was being said on the radio.

Simeon, on the *Pearl*, explained to the mayor what Domingo was doing and assured her that his ship was standing by, ready to use what weapons she had left.

Mayor Mossuril in turn urged Chakuchin not to fire at the downed berserker because of the danger of a secondary explosion. He should fire only at landers if they were deployed from the wreck, but none had been observed so far. He gave her assurances that he was not going to fire unless his captain ordered it; and that was the best that she could get.

The mayor in her deep shelter kept receiving discouraging reports from her tiny ground-based forces. They stated that they were unable to do very much at all about the berserker.

To begin with, there were no suitable all-terrain fighting vehicles available. With the artificial gravity gone, the surface atmosphere was being lost too rapidly to allow for the practical use of aircraft. And the assault force that was trying to reach the enemy on foot in space armor was bogged down in giant crevasses where the newly fractured and churned land kept slipping and sliding and piling up around them.

The mayor could hardly blame anyone for moving very deliberately in approaching the downed monster.

Even if—and this the mayor had not dared try to tell her allies out in space, for fear the berserker could be listening— even if there was a subshelter holding a thousand people almost underneath the thing.

Simeon's stock of missiles had been totally used up. All of the heavy weapon systems of the *Pearl* were virtually exhausted. She continued to move toward da Gama and Leviathan, but would be able to do little or nothing when she got there. It would be a couple of hours before another ship was in a good position to help.

Simeon and Branwen stayed at their battle stations and kept the ship going as best they could. There were still some light weapons in usable condition.

The Carmpan groaned in his berth, crying out with the psychic pain of singed and slaughtered Nebulons, and with his own untranslatable interior torment.

Iskander Baza in sickbay was nearly dead. The stunner at a range of only two meters had done to him what such supposedly non-lethal weapons all too often did.

And now a blood vessel broke inside the victim's brain.

Presently the machines gave up on his heart.

Minutes passed before any of his used-up shipmates noticed that he had died.

The launch with Domingo and Spence Benkovic aboard, descending swiftly and smoothly, came to a halt not quite touching the slabs of rock thrown up along the enemy's broken side. The little vessel came very close to docking against rock, even against the berserker's hull, but Domingo deliberately avoided solid contact.

Crisply the captain gave Benkovic his orders: to remain on the launch, to stay on guard and be ready to respond to whatever other orders might come from Domingo.

Judging from Spence's quiet, subdued response, and the fact that the simple orders had to be repeated, it was evident that he was in an increasingly odd mental state. But there was nothing to be done about that now.

As soon as the vessel was practically motionless relative to the ground, the captain in his armor, carrying weapons and tools, slipped out of a hatch and dropped lightly and slowly the few meters remaining.

The sprawled body of his archenemy towered over him, the broken ribs of the birdcage twisted into fantastic shapes. A gust of almost invisible blue flame played harmlessly from a rent in the berserker's hull. Another, larger rent nearby, one Domingo had already picked out as a good means of entering the body of his enemy, was dark and quiet.

After looking the scene over for only a few seconds, Domingo moved on alone. It did not seem particularly strange to him that he was about to carry out yet another boarding, though he supposed it was doubtful whether any other human being in history had invaded active berserkers so many times. The captain knew only that he must seek out the deadly life of this thing that had destroyed his own life, face it somehow in a final confrontation. After having come this far and been through this much, simply to destroy the hardware of it—to blast and burn its physical shape away—would no longer be enough. Whatever he needed to release him had not yet happened.

There were no immediate death traps ready for him as he went inside Leviathan's hull. There was no resistance of any kind.

More openings, some of them conveniently door-sized, were waiting ready-made in front of Domingo, and he moved deeper. As he moved, he took care to drop small radio-relay units at intervals, devices he hoped would keep him in contact with the human world outside.

Domingo remained on hair-trigger alert as he advanced, expecting at every moment to meet opposition from small maintenance machines at least. In his arms he carried a shoulder weapon connected to a thoughtsight on his helmet. It was much heavier, more powerful, than the handgun he had brought along the first time he boarded a berserker. Grenades, even more potent, hung on his belt. Let the androids come. Even the landers. He was ready.

A choice of ways lay ever open before him, and at each choice he went deeper still into the vitals of his enemy. And still the berserker had done nothing to dispute his progress. He moved in darkness now except for his suit lights.

The machinery by which the captain found himself surrounded was unlike any he had encountered aboard either of the two berserker research stations. This equipment was older, different in design and purpose. This was obviously all for weapons and defense. This must have come from a different factory, though there were a few general similarities in design.

Here there were plentiful signs that a great deal of repair and replacement had been carried out in the course of the centuries. Things had been moved, modified, disconnected and reconnected. There was evidence of a long ongoing effort to keep this engine of destruction in effective operation.

Domingo aimed his carbine at a fragile-looking device. Then he eased his mind away from the will-to-shoot that would have triggered a blast of destruction.

"Dead now," he muttered. "All this part. Where's your

brain? In deeper. In deeper, somewhere. Somewhere in there, you're still alive.''

Through misshapen, unmarked corridors, strange tunnels and ducts that no human being had ever seen before, he groped and climbed and walked in the direction of the berserker's core. His hands were trembling now, he noticed to his surprise. It was the first time his hands had trembled since . . . since he could not remember when. And the fact that he could not remember worried and puzzled him.

Meanwhile, down deep in the central core of the death-machine, the innermost surviving circuits still tried to compute some way of sterilizing the entire planetoid, destroying the thousands of badlife that were known to infest it. For the berserker to calculate anything now was very difficult, because its central processors were damaged and starting to fail, and its sensors had been beaten almost blind and deaf. But it was still trying.

Failing sterilization of the entire planetoid, perhaps it might destroy the underground shelter, crawling with badlife, that it could sense almost underneath its sprawling and half-crumpled bulk.

And failing even that, it ought to be possible to wipe out of existence at least the single specimen of human badlife vermin that had now come in contact with Leviathan itself.

Where exactly was the lone intruding badlife now? There. Approximately. The interior sensors, not meant for this kind of work, gave only the roughest readings. But there, somewhere, quite near a set of automatic doors . . .

With the abrupt removal of the artificial gravity field around da Gama, the upper atmosphere was peeling rapidly away, and the resulting depressurization of the lower air had brought on a fast chill as well as a fierce snowstorm. Not all of these changes were yet apparent among the huddled refugees sealed away down in the deep shelter. But one alarming fact was being quickly spread among them by word of mouth: Every exit from the shelter had been caved in or somehow blocked, either by the bombardment of the berserker's weapons as it approached from space or by the impact of the great mass itself.

Not that the lack of exits posed any immediate problem of survival for the thousand people who were here huddled underground. Their air supply was still secure. So the authorities in charge of the shelter kept repeating, in voices made as soothing as possible.

As matters stood at this moment, there was nowhere for the people in the shelter to go anyway.

Spence Benkovic sat, as he had been ordered, in the launch, gazing numbly out through one of the almost unbreakable windows. The autopilot was holding the launch just slightly above the surface of da Gama. Outside, snow was falling, drifting, accumulating a little here and there, on the rocks only about three meters below where Spence was sitting. A little higher in the howling, dissipating air, more snow was decorating the ancient black of Leviathan's metallic surface, for the first time in the centuries or perhaps millennia of the machine's existence.

Spence was watching the snow. He had gone beyond fear, beyond exhaustion. Only one other thing still bothered him, and if it were not for that, he had the feeling, a very profound feeling, that the best thing he could do would be to sit here and watch it snow forever.

He wasn't going to be allowed to do that, though.

Already the wind was blowing something like a gale. Benkovic could tell by the way the heavy rock outside was stirring and drifting now, mixing with the snow. Soon the atmosphere would begin to howl against the launch, maybe loud enough for him to hear it inside.

He had seen and heard all this before, somewhere else.

He watched snow vanish, steaming, in the blue flames that still came twisting out of one of the wounds in Old Blue's side. The sides of the cavity still glowed, where some kind of a beam weapon, most likely one fired from the *Pearl*, had probed and probed again.

Without consciously thinking much of anything, Spence sat in contemplation of that wound that was never going to heal.

Domingo, still advanced, looked around warily at every step, expecting at every moment to be attacked by landers, androids, or at least maintenance machines. The shape that had killed Maymyo might spring out on him at any moment . . .

Nothing sprang on him or at him. Nothing even got in his way. After one minor alarm from a set of automatic doors—the doors had closed sharply, perhaps trying to catch him—his progress had been unopposed.

The suspicious doors, well behind him now, would not be moving again for any reason. He knew he could no longer be far from his enemy's brain.

The captain was aware of the fact when he had reached his goal, though his opponent did nothing to mark the occasion for him. He was standing now in a large and fairly open interior space, enlarged at some time in the past, he supposed, by the removal of parts for use elsewhere, the cannibalization of redundant units for the front line, wherever that had been. There was plenty of room here for small fighting machines to get in and move around, but none of them came at him.

Deliberately, meticulously, Domingo had left his trail of radio relay devices. He could talk to the world outside if it became necessary. Later on, if he was still able to talk, no doubt he would. But there was another conversation he wanted to hold first.

Niles Domingo turned his radio off the regular channels and on a short-range mode that the berserker would certainly be able to hear, if it could hear anything. He wished that his hands would stop shaking now, but they did not.

He spoke to his enemy. "Where's the lander, Skullface? I want the one that you sent down on the world called Shubra. Bring it out here. Send it against me now."

The berserker heard him.

It had all of its functional maintenance machines at work inside another portion of its hull, preparing the sole remaining unit of its c-plus drive for detonation by a last suicidal application of power. It was now concentrating all its remaining energy and ability on this effort. The best calculations it was still capable of making indicated that here, in the planetoid's natural gravity, that unit would explode when power was applied, violently enough to cave in at least the roof of the shelter below, hardened or not. Caving in the shelter might well finish off all the badlife inside.

But the power mains leading to the c-plus unit had been broken in the crash, and there was much work yet for the little maintenance machines to do before that last killing surge of power could be applied. The machines needed more time to do their work. Unless the single badlife invader could be successfully delayed in its presumed mission of destruction, it was improbable that they were going to get it.

Destroy or delay the invading badlife then, somehow.

It would have been possible to divert some of the maintenance machines to attack this man, but the berserker decided against that course. The only machines it had available were certainly not meant for combat action. And it was easy to deduce that the life-unit must be heavily armored and armed, if it was here at all. Through battered and straining sensors, the berserker was barely able to perceive the presence of the lone invader. The trap with the doors had had a very low probability of success, but nothing better was available.

Time was needed. And when the man, the badlife unit, began to ask the berserker questions, a possible means of gaining time presented itself. The berserker knew the badlife language; it could improvise a speaker, a device to make sounds, and it did.

*   *   *

Domingo heard the machine speak. In a squeaking, inhuman but quite understandable voice it said to him: "I have no landers."

"Lying bastard," he told it, without much feeling in the words. He wanted the heart, the last drop of blood. He wanted reaction, acknowledgment that he had won. He needed to bring the dead soul of the damned thing somehow within his grasp.

"Liar," he muttered. "Liar."

He tuned the nozzle of his weapon to a fine jet and began burning and blasting one of the consoles holding the berserker's memory. When the console was open, he started in on the exposed memory units. They were small, no bigger than a fist, and he took them one at a time.

From one such unit his decoding equipment was able to pick out the coordinates of the hidden repair base that Leviathan had used for centuries. This was treasure. But to Domingo it was still unsatisfying.

The berserker's brain had now been fragmented, by combat damage and the captain's probing, until there was little left of it but mere data banks, incapable of planning or lying. Open books, waiting to be read or written in, indifferent to results and almost powerless to achieve them.

Domingo grabbed up another unit. This small portion of the machine held in its memory much of the research results from the berserker bioresearch stations. That research effort had finally succeeded in determining the form of the optimum anti-human life weapon—at least insofar as berserker machines were able to determine what that might be.

In the little image projected by Domingo's decoder, it looked very much like an ED human. But, Domingo thought, the berserkers had no real hope of developing one of those.

He dropped the memory unit. His sensitive suit mikes had picked up a sound twanging through the metal that surrounded him, and Domingo spun around, his weapon ready.

He waited on a hair-trigger, watching and listening, but

nothing happened. The sound had been that of something collapsing, something failing, or just metal cooling and contracting. There was no threat.

Leviathan would defend this place, its central brain, if it could still defend anything. There was plenty of room here for one of the landers, had there been any still working, to be able to get at an invader. The landers, at least the ones Domingo had seen depicted, weren't very large machines. When they came down on the surface of a planet or a planetoid to sterilize it, they had to be able to get into some fairly restricted spaces in one way or another. Caves, for example, under overhanging cliffs of rock.

But Domingo had faced no challenge since boarding Old Blue, except possibly for the puny effort of the doors. It was almost as if he were being welcomed as a friend.

Was Leviathan really helpless? Or might all the small machines be doing something else?

"I say again, you lying bastard, bring on your machines. Where are they?"

Now even the core of Leviathan's brain was failing rapidly. Domingo's probing dissection had provided a finishing stroke.

The malignant purpose of the fundamental programming had now been almost entirely erased. Only the c-plus detonation project was being continued, and that by machines that neither knew nor cared what they were doing.

What was left of the berserker's intelligence pondered whether or not to answer this most recently asked question and why.

Domingo was not waiting for an answer. He forced open another console that almost certainly had part of Leviathan's brain inside it.

Still the final satisfaction of victory, of revenge, eluded him.

"Do you remember, damned machine—do you remember a planetoid, a colony, called Shubra?"

The fading berserker intelligence had now lost, along with much else, the ability to lie. Ongoing damage was steadily consuming everything. But for the moment the ability to answer questions still remained.

It said, in its squeaking, erratic voice: "I remember that."

"The day that you destroyed life on that planetoid, you sent down some of your small lander machines to make sure—remember? Remember? To make sure that you had done a thorough job. You sent one lander to a particular cave—"

The relevant memory units were still intact and were quickly examined. The berserker responded: "No."

The voice of the life-unit was changing, becoming ragged, too. Its breathing was hard inside its helmet. "—in a particular cliff. Your lander went there and killed a particular young human being. It—"

"No."

"—it killed, it . . ." Domingo could hear the pulse beating in his ears. He could hear his own breathing inside his helmet. He wondered if something was happening to his heart. "What do you mean, 'no'?" He wondered if he was going to hyperventilate and fall helpless here in the face of the enemy. No. He would not.

The berserker said: "In the attack on Shubra I employed no landers. I had none available. The last had been destroyed on the colony of Liaoning."

"You lie."

"No."

The captain drew a deep breath. It was almost a sob. "Ten years ago," he said. "More like eleven. You killed a transport ship." He named the ship. "You left no survivors. My wife was on that, and my children. Can you know, can you understand—"

"When and where?"

Domingo gave the information.

"No. I did not destroy that ship."

"Lying bastard."

"No. Accidents are common."

There was a metal sound again, a clanging somewhere off in the middle distance. Again Domingo spun around, ready to fire. Again there was nothing to aim at.

He turned up the sensitivity on his suit microphones. Ah, something. A steady working, murmuring . . .

"You lying bastard, lying, lying . . ." He was almost in tears. *"Where are your small machines?"*

"They are at work preparing a—" There was a pause, then the same unemotional voice resumed. "Preparing a c-plus detonation that will—that will cave in the roof. Of the badlife shelter. The badlife shelter below. The shelter below the—"

"Stop them!"

Pause again. "The effort has been. Has been stopped. The life-units . . ."

That was all. There was no more.

The distant murmuring had stopped.

Domingo, suspicious, began ransacking what was left of his enemy's brain.

"Damned treacherous . . . I don't believe you yet."

Only silence answered him.

"Not an accident, that transport ship. No." He paused. "An accident?"

The machine no longer answered him. He probed and probed, but he could find no evidence that it was still alive at all. Stray voltage and current here and there within its brain, charges not yet dissipated. Memory of this and that. If he were to probe long and hard enough, he might be able to find the memories he wanted. Where would he find the dead damned soul?

No landers were here now. No landers had been sent down on Shubra. No landers . . .

The c-plus drive unit. He would look at that, to be sure.

He thought he knew where that would have to be, on a berserker built like this.

It took the captain a minute or two to get there, climbing through the unfamiliar hardware.

The c-plus unit when he found it was surrounded with little maintenance machines. All of them were now immobile. Domingo stared at them for some time, then with his fine-tuned weapon he burned them, one at a time, into permanent immobility. Just in case.

He made his way back to the central chamber housing the now-dead brain and sat there. No landers had come down on Shubra. His hands were shaking worse than ever now.

CHAPTER 24

Down one of the long, sloping half-open aisles that converged on the place where Domingo waited, through one of the passages never meant for humans and clogged now with machinery dislodged and broken in Leviathan's dying crash, the captain saw a new light. It was bright and it came waving shadows ahead of it with its own approaching motion.

He suppressed the urge to cry out. Instead he stepped back silently, the weapon that had been slung over his shoulder coming up smoothly into his two-handed grip.

For a moment wild suspicion returned. But the approaching shape was too small to be that of a lander. Maybe an android, it was the right size for that . . .

But it was not an android. Instead the light-bearing shadow became a shambling human figure, wearing space armor belonging to the *Pearl*.

Spence Benkovic stumbled to a halt when he saw the captain leveling a heavy weapon at him.

For a moment there was silence. Then Benkovic said on

the short-range radio: "I came to find you. I had to see what you were doing."

"Your orders were to stay on the launch." But the rebuke was no more than mechanical.

"I couldn't do that," Benkovic said simply. "I had to see what you were doing here."

They looked at each other.

Domingo said: "I was wondering about you, too. About why you signed on my ship. The real reason."

"It was like I couldn't keep away. I had to come along to see what you were doing. What you were going to find out."

"Are you goodlife, Spence? Is that it?"

Benkovic's face inside his helmet, plainly visible in the center of Domingo's light, showed nothing but bewilderment. Whatever he had been expecting from Domingo, it wasn't that at all. "Goodlife? What the hell kind of a thing is that to say?" But the protest was weak. Benkovic appeared to be on the verge of laughing or crying.

"Are you?"

"Nothing like that, Captain. No, nothing like that." Spence gestured toward the components of the disassembled brain that were lying at Domingo's feet. "Is it dead now?"

"It's been dead all along, Spence. Now it's pretty well turned off."

Benkovic nodded. There was silence, for a moment, as if there might be nothing more to be said between the two men.

Then mechanical sounds came echoing from somewhere within the nearby metal caverns as before. Spence grabbed for the holster at his belt, then realized that he had come here unarmed. He looked down, perhaps marveling silently that he should have forgotten such a thing; or perhaps he knew the reason for his forgetfulness. Then again only tiredness showed in his face.

Domingo hadn't turned or raised his weapon this time. Now he said: "Pretty well turned off, but it still talked to me there for a while. I got some truth out of it. There aren't any landers here. This berserker hasn't had any landers or androids for months."

The other was looking at him. Looking and listening intently, like someone hoping for a message that would mean rescue.

"Not since Liaoning," Domingo said. "Not since before Shubra."

Branwen Galway, groaning, semiconscious, lay in her berth aboard ship. She'd had to abandon her battle station because her mind seemed to be fogging up again. She knew she needed medical help. She was going to hang on somehow and do what she had to do until she got it. She was going to shoot Spence Benkovic if he came through her door again.

Fourth Adventurer was still living, but almost inert.

Simeon, virtually alone now on the *Pearl*, was himself on his last legs. Duty held him to his post.

Back in the central cave of the devastated berserker, Benkovic sat down slowly on a projecting ledge of metal that had been designed for some totally different purpose. Presently he let his helmeted head fall forward into his hands.

The captain remained standing. Even in the light natural gravity, he swayed. The mechanical sounds out in the caves of machinery had stopped, but there was still a roaring in his mind. A rushing and a roaring, like a prolonged explosion. It seemed to have been going on forever, like the space battle with Leviathan. He could feel it all, everything, catching up with him at once.

His weapon no longer pointed at Benkovic, but still the captain held it in both hands. His hands holding the heavy carbine were shaking more than ever, uncontrollably.

"Tell me what happened on that day." Domingo's voice, asking the question, sounded like that of a man trying to memorize a line that he was going to have to deliver in a play.

Spence raised his head and nodded, making his helmet

light bob up and down. He didn't look at Domingo at all now, but instead gazed off into the shadowed recesses of the ruined machinery.

"What I told you before, a lot of that was true," he said. "The first part of the story I told everybody, that was true."

"Tell me again. The whole thing now. I want to know all the truth."

Once more Benkovic nodded. He spoke as if he were remembering something from long years before, or maybe even from an earlier lifetime. "There at the wedding, after the alert was called, I ran along with everyone else and got into my ship. I didn't have any idea then . . ." The recital stalled.

"Go on."

Spence went on. He described how, when the other ships lifted off, he too had launched from Shubra in his one-seater battler, headed back for the moon.

From space he had seen the relief squadron, led by Domingo, depart for Liaoning.

"Then I sort of wished I'd gone with you. Wanted t'be in on the action, y'know? But by then it was too late."

"Go on."

At that point, Benkovic said, he had changed the objective of his own flight, deciding to do some scouting on his own. He had radioed first to his three women companions on the moon, telling them to go into the shelter and lie low.

The moon's orbit brought it within only the outer limit of the effective range of the Shubran ground defenses. But Spence had had no reason when he made the call to expect that there was really going to be a berserker attack on Shubra almost at once. So presumably the women would be just about as safe in the little shelter on the moon as they would have been taking flight in a ship or coming down to take shelter on the planetoid—that last assessment had turned out, grimly, to be all too accurate.

"I should have gone back and picked them up in a ship, I guess. Got 'em the hell outta there. But I didn't." He shrugged. "Everybody else should have done something different, too."

"Go on."

After making the call to warn his girlfriends, Benkovic had zoomed away for a few hours, scouting. He'd had no success, even though he was a good pilot. Anyone could testify to that.

"And I've never been afraid to do things." Spence raised his head all the way and looked around him when he said that, as if to say that his presence here on this boarded berserker justified that claim.

Giving up on the fruitless scouting expedition, he had returned to within visual range of Shubra in time to see Leviathan in the process of attacking the colony.

"You told all of this before."

"Yeah. And up to that point, up to what I'm telling you now, everything I told you before was the truth."

"And now. Tell me the rest of the truth." Domingo was still on his feet. He was resting his weapon on the machinery in front of him, trying to stop the trembling in his hands.

"Yeah. I want to do that." Spence's voice fell lower and lower. He swayed as if he might be going to topple from where he was sitting. "God, what a ride you put us through, chasing this thing. I can still feel it. It's all still coming at me."

Domingo waited.

"What really happened. Yeah." Benkovic paused for a long time. "But it's like none of that part is real."

"It was real enough. It was as bloody real as anything. Go on."

Benkovic went on. Actually, as he related the story now, he had not seen the berserker send down any small machines to devastate the individual defensive outposts. But he had assumed that Leviathan had landers and androids; they were practically standard equipment on large berserkers. "And I never guessed . . . I'd be here finding out different."

"Go on."

Benkovic wasn't sure now how long he'd drifted in space in his little one-seater, watching the slaughter, the destruction, from a safe distance, far beyond the orbit of the moon. But eventually Leviathan had completed its programmed task and had departed the vicinity of Shubra, leaving nothing but smoking ruin on what a few hours before had been an inhabited surface.

Benkovic had returned to his moon to find his colony destroyed by a few touches of the enemy weapons with only one of his women still alive. He had given her what help he could. She was seriously injured but seemed likely to survive, and he had left her there alone in the charge of the medical robot, which was about the only useful machine to have survived the attack.

Fascinated as always by destruction, he had then flown down to the Shubran surface.

"I could see that just about everything was ruined. There were no radio signals. I told myself that when I landed I was going to see if there were any survivors—anyone I could help. That's what I kept thinking most of the way.

"Then I saw—I really started to see—what had happened. I don't know. All gone. Destruction. That kind of thing. It turns me on in some way . . . you know? I guess you don't know."

"Tell me. I want to hear."

"You already know, don't you? I'm so bloody tired now. So damned . . . there's no way out. But first I'll tell you."

"Yeah."

"At last I picked up one little local radio signal, because I was so close; it never got out to anywhere else because of all the ionization around. A distress call. I followed it, and answered. She said . . . who she was."

"My daughter."

"Yeah—it was Maymyo. I don't know if she knew my voice. I don't think so. I never said who I was. But she gave me enough directions so I could find the cave. The airlock was still holding. She—she saw me outside. When she was sure it was a man and not a machine talking to her, she let me in.''

"The door, the big door to the cave, was blasted open.''

"I did that, later. With the cannon on my little battler. To make it look like berserkers, see.''

"I see. Go on.''

"I told her that the attack was over, but she wouldn't believe me at first. I don't think she knew who I was, even then. She was in a kind of daze. Combat fatigue. I don't think she was hurt otherwise. Maybe a little concussion.''

"Like Galway.''

"Yeah . . . yeah. Then it came over me what I had to do.

"I told her to take her armor off, and she did. Just like that. She was in a total daze, following orders. I told her to take her armor off, and then that white dress, and then to lie down. Then she struggled, but I . . .

"Then—after—I thought I couldn't just leave her. Because, you know, she'd probably remember.'' There was a pause long enough for two breaths. Domingo could hear them distinctly on the radio. Then Benkovic concluded: "And if she remembered, she'd tell.''

Having said that, Benkovic nodded sagely. He appeared to be considering the human condition, himself as an example of it.

"You killed her.''

Benkovic looked up. "I couldn't just leave her. Yeah.'' It was a simple truth; he looked afraid of it. But he was not really frightened of Domingo's gun. He looked yearningly at the big bore of the carbine as it leveled steadily at his helmet.

Domingo was still sitting there when Polly and Gujar came in.

There were other people with them, people from the crew of Gujar's ship, and they were going through the motions of trying to rescue Captain Domingo, not really expecting to find him or anyone else in Leviathan's guts alive.

The new arrivals took note of Benkovic's headless body

but were not much surprised. They assumed that the berserker had somehow killed him.

Simeon, Fourth Adventurer, Branwen Galway—all of them had already spoken to the rescuers on radio, and all three welcomed them back to the ship a little later when they came bringing Domingo with them. But none of the crew members who had stayed aboard the *Pearl* could tell the tale of what had passed between Benkovic and Domingo on the wreck.

Niles Domingo was to tell that story once, to one person only, and much later in his life.

The captain and Polly Suslova were side by side, more or less in each other's company, as they left the dead berserker on their way to find her children.

Domingo looked around him before he left, as if he had never seen this place until this moment.

FRED SABERHAGEN

POUL ANDERSON
Winner of 7 Hugos and 3 Nebulas

☐	53088-8	CONFLICT	$2.95
	53089-6		Canada $3.50
☐	48527-1	COLD VICTORY	$2.75
☐	48517-4	EXPLORATIONS.	$2.50
☐	48515-8	FANTASY	$2.50
☐	48550-6	THE GODS LAUGHED	$2.95
☐	48579-4	GUARDIANS OF TIME	$2.95
☐	53567-7	HOKA! (with Gordon R. Dickson)	$2.75
	53568-5		Canada $3.25
☐	48582-4	LONG NIGHT	$2.95
☐	53079-9	A MIDSUMMER TEMPEST	$2.95
	53080-2		Canada $3.50
☐	48553-0	NEW AMERICA	$2.95
☐	48596-4	PSYCHOTECHNIC LEAGUE	$2.95
☐	48533-6	STARSHIP	$2.75
☐	53073-X	TALES OF THE FLYING MOUNTAINS	$2.95
	53074-8		Canada $3.50
☐	53076-4	TIME PATROLMAN	$2.95
	53077-2		Canada $3.50
☐	48561-1	TWILIGHT WORLD	$2.75
☐	53085-3	THE UNICORN TRADE	$2.95
	53086-1		Canada $3.50
☐	53081-0	PAST TIMES	$2.95
	53082-9		Canada $3.50

Buy them at your local bookstore or use this handy coupon:
Clip and mail this page with your order

TOR BOOKS—Reader Service Dept.
49 W. 24 Street, 9th Floor, New York, NY 10010

Please send me the book(s) I have checked above. I am enclosing
$_____ (please add $1.00 to cover postage and handling).
Send check or money order only—no cash or C.O.D.'s.

Mr./Mrs./Miss _____
Address _____
City _____ State/Zip _____
Please allow six weeks for delivery. Prices subject to change without
notice.